THE ENCOUNTER

GABRIELA
ADAMEȘTEANU

THE ENCOUNTER

Translated by
Alistair Ian Blyth

WITHDRAWN

DALKEY ARCHIVE PRESS

First published in Romanian as *Intalnirea* in 2013.

© 2013 by Gabriela Adamesteanu
Translation copyright © 2016 Alistair Ian Blyth

First edition, 2016
All rights reserved

CATALOGING-IN-PUBLICATION DATA
Names: Adamesteanu, Gabriela, author. | Blyth, Alistair Ian, translator.
Title: The encounter / by Gabriela Adamesteanu ; translated by Alistair Ian
Blyth.
Other titles: ălntăalnirea. English
Description: First edition. | Victoria, TX : Dalkey Archive Press, 2016.
Identifiers: LCCN 2015040724 | ISBN 9781564789532 (pbk. : acid-free paper)
Classification: LCC PC840.1.D34 I5813 2016 | DDC 859/.334--dc23
LC record available at http://lccn.loc.gov/2015040724

ROMANIAN
CULTURAL
INSTITUTE

Partially funded by the Illinois Arts Council, a state agency, and by the Translation
and Publication Support Program of the Romanian Cultural Institute.

www.dalkeyarchive.com
Victoria, TX / McLean, IL / London / Dublin

Dalkey Archive Press publications are, in part, made possible through the support of
the University of Houston-Victoria and its programs in creative writing, publishing,
and translation.

Printed on permanent/durable acid-free paper

To my uncle, archaeologist Dinu Adameșteanu, who, without knowing (me), shaped my life from afar.

Every exile is a Ulysses traveling toward Ithaca . . . The path toward Ithaca, toward the center. I had known all that for a long time. What I have just discovered is that the chance to become a new Ulysses is given to any exile whatsoever (precisely because he has been condemned by the gods, that is, by the "powers" which decide historical, earthly destinies).

But to realize this, the exile must be capable of penetrating the hidden meaning of his wanderings, and of understanding them as a long series of initiation trials (willed by the gods) and as so many obstacles on the path which brings him back to the hearth (toward the center).

That means: seeing signs, hidden meanings, symbols, in the sufferings, the depressions, the dry periods in everyday life.

Seeing them and reading them even if they aren't there; if one sees them, one can build a structure and read a message in the formless flow of things and the monotonous flux of historical facts.

Mircea Eliade

Part One
The Departure

CHAPTER ONE
The Journey Home

WAS THAT THE door to the next compartment opening? A conductor, who else could utter the words so clearly, so curtly:

—*Guten Tag, geben Sie mir, bitte!*

You are tense, you are feverish, you force yourself to calm your quickened breathing. You keep your eyes turned to the dark, shiny window, but you cannot see the landscapes that race in the night, you are on an express, an inter-city.

—*Den Fahrschein, bitte!*

You pat your pockets as if wishing to step into the corridor to have a smoke, the eyes of the people in the compartment are fixed on you, are they looking? Are they not looking?

—*Bonjour, mesdames, messieurs! Vos billets, s'il vous plaît!*

You rise slowly from the bench seat, you see your rigid face flash in the void of a mirror, is it your face? It is as if it is not.

—*Your ticket please!*

You edge past raincoats, jackets, hats, past lustrously shined shoes on which you try carefully not to tread, you sidle down the corridor, you hope that the motionless faces behind the windows across which your shadow smoothly slides will think that you must be going to the restaurant, the buffet car, the toilet, quickly, quicker and quicker, quicker and quicker, quicker and quicker, quicker and . . .

—*Den Fahrschein, bitte!*

The speed of the train makes you bump against the walls, you are on an express, on a TGV, you are on the Drăgăşani train, third class, you choke on the fluffy black swirls of smoke and a bee has been buzzing around for a long time. But look, two paces away, the railway official's uniform, the conductor's cap, his hand outstretched to punch your ticket.

—*Good morning, sir! Your ticket please!*

A trapdoor is about to open under your feet and, while you

repeatedly try to explain, embarrassed, sweating, jumbling the pronunciations, declensions, conjugations, you are about to tumble between the swift wheels into the damp blackness . . .

*

What luck, the conductor was standing two paces away from you, but he did not see you! What luck that nobody can see you floundering beneath the heap of coats, heavy overcoats, uniforms, smoking jackets, swishing trench coats, white sheets, the shrouds from which rise a cloud of moths. But no, it is always the same moth.

—*Den Fahrschein, bitte!*

You burst out of the compartment and break into a run, behind you, you hear the soldiers' boots, your pajamas are unbuttoned and your half-shaven face is lathered with foam. At speed you bump into the walls with their shiny, smoky, dark windows, you are on a TGV, on a freight train, in an inter-city, and the strange faces gaze at you tensely, you are running, running, running! Look, an empty compartment, he opens the door with a confident hand, utters curtly:

—*I biglietti, prego!*

The suspicious faces in the corridor are going to think that he went into the empty compartment, his cap glints in the mirror of the window, it is his cap, it is your face, hide quickly, where?

*

Calm down, it is the same old dream, it happened before, you have experienced it before, where? You cannot remember when, you cannot remember where, ah, how tedious . . . You rummage through your pockets for your blood pressure pills, you find cigarettes, hard candies, crumpled pieces of paper, but you do not recognize the language in which you wrote the text of your lecture, you do not recognize the alphabet. What then are you going to read to the audience? You do not know.

You have risen from your seat by the window, you make a

show of cleaning your pipe, as if you were about to step into the corridor, but why this disapproving silence? Ah, yes! It is a non-smoking carriage! You have crawled under the bench seat, you huddle up, as small as you can, smaller and smaller, smaller and smaller, between the revolving wheels. You crouch on all fours and hold your breath, from up there, from the baggage rack onto which you have climbed, you see the shadow darken the window:

—*Good morning, bitte! Vos billets, mesdames, messieurs, s'il vous plaît!*

Now he is going to open the door to the compartment and you, huddled up, frightened, you are going to tumble into blackness slashed by blinding whorls of light.

Up on the walkway, look, the soldier aiming his rifle, as stock-still as a statue.

—Who are you? Where are you from? Where are you going? Your papers! Answer!

You burst from under the bench seat, your horrified face flashes in the void of a mirror.

—Your papers! shout the customs officers, the border guards, and they bang the door to the compartment with their rifle butts.

—Your papers! Who are you?

—Where are you going?

—What are you doing here?

—Answer or I'll shoot!

*

Don't be frightened, keep calm, it's the same nagging dream. To wake yourself up, you dig your fingernails into the soft flesh, you try to clench your limp hand into a fist, but you are still here. Whatever you do, it is in vain, you cannot escape, you run madly, look, the uniform of the conductor at the end of the corridor, you run towards him madly, it is too late to turn your back, it is too late to pretend you don't see him, he is in front of you, two paces away.

—Your papers! you hear from behind.

*

How many times you have stood like this, in the deserted station, ready to depart, coming from school, with a trembling hand you mop your brow, your damp cheeks, a good job you managed to escape from the train full of conductors and armed soldiers! If only those red, blood-like stains would vanish from the damp cement, and the whining noise that bores into your temples, the back of your neck . . . You cast an idle glance at the young, russet fur gliding over the railway sleepers, over the tracks, under the train, that dog holding its bushy tail between its tensed legs, what a good resemblance it bears with Federigo, your dog at home!

—Fed! Fed! you call, but the dog growls beneath the train and snuffles.

What scent is it tracking? Might it be yours? You have turned your back, so that they will not recognize you, the two surly soldiers whose hands are grasping their rifles.

—Your papers!

—Where are you going? Answer!

—Where are you from? Show your papers!

—Stop! Stop or I'll shoot!

*

You walk quickly, you run, fast, faster and faster, faster and faster, you sense the station growing smaller and smaller behind you, and the red blotches, like fresh blood, pulsate on the foggy path down which you advance on legs limper and limper, your shoes wet with dew.

A sudden shift in sounds, colors, light. The deep green of the pines ascends to the mist-enveloped summit, the soft green of the meadow below, the sticky path on which you crush fibrous clumps of gypsophila under boots that are too tight, careful you don't slip! Careful you don't . . .

How many times you have walked here, the same way, the

same way, alongside you countless other feet climb the cement steps of the bridge, beneath flow three trickles of water, absorbed by the sandbanks, by the large, round boulders, on which sit homely vacationers, soft, whitish corpses, waiting in vain for the sun to emerge above the shadow-strewn earth. *Then to the bounds of deep-flowing Ocean we came, / Where lies the city of the Cimmerian race, / Forever enveloped in mist and darkness deep, / Upon whom the bright Sun his rays doth never cast.* Look, DRY CLEANER'S, the sign fixed to the dirty-white wall rising from the sandy earth, look, the duvet covers, harsh yellowish-white shrouds, hung up to dry, above them black, puffy whirls of smoke settle on the heads of those endlessly ascending and descending with suitcases, shopping bags, sacks, valises, candles decked with paper flowers, large wooden boxes, coffins. You are panting, with trembling hand you wipe your damp cheeks, your palm grips the handrail, you dare not look into the dizzying void lest you slip on the cement steps down into the cold blackness.

*

Precisely because you know the line very well, you realize that you have got it wrong, *who, o stranger, made thee embark on such a journey into mist and darkness,* but what comes next? Your desk is right next to the open window, the blossoming branch of the apple tree brushes the sill, clusters of furry bees and pink flowers swarm between the little green leaves.

Come inside, you whisper to your bee, come inside and sting Teacher.

—Instead of talking to yourself in the corner, why not come to the front of the class and recite? says Teacher and arms himself with the ruler from his desk.

You are not afraid of Teacher's ruler, for twenty-lei coins you do interlinear translations from ancient Greek, from Latin, for the boys in the years above you, but now you have a memory lapse, which is why on your way to Teacher's desk you keep repeating the poem to yourself in a whisper, *but in this life is there*

*anything more onerous than the journey thou thyself hast chosen
through mist and darkness?*

On the diesel-blackened floorboards between the two rows
of desks, pink blotches pulsate beneath your boots, they are the
pink flowers of the blossoming apple tree outside, a breath of
wind cast them through the window, you walk feverishly, tense,
over the glossy floorboards, a mirror, careful you don't slip, careful you don't slip! You clear your throat, you compose your face,
which flashes in the void of the open window. Is it your face? It
is as if it is not. You recite: *Better to abandon the voyage to stony
Ithaca, poor wretch, than to wander long years through the darkness
and mist thither where none awaits thee . . .*

You have made a mistake, the word is on the tip of your
tongue, but you cannot remember it, you have a memory lapse
and your tongue is tied, you hastily search your inside pocket,
where you keep your purse, it is empty, nothing but a small black
coin with a hole in the middle, a Mycenaean, Assyrian, Egyptian
coin, you hold it in your clenched fist, they will ask you for it in
the parking lot, after you cross the bridge. You cannot find the
crumpled sheets of paper with the text of your lecture, which
would have allowed you to see where you went wrong, but what
luck! Teacher is deaf, he cannot hear, he too has grown old in
the meantime.

—*Good morning, mesdames, messieurs, vos billets, s'il vous plaît,*
intones Sir, in a melodious bass-baritone voice.

He has put his cap on and gone out, rapping the door with
his ruler. You stand in the empty classroom, alone, you cannot
leave unless you remember the line from the poem, although
they are waiting for you at home with the table laid.

*

Look, the spire of the church in the valley, when you reach the
church all you have to do is cross the road and you will be home.
What astonished faces they will have, what cries of joy they will
raise when they see you! Will they recognize you? Will they
recognize you after all your years of wandering alone *through*

the darkness and mist? So many years have passed since you left, yesterday evening they saw you off at the station.

You try to espy something between the old fence pales, you stand on tiptoes, trying to peer into the yard, but the fence is too high and the green paint sticks to your fingertips. The fence is freshly painted, you yourself painted it only yesterday, before you went to the station. The house is made of red brick, they did not manage to finish it, because the bank went bust. The banks were nationalized, all of them. The bank refused to grant them a loan, because you had left the country.

Now you stand beneath the cypress by the gate and wonder: shall you open it? Shall you lift the latch? Look, what a meal they have laid out in the yard, a wedding, baptism, funeral repast.

*

How tedious, how heartrending! How many times you have stood here, beneath the plum tree, with your hand on the half-opened gate, ready to fling it wide!

A child with a dirty face and a bare bottom rises from next to the fence and pulls his pants up. Whose might this child be, with snot glistening silvery on his cheeks, like snail slobber desiccated by the sun? You have lost sight of him in the courtyard filled with the bees' buzzing, filled with sunlight, it is summer, it is spring . . .

And that child, left to grow up unsupervised, like a weed, you know him, you have seen him somewhere before, but where? Ah, yes! Mother always kept a photograph of him in her handbag, a sepia photograph, specked with coffee or cooking oil, its corners curling.

*

You tread heavily on the gravel with your stiff, cracked shoes, you would like them all to lift their eyes to you, to see you, to listen to you. They are sitting at the table and the shade of the fir tree obscures their faces—but was there a fir tree? Was there a cypress in your yard? A fir tree in the yard brings misfortune, so they say, and the only place you have seen cypresses was in Rome.

You clomp over the gravel with your cracked, dusty shoes, you tread heavily, just maybe you will see their eyes turning towards you, so that you will be able to say to them: Good to see you again! *Bon appetit*!

But they carry on eating, they do not even look at you.

Nonetheless, they must have known you were coming, otherwise they would not all be here. All of them, all of them! So, they are all alive; none have died. So, the letters, the telegrams, the obituaries were all lies! What happiness, what a relief, Lord! There are Mother and Father, look, sitting at the head of the table the same as ever. And Mother, who keeps getting up from the table, the same as she usually does, to fetch a mug of wine or a basket of bread! So, they are alive, they are among the living! Lord God, what a miracle, what happiness, how good! The rest was just a lie, a dream, an illusion . . . Everything that you believed, everything that you suffered all those years, was for nothing . . .

*

You approach, smiling broadly, happily, even if they do continue to talk among themselves in low voices, as if they had not seen you, as if they had not heard your footfalls . . . None look up at you, they merely pour wine, water, in each other's glasses.

And you, who have journeyed hither so long, so many tormented nights you fled through trains full of conductors and soldiers, you are too tired to appreciate the joke they are playing on you. And if they do not understand that, then let her, at least her, understand!

—Mother! you call softly.

But it is plain that she has not heard you, she is old, the poor woman, her senses have dulled.

—Mother!

You force yourself, you strain, desperately, but you cannot hear your own voice and nor do you cast any shadow on the grass. How can it be that not even she will turn her head towards you?

How can it be that not even she will pay you any heed? And you, who spent the whole night leaping out of one train and onto another, hiding under the bench seats, in trains guarded by armed soldiers, you have come hither in your pajamas, unshod, your cheeks lathered with foam, only half-shaven! As if from another life, as if from a dream, you remember all you have suffered on this endless journey, and not even she will ask you: Is that you, my dear? Not even she will cry out: It is he! It is he, Lord God, how can I thank You for letting me live to see this day and him here with us, among us? Come over here, beside me, dearest of all, so many people have been waiting for you for so long! Are you thirsty? Are you hungry? Are you tired? Come on: say something! *For, there is nothing harder than to come hither, through the mist and the darkness . . .*

But she is silent. She sits motionless, her head turned, the cypress casts its shadow over her face and what else can you do except call out to her yet again:

—Mother!

*

She looks at you in amazement.

—What do you want, stranger?

Have you really changed so much that she is no longer able to recognize you?

—Mother, it is I! I, your son! Why do you call me *stranger*?

How badly you must look if her eyes fill with pity and her voice softens all of a sudden:

—You poor man! Who knows where you have come from! How much you must have suffered, if not even your own mother can recognize you! Come, sit down, have a glass of wine, a piece of bread! It won't be the death of anyone if, before you go back, you stop to catch your breath!

—Go back where? you whisper, exhausted.

—What do you mean where? To your own country, whence you came! It's plain to see that you are not one of us . . .

—How is it plain to see?

—What do you mean how? By your walk, by your clothes . . .

—That's enough joking, Mother! You can see I'm too tired and I'm not in the mood for jokes!

—Poor man! You must have been in prison and lost your mind because of how much you suffered there, if you keep insisting that I'm your mother!

No, she is not joking! She really has not recognized you, poor woman! What a sorry state old age has reduced her to, if she cannot tell that yours is this voice trembling with impatience, with annoyance.

—What else do you want me to call you? I've never called you anything but Mother!

—You must be ill, very ill, poor man, if you don't even know when you are asleep and when you are dreaming, things so simple that even a child knows them! It's a serious illness not to know who you are!

*

—Who else could I be? It's me!

They have all lifted their heads; they are looking at you.

—It is me, what the hell! Can't you see it is me? Me, me, me!

They are silent.

—It is me, your son, brother, nephew, uncle, son-in-law!

The tense faces around the table peer at you as if through glass. She smiles sadly, waves her hand in disgust:

—How good it would be if it were you, but it cannot be you! If it were you, you would not be here, with us, you would be far away! If it were you, you would be on the *Other Side*! You would be as if dead!

—Take a good look at me, you shout at them. It is still I, except that seven, fourteen, twenty years have passed since I left! How could I still be like in the photograph? I am thinner, older, and the journey here was long! I am unwashed, unrested, unshaven! And I can't tell how much I have changed, because here in your house all the mirrors are shrouded . . .

How tedious, how heartrending! How many times you have

lived this same scene! They are sitting around the table, which is laid for a baptism, for a wake, for a wedding, they are smiling in awkward silence, and you cry out, angrily:

—It is me, except that I have put on a few pounds since I switched from cigarettes to a pipe! But I'm hardly so fat that you can't recognize me!

*

They have risen from their chairs, they make to approach, they whisper among themselves, suddenly they all cry out, their voices overlapping:

—Whose son do you say you are?

—He claims to be one of the family!

—But where are your suitcases?

—If you were he, you wouldn't have turned up unshaven and unshod to the wedding.

—Whom did you say he was related to?

—If you were he, you'd have a Rolex on your wrist and a great big Mercedes parked by the gate!

—It's not him: can't you see how shiny his shoes are? Can't you see what an expensive coat he's got on?

—You're an imposter. Mind your own business!

—Where are you from? What are you doing here?

—Where are you from, answer!

—Shush! Leave him be! Can't you see? He's with the Securitate!

—A poor madman! Look at the state he's in! A poor madman, escaped from the asylum!

—A dangerous madman!

—Beware of him, I told you where he's from!

—They sent him here to test us! He wants to hear what we say, what we talk about, so that he can inform on us.

—Shush! We don't have any relatives on the *Other Side*, stranger!

—We have just one, who is long dead.

—We held the seventh-year memorial service for him.

—The fourteenth-year memorial service.

—The twenty-first-year memorial service.

—None of our kin has gone *Over There*, understand that, stranger!

—We have no kin on the *Other Side*.

—We don't need to leave the country.

—We've never gone further than our own backyard.

—Beware! He's just acting the madman, so that he can hear what we're saying and then inform on us afterwards.

—An imposter!

—An informer!

—Can't you see how he's looking about the place? How . . .

—If you were he, they wouldn't have allowed you to cross the border!

—If you were he, you wouldn't be carrying suitcases with broken zippers and tied up with string!

—If you were he, you would have been dead in the Donbas!

—At Stalingrad!

—What the hell, I thought we agreed to say that he'd died on the western front, in the Tatras!

—Did anybody see you, stranger, when you entered our yard?

—Let him leave, let him be on his way! People have gathered in the street outside, by our fence, to gawp.

—Give him some food for the journey, stop shillyshallying like that! Look, here's a plastic bag with some apples and bread, take what you have to take and get out of here!

*

They have turned their backs on you, they are eating peacefully, their eyes fixed on their plates, they obligingly pour wine, water, into each other's glasses.

—It is me! I am one of you! Take a good look at me, you cry out to them, I am your son, brother, nephew, cousin! We were together, all of us, three months ago, thirty years ago. We have known each other since the cradle, since we were little, we slept in the same bed, we ate from the same dish, we were in love with the same girl. I have travelled so long to tell you that if I had known what I would have to suffer, I would never have left our yard. I travelled so long just because I promised you that I would return, otherwise I would never have set foot here, in this yard.

Your lips are moving, but from your throat there comes a halting croak, a bee is flying around above you and the cypress casts its shadow over your face. Your voice is inaudible and your body leaves no shadow on the grass.

Calm down, never mind, it is just a dream, the same nagging, tedious dream . . .

CHAPTER TWO
The Motorway to Rome

—Wake up, Traian! Come on: wake up! Sleep is contagious, you know! Come on, make a little effort to wake up! You don't want to make me fall asleep at the wheel, do you? There's going to be a short delay. I turned off at the wrong exit, but if we take the next right, we'll be at the hotel in three hours.

Groggy, he opens his bleary eyes. He swallows. His neck is stiff and his left arm is tingling.

—You're exaggerating . . . You can hardly call this . . . sleep . . .

His tongue is furred, as if he had been drinking all night.

—Maybe I dozed off for a minute . . . but don't tell me I was asleep . . .

In his mouth, the metallic taste of old age. He reaches for the box of Tic-Tacs and places a minty pill on his numbed tongue. If he dozed off it was only because of the blinding light and the heat coming through the open window in a scorching blast. On each side of the motorway, the hills are covered with gnarled, silvery olive trees. The white blotches of ancient villages perching on the hilltops.

—Dozed off? Really! You were fast asleep. I think you must have been dreaming . . . You were muttering something, the same as when you talk Romanian in your sleep . . .

Did he really talk Romanian in his sleep, as Christa believed? *What are you saying darling? What are you saying? Tell me . . . speak louder . . . so that I can understand what you are saying . . .*

How long had it been since he had spoken Romanian when he made love to a woman? How long had it been since he had stopped speaking Romanian altogether? Forty-five years? Less, more? Nothing but inarticulate sounds, a cry from the body's depths . . .

*

—Maybe I was dreaming after all, why not . . .

He concedes, to get off the topic as quickly as possible. What might Christa have heard him saying? He is still groping for the dream, but he opened his eyes to the light too quickly and the film sequence faded away. Blackened pieces of paper that crumble with a dry rustling noise when you touch them.

—I drifted off, because of the heat . . .

He unbuckles and then refastens his seatbelt, in which he had fallen asleep, like a horse in the harness. Incomprehensible tatters from the dream flutter in front of his eyes, while the silent cries languish, floundering in saliva, among the paralyzed muscles of his throat, his tongue.

He does have a suspicion as to what the dream was about. It keeps recurring whenever his leg aches, whenever he is ill or sleeps in some uncomfortable position. And besides, he has heard it told hundreds and hundreds of times, in so many different versions. He shares the nightmares of the exile with all those like him, who dream the same perilous journey, some of them are captured in their former countries and are unable to return, others are happy because their friends and relatives are waiting for them at the station, with flowers. Ever since he came to live in this country, a country for whose sake he had to suffer before it accepted him as one of its own, he has dreamed the same dream in countless versions. But which version was today's dream?

—It's hot because you keep turning the air conditioner off! Who else has to keep the window open when it's more than forty degrees outside? Don't other people risk coming down with sinusitis, otitis, rhinitis and all the other illnesses you're afraid of? But if you can avoid modern technology, you're the happiest man in the world . . . Your Balkan archaism . . .

*

Christa and her modern technology! There had been a time when she wouldn't move so much as a test tube without casting him a glance to check it was all right! How far would Christa have got on her own, if her Teutonic perseverance had not led her to wait outside his locked door for almost an hour that time, sitting on her cheap canvas handbag, tearing off her cuticles, a bad habit from a stressful childhood, but with her thick-soled string sandals placed neatly beside her? Back then, she still looked like an anorexic teenager, but how incredibly supple, almost boneless, her body had been! Ashamed at having forgotten their date, he had bent to pick her up, but she had coiled up in his arms like a cat, and in his arms he had carried her to the bed, barefoot, her hair undone. Where else could he have put her? The table, the chairs, the floor were covered with open books, typewritten pieces of paper, laboratory samples, glasses of cheap wine, cups with traces of coffee, and curling sandwiches. Her small, firm buttocks, which squirmed on feeling his erection, and the cheap Chianti he had drunk in the *trattoria*, where for almost ten years he ritually met other exiles like himself, excited him so much that as he was ripping off her clothes, he told her, his voice unsteady, impassioned, about the wedding rituals of the country he had left behind. About how the groom carries the bride in his arms, because she must not step across the threshold.

Why had he done that? Had he been flattered at how the scion of a family with three-hundred-year-old diplomas and coats of arms had surrendered to the outsider, the *Ausländer*? Or had he felt a surge of nostalgia after the party with his old friends and would have liked to cross the threshold of his old house in Cărbuneşti carrying a bride in his arms, no matter who she might be?

*

He had long since stopped thinking about Ana Maria, left behind in his former country, on the *Other Side*, about how he used to watch her as she practiced the piano: she was as if dead.

But nonetheless, perhaps while he was carrying Christa to the bed and sliding his hand towards her burning sex, which nestled between her slender thighs, he had glimpsed the him of times past, the private tutor teaching Greek and Latin to Anton

Dobrotă, sitting stiffly on a sofa spread with a coarse carpet, an illustrated book about Rome open on his lap. The thin leaf rasped harshly when he turned it to reveal a yellowing engraving of cypresses and ruins. Ana Maria rehearsed her concerts in that spacious house he entered twice a week. While he listened to her play Brahms, he used to rejoice at the thought of the coffee and the bitter cherry preserve and the plate of almond cakes that were to come afterwards. Those had been the only moments when he allowed himself to waste time back then. He had to save up money by giving private lessons, so that he could pay the rest of his lycée fees and, perhaps (why not?), so that he could finally pay a visit to the whores at Crucea de Piatră, since he was the only one in his class yet to set foot there. Or perhaps he was the only one brave enough to admit that he had not set foot there.

*

Avoiding the reflection of his ruddy, morose face in the huge mirror with the gilded frame, he looked around him frowning. His only suit was covered in hair from the cumbersome ginger cat, whose belly was swollen with kittens, and which he would awkwardly try to stroke until, as irritated as any other female in her condition, she would spit at him or silently drag a thorny claw across the cheap fabric. He ceased to hear Brahms' Sonata, but at least the avalanche of sounds drowned out the shameful rumbling of his stomach, wracked by the long summer fasts of cabbage and beans at the canteen of the Theological Seminary. And he continued to watch the narrow, increasingly febrile face of Ana Maria, which was bared now that her thick hair was tied in a bun at her nape, and the outline of her pointed breasts through her pink, vaporous blouse. It seemed to him indecent that she could allow herself to be gazed at like that, arched above the black and white keys, her every muscle writhing blindly. He would have liked to strip bare that fragile body and to enter it slowly, with maddening slowness, until it arched feverishly, until her muscles writhed rhythmically, while he watched her from between half-closed eyelids, waiting to detect on her increasingly unfamiliar face the moment of release, the indecent spasm, the frozen rictus, and the bags under her eyes that abruptly aged her features.

How easily he grew excited back then, how embarrassing it would be if the people around him glimpsed the bulge in his pants, and sometimes, when he could no longer bear it, he would go to the perfumed bathroom of the Dobrotă house and ease himself, having first anxiously made sure of the lock on the door. Then he would go back in on tiptoes and doze, exhausted by the shameful pleasure, by the pointlessly wasted energy, and he would awake on the final chord and applaud mechanically.

*

Was it that he remembered Ana Maria on the evening when in his arms he carried Christa across the threshold? His mind was too tenebrous to remember the next day, in the light of morning, but Christa's mind was as awake and alert as ever.

When she came back from the bathroom down the passage, while he was trying to apologize for the mess in his room, Christa burst out laughing and reminded him of his mumbling about archaic rituals in his native land, which she had taken as a proposal of marriage. And without giving him time to come to his senses, she nimbly clambered onto him, wrapping her arms and legs around him and "I am a spider and I've caught a little beetle in my web!" and "Don't you want to be my fly?" she sang to him. Was it some unfamiliar lullaby or had she made it up? And with the same directness that even now still shocked him, she confessed that she had singled him out on the very first day she had set foot in the laboratory. Not as a passing lover, but as a successor to Hermann.

It boded well for his career.

He had always shared the opinion of those who believe that women weigh up in an instant not only the masculinity of their future partners, but also their social status: that is how they choose, even the ones who from an excessive or deviated maternal instinct devote themselves to life's failures, to life's invalids.

But that was not the case with Christa, who, wearing nothing but one of his shirts, buttoned up crookedly over her small, slightly sagging breasts (she had breastfed two children already), opened the windows wide, careless of whomever might have seen her from the mansard opposite, and as she picked up the overflowing ashtrays, the dirty plates, the chipped cups, she rattled on and on about her plans for their future house, about their future life together.

And he listened, flattered, as if being given the news that he was to be promoted: had he confused Christa's perseverance with devotion, had he confused love with his desire for legitimacy in his adopted country?

*

—This trip has put you out of sorts, your sleep has been disrupted, I'm positive you've been having nightmares . . .

He mutters something, no, yes, maybe. He coughs for a while, the minty pill has gone down the wrong way, and then he sits motionless, his eyes on the monotonous motorway, sliced down the middle by a little hedge of white and pink oleanders, which curves and vanishes in the wake of the car, concealing itself behind the rocky hills with their gnarled olive trees and undulating juniper bushes.

—I don't expect you to admit it to my face, but at least admit it to yourself, that you have been torturing yourself ever since you decided to make this trip. Elementary caution ought to stop you from taking such a risk, even if it is your country, the country which . . .

His country? That country of stupid people he was embarrassed to be seen with in public? All those paunchy officials and their drooping jowls and chops, their swarthy faces pocked with greasy pores, their eternally crumpled clothes, the officials his friend Alexandru Stan always insists on introducing to him? Who disgusted him all the more when they opened their mouths and he heard them speaking that no longer familiar, ungrammatical, belabored, vulgar language? How low they had dragged his poor native tongue, the same as his poor, barbarized native land!

Their land, theirs. Not his. *It's the country that was ours, but now it belongs to nobody* . . . That is what he might reply to Christa, but if he told her the story of the letter that Cioran sent from Paris to a friend in Romania and how everybody who read it ended up in prison, he would just add more grist to the mill of her worries. And how could Christa understand such things? How, for example, could she understand that although they mangle the language in such a vulgar fashion, he is drawn like a magnet to wherever he can hear it? He makes a beeline to those sounds, which come from somewhere deep within him and instantly turn the world into something captivating and clear. What is that language and why do I understand it so well? Why do I suddenly relax when I hear it? Could that language be my true native land?

But he would at least see the smoke from the hearths of his native land before he died . . .

Might Homer and Christa know him better than he knows himself?

*

—No matter how long you have lived here, your country will always be the one you left! It's still your country, even if you never see it again, which would be advisable! You know it yourself, even if you contradict me, even if you say nothing. But after all these years we have been together, I can guess what lies beneath your silences . . .

Can she really guess what lies beneath his silence, when he himself would find it hard to say? And would his country forever be that faraway region peopled by mutants? What then was the good of all the years he had worked in his adopted country? What was the good of the awards he had received here, the esteem of his peers, the recognition of the state, the affection of his assistants and students, if by just two words—*your country*—Christa could send him back, exile him to that barbarous and barbarized land? *In the country that was ours and now belongs to nobody*, wrote Cioran to the friend who paid for it with beatings on the soles of his feet and long years in prison.

—Believe what you like, my dear . . . but the people who decorated me just last month, the people who invited me to the Academy think otherwise . . .

His conciliatory tone of voice and the way he looks straight ahead, through the windscreen, without saying a word, are merely the first phase of his obstinacy. Christa knows that in the next phase he might have a choleric outburst, that he might start shouting and waving his arms. But nonetheless she does not give up. She keeps at it:

—You still have time to change your mind, you can say you don't feel well . . .

Christa keeps trying, although she knows that there is now no way to prevent the trip, she keeps trying, in a voice increasingly brittle the older she gets. They are both getting older, but she more quickly than he. Despite her coat of arms and the difference in age between them, despite her aerobics classes and massage sessions, her buttocks have sagged, her breasts and her belly droop like limp, half-empty bags.

Her body grows fuller and fuller, but her gaze is more and more self-confident. Why? Is it merely because she was born in the world over here and thinks she knows its rules much better than he, who, coming from afar, had to learn them laboriously, as if from a textbook? But how far have each of them come to get where they are now? How far has Christa got and how far has he, the outsider, the *Ausländer*, the foreigner, got?

After such thoughts pass through her mind, she feels guilty, as if she were witness to moments of unfaithfulness. She sits up straighter in her seat.

*

—I'm not stopping you from taking this trip! I couldn't even if I tried! But I am warning you that you will regret it . . .

He does not like to see her angry when she is at the wheel of the car, and so he tries to smooth her furrowed brow. Hunched in his seat, he recites:

—*And so now you wish to return to your native land? May you go in peace! But if you knew how much you will suffer / Before you arrive in your own land / You would stay with me, here in this house* . . . Why are you looking at me suspiciously like that? That's what Calypso says, darling, not you! The nymph Calypso! In *The Odyssey. Gods you are malevolent and more jealous than any other creature! / You are merciless toward a goddess who openly / Loved a mortal man and kept him as her companion. / For, I myself saved him from death in the waves / When on a boat shattered by the thunderbolt of great Zeus / He wandered adrift on the wine-dark sea / And all his trusty comrades had drowned. / He alone was brought safely hither from wind and wave. / I received him lovingly and joyfully did regale him. / Even would I have given him undying youth or immortality. / But alas none of the other gods may defy / Zeus the thunderer or try to thwart him! / Let him go whither the god wills to send him!*

*

—That's ancient Greek, isn't it? An insufferable subject! But I don't advise you to start with your eternal *Odyssey* in the place where you're going!

He gives a strained, rueful smile. Why did he have to show off in front of Christa, when he knows she is lacking in all literary sensibility?

—His secret services . . . What do they call him? Ce-o-ces-co? What an impossible name! The man seems just as impossible, by all accounts. But anyway. It doesn't matter what he's called. What matters is that the people there will become even more suspicious if they can't understand what language you're speaking. I'm serious, it's no joke . . .

He says nothing still, staring fixedly at the windscreen. Unseeing, he looks at the sandy hills with their sparse tufts of grass. Yellowish-white dunes of petrified sand with shells embedded in the porous stone, upon which descends violet light. The wine-dark expanse of a sea of long ago. He might avenge himself by continuing to recite: *Pining away he wasted his sweet life and sighed with longing for his native land after he tired of the goddess.* Except that he no longer pines for anything and he cannot imagine his work or his life without Christa, even if she does sometimes nag him so much.

But hasn't he been moody or absent the whole journey?

Inexplicably to her, his voice suddenly softens.

*

—Ancient Greek and Latin were my life belt when I was a teenager! I dreamed of passing my lycée exams and becoming a teacher of Greek and Latin. My poor father—I've never told you about this, darling—forced me to go to the school for priests because you didn't have to pay a fee to get in . . .

—Have you ever told me anything about your life there?

—I'm telling you now . . . I was dead set against going to the Theological Seminary but my poor father dragged me there by force! He thrashed me with his belt. I can remember it even now. I couldn't sit down for a week!

—How barbarous!

—But you see, in the end, it did me more good than if I had stayed at home and worked in the fields. My father dragged me there to enroll me, and I wept in desperation all the way to the station. He didn't have the money for lycée fees, but nor did I have any vocation to be a priest. I never resigned myself to the life the Seminary had in store for me. And at the age of sixteen and seventeen, my favorite reading was *The Odyssey*. I knew it by heart and as you can see I still know it . . . Before I finished seminary school, I passed the lycée exams, I had saved up the money by giving private lessons to a schoolmate, Anton Dobrotă, whose parents were wealthy and who was only interested in getting up to mischief. At the lycée I was awarded a scholarship, but once I got in, I did a 180-degree turn, to biology, physics and chemistry . . .

*

What a torrent of words! What has got into him? His reactions never cease to amaze her, such as his tender understanding towards the father who humiliated and beat him. A brilliant mind wrapped up in an archaic attitude . . . And obviously that mind is now completely focused on this pointless journey, on that barbarous land, a place whither she has no desire to accompany him. But at least his talking keeps him awake: it will take another two hours to get to Rome . . .

With a determined gesture, Christa rolls up the window and turns on the air conditioning. She will leave it on while she fills the car with petrol and they drink an espresso in a bar.

And Traian looks impatiently out of the window. In five minutes they will stop at a petrol station, at a tourist market. An espresso, a *té freddo*, and young women with breasts jiggling under their t-shirts.

CHAPTER THREE
The Visit to Our Academician

HE YANKED THE cord a few times, but as the drape would not budge, he grasped a fold of thick damask at random and tugged, his hand clenched in a claw. The drape still refused to glide along the rail at the top, and he found himself clasping one of the dusty tassels between his painfully stiff arthritic fingers.

Just as he was about to toss the tassel aside, he recalled that the other man was watching his annoyance and smiling, and so he carefully placed it on the dark wood of the windowsill.

—Like I told you, comrade academician, there's no need to bother yourself! I don't need no more light. I can see! My eyes is still quite good! (*He chortles*) Don't you think there's some moron who goes round turning the electricity off where we are, too? When we found ourselves twiddling our thumbs because all the equipment had gone off, they dragged him in front of me! A chucklehead! He says that every morning between ten and two he has orders from above to turn off the electricity, to economize all over the city, because it's all part of the same network, and even if we were God, he couldn't turn it back on just for us! Nothing you can do about it my ass! Get out! I told him. I made a meal of him, I can tell you . . .

The man was chattering away, puffing himself up. The joviality of a cunning scoundrel. In vain had he told him he had a meeting at the Institute; in vain had he looked up at the clock twice. The other man was sprawled on the couch, his briefcase between his legs, his glass always empty. He moved to refill his glass, but when he stretched the crooked fingers of his small hand towards the crystal decanter, hoping that the other man would make a sign to say he had had enough, the scoundrel grabbed it from him and poured a drink for himself, smiling contentedly.

—Didn't I tell you from the start not to bother yourself and

that I can refill my own glass? Pour, pour, brother, ha-ha!* he
brayed. No ice. You know I've got problems with me throat . . .
The ice cubes were already floating in melted water on the
tray: he had shown up more than an hour ago, unexpectedly, as
was their wont, they popped up out of nowhere and when they
decided to vanish, they also took you by surprise, without fail.
Until then, he helps himself to your booze and when he thinks
you are not looking, he quickly casts his eyes around your room.

They have been stalking each other for years and every match
they have played has ended in a draw. The next time he comes
here to his office, he will try to catch him out again. But with
what? What could the likes of him possibly understand from
foreign journals and books on biochemistry? When he wants to
show off, his type slips in a word or two of Russian. He doesn't
have the courage to open his mouth in any other foreign language. How then, you might ask yourself, does he do the job he
does? How has he forged a career for himself? Simple: he was
head of the Department of Security and the Madman's Guard!
He keeps going on about having a Degree in History, but he has
winkled out that he took his diploma at the age of forty, and
how! He took it when he was head of the whole region and the
lycée headmasters came crawling to him on their knees!

Might he be unhappy about something in his report? He
holds the page in his left hand, at a large distance from his eyes.
He keeps sipping from the glass in his right hand. He grips the
briefcase between his knees.

* In Romanian: toarnă, toarnă, frate (pour, pour, brother), with a punning allusion to torna, torna, fratre (turn, turn, brother), supposedly the earliest recorded
instance of the Romanian language, the words of a soldier quoted in a Greek
chronicle of the Byzantine period, dating from A.D. 587 A.D. The words in
question are in fact Vulgar Latin, the lingua franca of the Roman Empire. The
earliest known document in Romanian dates from almost one thousand years
later (1521). The claim that torna, torna, fratre is Romanian is a typical example
of "protochronism," the nationalist pseudo-scholarship of the Ceauşescu period
(and afterwards), which aimed to prove the historical anteriority of the Romanian
people (extreme protochronism goes so far as to claim that the Romanians, or
rather Dacians, invented writing, the wheel, philosophy, etc.). There is also a pun
here on the slang meaning of the verb a turna (to pour, to cast [metal]) during
the Communist period; i.e., to inform on or denounce somebody.

Is he frowning because he is reading without his glasses or because something he has written has put him out of sorts?

*

4 March 1986

REPORT

On the occasion of the visit I made to Italy between 19 January and 21 February 1986, at the invitation of the universities of Rome and Milan, I also had the opportunity to meet some Romanian fugitives living in that country. Returning to Rome from Milan on 9 February 1986, it was proposed to me by comrade Minister Constantin Pleja that I should pay a visit to the European Institute for Research into the Mediterranean Environment in Naples, headed by MANU TRAIAN, given that we had studied at the same university in our youth. Comrade Pleja wanted to determine whether TRAIAN MANU enjoys a good reputation among western researchers. I accepted, happy to be able to visit that institute and laboratory about which I had heard so much in specialist publications.

In joint agreement with comrade lieutenant Matei Silviu, I sent MANU a telegram, asking him whether he had anything against my visiting him in Naples. By telegram I received his affirmative response, and so on 13 February of the year in progress we had the meeting. Of course, in order not to be suspected of talking to a representative of our regime, MANU TRAIAN preferred that we talk in Italian, as one of his assistants was present the whole time. But one evening we were able to talk for around 2 hours, during which time he told me about his usually very busy working schedule.

He has been able to conduct recent research in
partnership with SCHMIDT HEINRICH, the director of
a similar European Institute in Hamburg, an important specialist. As I laid out in the detailed
report submitted in accordance with regulations to
lieutenant Matei Silviu, TRAIAN MANU would be an
important acquisition to the benefit of our cause.

"EMILIAN"

*

His thin lips had become pursed while he was reading, but as he
laid the page to one side, his face brightened. The deceptively
easygoing smile that bared a disquieting gap in his broad front
teeth.

—You took your time about it, didn't you, comrade academician! A whole month is a bit much, isn't it? A whole month
in Italy! No, don't take it like that, I didn't mean you were having fun! Who could know better than me that you were there
on business? But what about the Institute? What about the
Academy? Did everything go smoothly while you were gone or
when you got back did you have to take your broom and bat
away the fat rats that had climbed up on the table? A broom, I
say? A machine-gun more like! You had to turn the cannon on
them, didn't you? There, you see, we know more than you think!
When they celebrated your sixtieth birthday, I wish I'd had a
dollar for every one of the thousands of people who praised you
while wishing you ill! They was sniffing around our department
to see whether there was any heads to be chopped, 'cause even
the Comrade himself said that in this country there's nobody
that's not replaceable! Get out of here, you jackals! I gave them
jackals a boot in the teeth like you've never seen! Well, we put
our shoulders to the wheel too when need be! That troublemaker
Matei, your contact, told me, he's not daft, even if he's still green
behind the ears, as the saying goes: comrade colonel, what are
them curs working on our academician for? We support you and

I think you won't take it amiss if I tell you all this bluntly, out of friendship, if you'll permit me, comrade academician!

—It's a comfort to me to know that I have the Institute's support! That is, trustworthy people who recognize my worth and my devotion! Even friendship, as you yourself said . . .

Friendship with Satan in person! Who looks like an easygoing accountant, with his round little paunch under his *first-class* grey civilian suit from the APACA factory, with his pale blond curly hair. It's obvious that he doesn't go out in the field anymore, that he doesn't roam the wilderness when the Madman goes on his hunting trips! An accountant at the collective farm in his native village: that's what would have become of him, if he hadn't ended up fighting the Legionnaires in the mountains when he was doing his national service; he made mincemeat of them and after that he rose through the ranks like he had a rocket in the seat of his pants. Might it have been a warning when he alluded to his enemies in the Institute, to those bastard chirpers who gave him a dressing down at the general meeting?

—The problem would be that it didn't all come out like we'd planned, growls the visitor. I got the other report, I saw that your Italian counterparts didn't make you an offer, as yet I haven't got the conclusions, they're in the pipeline, but I wouldn't say that it intoxicated us. I'm not completely ignorant, I've read books, I've heard what other people have to say, I haven't passed through life like a suitcase through the train station. You yourself, comrade academician, confirmed that last time you sensed their people were hovering ready to recruit you, that's why I briefed you. I won't hasten to say that it was a waste of time, there are other days in the year and that bunch are desperate to bag us . . . But I wouldn't rule out that there's a traitor, you yourself pointed out that there might be leaks somewhere. Besides the pleasure of having a chat over a Johnny Walker, which is why I came over, we can talk differently here, but do you mind, comrade academician, if I light up a cigarette?

—Not at all, not at all . . . Just let me open the window a crack.

—Doesn't bother me, go ahead, I've got me sheepskin coat, but you're a bit delicate.

*

He let it slip out, while he was waving the packet of Dunhill under his nose, so that you would know what to bring him the next time. Each sentence uttered by a man so two-faced had to be interpreted like it was a pronouncement of the Pythian oracle! Pathological secrecy at war with vanity, to make you believe you're at their mercy! And besides anything else, these unseasonal early March days depress him.

If you look, as he is doing now, at the anemic tongues of snow that fell overnight on the flowerbeds in the garden, where all that remain are the blackened stumps of the soggy-thorned rose bushes, you might well think it were November or January. Denuded of leaves, the linden is outlined stark and black against a leaden sky that is as dirty as the façade of the building opposite. On the pavement, the wind has arranged the fine dust in strange figures, like seawater ebbing from the sand.

The intense blue of the Mediterranean is still fresh in his memory . . .

—You say you met a few of them Romanian fugitives that denigrate our country and you had a look at this . . . this Manu Traian. Did you really get the impression he's a big wheel over there, to make it worth our while doing something with him? I had the files section check him out, asking them to gather all the information on what's known about him, but they reported back to me that they haven't got anything on him!

The colonel had waited for him to close the window before getting to the point at last. And when the academician went to fill his glass he put his hand on top of it and uttered his classic *uh-hic!* Codename "Emilian" quickly answered, in the hope of finally getting rid of his visitor:

—Ah! Categorically! Categorically, comrade Ispas! Comrade colonel! The very position that Traian Manu holds gives us sufficient information about the high-level connections he has! And as I said in the detailed report I submitted to the embassy, Traian

Manu needs to be exploited at all cost! At all cost! I insist on reading you the reference sheet right now! —You insist because you want to get rid of me! Well, all right, I'm listening.

*

4 March 1986

Reference: Traian Manu

A meritorious researcher, MANU TRAIAN stood out as a student thanks to his remarkable intelligence, particularly his thorough training in chemistry, he demonstrated great skill in biology and the natural sciences, but also in Latin and Greek. He took courses at the University of Bucharest in both departments, Natural Sciences and Classics, at the same time as when I was a student, which is how we met, and we continued to be acquainted when studying abroad, in Montpellier. Upstanding. Self-effacing. An excellent fellow student, jovial, communicative, obliging. Highly discreet in his political attitudes. He refused to return to Romania after the war, for which reason his citizenship was revoked. Over the last decade he has made a name for himself among French and Italian biologists, who have entrusted him with important missions. He also carries out important missions for UNESCO.

I have undertaken extensive explanatory work with him in order to persuade him to agree to enter into relations with the Romanian authorities and to agree to visit our country, although the invitation will come not from us but from the German Cultural Center.

"EMILIAN"

*

—What connections does he have over here?

—He claims that he hasn't had any connections for the last thirty years.

—On the other hand, he's in with that vipers' nest at Radio Free Europe! Don't you try and deny it!

—From what I've been able to deduce, he frequents scientific circles and even high official circles . . . But naturally, like other people of his generation, he also has connections with hostile émigré circles. He tried to avoid the subject, but I wouldn't let it go . . .

—What about his citizenship? Under what circumstances was it revoked?

—Unlike me, he refused to come back after the war.

—He's dyed in the wool, venomous, reactionary, isn't he?

—How should I know? True, I found him reticent, wary.

—If you didn't find a chance to talk to him privately, I'd say there's no real hope that his coming here will achieve anything. Now he has the brass-faced nerve to bare his fangs openly! Tomorrow, without fail, he will go to the Chancellery of the Central Committee, to the Bureau of Research and Information, and file his own reports, as a way of making sure they will counterbalance this scoundrel's report: God knows what observations the colonel will make in the margins of his briefings! But in the meantime, the academician quickly answers:

—It was just a preliminary interview, comrade colonel! Despite Traian Manu's wariness, the mission was accomplished. On the first evening I heard his assistant asking for the day off. And so the next day I turned up unannounced. I told Traian Manu that I had been in the area, that I wanted to visit some museums and needed his advice . . .

—Hogwash! And? Did he take the bait? It says something about an invitation in the report. Is he coming or isn't he?

—I undertook extensive explanatory work with him in order to persuade him to accept the invitation to visit. I reminded him of shared experiences in our youth, he began to relax and open up. The argument was that it was the German Cultural Center rather than we who were inviting him. Come on, Traian, I said, stop being more Catholic than the Pope! Don't you trust your own people?

—But does he trust you?

—He ended up telling me (*he laughs*) that he had read some of the articles I had published, that he sometimes reads the Romanian press. And he put his arm around my shoulders and whispered that I shouldn't dabble in politics. (*Haughtily*) I replied that I write as a committed scientist . . .

—Next time, tell me what's new at the Academy! Oh, I almost forget. Take your hard currency expenses claim to the cashier's office!

*

—You look a bit downcast, Daddy! That man wore you out. Who is he? If you'd stepped out of the office and told me, I'd have got him to leave . . . Why did you open the window again? The radiators don't work as it is . . .

—Teodora, be so good as to tell the chauffeur to have the car ready in a quarter of an hour. In ten minutes! And leave the window open, darling! To get the smell of that scoundrel out of the room!

CHAPTER FOUR
The House Where We All Used to Be Cold

—NOBODY UNDERSTANDS BETTER than I do your nostalgia for that place, that is, for childhood . . . You would give anything to wake up and find yourself back in those years when your parents were alive, even if they sometimes forced you to travel a different road than the one you would have wanted . . . But all the same, they were the ones who bore life's hardships . . .

And what about her? What is she doing here, seven years later? Why has she come down the old road, like a somnambulist, the road from school to her old house? Why is she reaching out her hand to the freshly plastered wall on which no trace of the old doorbell can now be seen, and why is she waiting for her father or her mother or Klara or Walter to open the door and for the strains of a piano and a violin to pour onto Hauptstraße from the salon, where the fire is lit because today it is the musical soirée?

—But to expose yourself to risk, like you are doing, and to be burdened by so many emotions! For what? You can't go back to a place hoping that you will go back in time, believe me, darling! What you want to find again exists nowhere except in your own mind.

The red, green, white flash as the bicycle speeds past, red and white corollas, Japanese cherry trees, magnolias, fruit trees blossoming in the gardens, and now she pedals without haste, because it is too beautiful outside to be in a hurry. From the bridge she sees the green Rhine, stretching into the distance, the white foam rising above the locks, the white trees in blossom on the green hills, she hears the cathedral bell.

Even blindfolded she would still know the way from school to the house on Hauptstraße.

*

—Do you remember when you came to my little hometown for the first time? I waited for you at the station and we walked the streets. When we sat down outside, in the courtyard of a café on Hauptstraße, you were amazed when I told you that I had been born in that building. I showed you the window of my old bedroom and told you about how seven years after we moved from there to the edge of town, on Bergstraße, I went from school on my bicycle, like a somnambulist, to our old house on Hauptstraße . . .

And why does she still reach out her hand to the doorbell that was ripped from the wall years ago, leaving a hole that has been filled in and plastered over, to the door by which they all used to enter and leave, but which is now locked and unlocked by strangers' hands?

What is she doing there, twenty years later?

—I was cold in that house throughout my childhood! It was too costly to heat those large rooms with their very high ceilings. Except when there were musical soirées and on holidays, in winter they used to light the fire only in the living room where we all sat. Father had refused to join the National Socialists and his salary as a lawyer now barely covered our school fees, Klara and Hermann's engagement . . .

Her father's hand, gripping the handle of the cafetière as he carefully pours a slender stream of brown liquid.

—Add as much milk as you like today, Christa! The prince has sent us two bottles as a present.

The five porcelain cups placed at equal distances next to the thin slice of moistened bread.

—Don't waste a single crumb, children! Be thrifty!

Walter's patched boot touches her patched boot under the table, yesterday morning they drew on the flagstones in the courtyard with colored chalk, they drew defecating bottoms, how upset Mother was when she saw it! But tomorrow the fires will be lit throughout the house, because it is Saturday and there will be a musical soirée . . .

—When I went to our old house on my bicycle that time,

Father was away at the front. Mother's depression had grown worse. Maybe I wanted to go back to a time years before, when our only problems were shortages and poverty. Or maybe I had not yet grown used to living in Bergstraße and I felt embarrassed in front of the other girls, who knew that I had to come all the way from the edge of town on my bicycle. Anyway, when I found myself there, stretching my hand towards the doorbell that had not existed for years, it was difficult even for me to explain why I had come.

Why is she standing in the street and gazing in puzzlement at the window that the plane tree used to touch with its branches? How well she knows the hourly progress of the shadow cast by the leafy branches, which in late April bathes each corner of her room in turn . . . When she opens the window, the leafy branches enter her room with a green, melodious scent, with a golden, velvety light *Sonate für Klavier und Violine nr. 1, G-dur, op. 78 vom Johannes Brahms*, she closes the piano lid, she goes to the window and gazes as if asleep at the white trees in blossom on the green hills, until the sun sets behind them and they turn yellow, red, black.

*

—After much hesitation my parents decided to sell the house on Hauptstraße, which had been in the family for generations, and to move to a smaller house, at the edge of town, on Bergstraße. It was something common at the time. After defeat in the war came the depression. Old properties, even castles, were being sold all the time. The stationery shop next door belonged to a prince who had ended up serving the customers himself and who sometimes used to give us bottles of milk. One day he closed up shop, he sold it and moved to Switzerland. He was a gentleman, but very prudent. He sensed what was coming and did not want to endure another war . . . After my parents sold our house, the new owner, a man who had got rich from the war, began to renovate it: he tore down the inside walls, he moved the doors, he installed white cake-shop furniture, and he turned our garden into a courtyard, where people ate ice cream in summer. He chopped down the trees, but the plane tree in front of my window survived.

Why was she looking in bewilderment at their former garden, now full of ladies with children, the crystal glasses and silver teaspoons glint in the sunlight and seated at stylish white tables they guzzle down huge portions of ice cream with golden sponge fingers protruding from mounds of whipped cream, unaware, just as she, who is looking at them with envy, is unaware that three months later the bombing raids will begin?

—The new owner, the proprietor of the cake shop, was lucky. As if by miracle, the house on Hauptstraße escaped the bombing unscathed, unlike the house on Bergstraße, where she lived with her mother and Klara. A bomb blast shattered the windows and tore the front door off. The other house is still a cake shop to this day, although it has changed hands many times.

What else can you do but take your bicycle, which you have leaned against the alien wall, and slowly, as if in your sleep, ride along Haupstraße, looking neither left nor right, looking straight ahead? What do you see there? Nothing but an immense chocolate egg, covered in a multicolored red and white and pistachio glaze, adorned with pink ribbons and crowned with a chocolate Easter bunny, in the window of the cake shop that used to be our house. For, it is only a week until Easter and just three weeks until the bombing raids.

—It must have been almost a year after Father was called up. I remember the envelope. It was a dirty yellow color and changed the atmosphere at home. I remember how Walter and I went with him to the station. You received permission to take the day off school if a family member was leaving for the front. Only the three of us went, because Mother was taken ill just as we were going out of the door, and we left her at home . . .

And so every Easter thereafter you will be the only one left to see the huge chocolate egg among the marzipan bunnies in the window of the cake shop in your old house, where you were all so cold together. And perhaps your arguments of late were the arguments of maddened creatures that had a presentiment

they were about to die. Mother and Klara were to die in the
bombing. Walter was to die near Berlin, without knowing why
he was so frenzied, without managing to throw at any tank the
grenade he gripped in his narrow, sweating hand. But you will
never find out exactly how and exactly when Walter died. You
will never know whether your father was executed as a deserter
or whether he died in a Siberian mine, a vile-smelling skeleton
with gangrened hands and feet. His exhausted footsteps, falter-
ing through the snow, the excrement, the blood, the barbed
wire . . . Father . . . The warmth of his large, protective body
as he carried you sleeping in his arms, the creak of the snow
beneath Father's heavy footsteps.

*

We are different people and we are living a different life,
Hermann used to say when she tried to make him tell the story.
He avoided his memories of the Ukraine, of the executions of
the local Jews by the Einsatzgruppe, which he, like others in the
Wehrmacht, had witnessed. Perhaps he had sometimes even lent
them a helping hand? Had he his own nightmares to forget, the
out-of-date tins of food, the diarrhea and the inhuman cold of
the trenches at Stalingrad, which he sometimes remembered,
the tooth-and-claw battles for a place in the trucks during the
retreat, in the midst of a crowd of soldiers reduced to savages,
the leg amputated at the knee in the hospital car of the train that
missed by just two days the coup d'état the English engineered
with Russian connivance in Bucharest? Had he swallowed his
memories, the same as she had swallowed hers? Or did they not
have enough years of living together to make the memories lose
their sharp edge in the telling, to make them cease to ache?

    And if not even Hermann had been able to tell her every-
thing, absolutely everything, why then does she strive to tell
Traian, who is dozing, his mind elsewhere, his eyes on the
motorway?

    —This road is getting to be too long for how old we are.
There's not long to go and I wouldn't like to fall asleep at the

wheel having come this far. But try to stay awake, will you? In two hours we will be at our hotel having dinner, I promise. Unless I take the wrong exit, of course . . .

Through the car windows, the same monotonous, endless motorway. The man and woman dressed in black pass through the blindingly white sunlight: two eternally frozen, solemn silhouettes. They are the same as when he arrived here, but Lord, how the country has changed! He has lived here long enough to remember what that country, his new country, was like when he first arrived . . . *Cristo si è fermato a Eboli.* Back then, before the war, Christ had stopped at Eboli, but then he had gone on his way . . . Where were the marshes, where were the mosquitoes, the landed properties and the malaria? Look, yards with two automobiles, orange and olive groves where once there were rushes, carefully tended fields . . .

He delights in them, because now it is his country, but why is Christa so gloomy? She is lost in her memories, which is what always happens when she leaves the motorway and misses the exit into town.

CHAPTER FIVE
Nobody Will Ever Hear His Story

—So you see, I know too what the lure of the past means. But sleepwalking your way to somebody else's house makes you ridiculous, whereas a journey to a land at the ends of the earth . . .

—The ends of the earth! Don't exaggerate! It's a two-hour flight away, that's all! You can come and see for yourself. We'll phone from the hotel to book another ticket.

—It's not the ticket that's the problem, my dear! And nor the distance on the map! The problem is the country itself, which isn't like anything in our world here. And I am prepared to accept a lot of things for your sake, but not that. Wasn't that how I grew up, listening to my parents whispering about which of the people who crossed our threshold that day might denounce us the next day?

Calmly wheel your bicycle away, you have nothing to see here except the reflections of the same SS uniforms in the same familiar shop windows, go without fear, you have nothing to hear except the rhythmic tread of the boots, the clicking heels, the curt shout, the car with the loudspeakers has turned the corner, a white glove directs the surging crowd on the pavement towards which you wheel your bicycle, pretend you don't notice the civilian standing by the window of the cake shop holding his hands behind his back, push your bicycle towards the place indicated, quickly now, hurry, hurry . . .

—At the time, few thought that the war was a venture that would turn out badly for us. And ever since I was little I had been taught not to join in such discussions. But after the trial of Dr. Geiger, one of my father's friends, whom a client had denounced for not believing in Germany's victory, it became a real obsession for me. If I opened my mouth at school or in the shelter, for hours on end I would chide myself for imagined inadvertencies. I would go over all the people who had been around me at the time: had they been trying to provoke me? Which of them was trustworthy, which not?

It is nothing but the usual silence, the deafening rumble of the open-topped armored cars approaching: can you feel the trepidation in the air, on the asphalt, can you see our eyes greedily straining? Where is he? Where is he? Where is he?

The Führer! The Leader!

And our hands lifting up, hastening to uncover our heads, and our mouths opening wide, to acclaim him . . .

*

—We had already moved to the house on Bergstraße when Dr. Aloys Geiger was arrested. Father lost the trial at which he defended him and very soon thereafter he was called up. Maybe they wouldn't have sent him to the front so quickly if he had not been Dr. Geiger's lawyer. If he had judged it coolly, Father would have seen that Dr. Geiger would not be able to help him, but that he could do him harm, and us too. Poor Mother warned him . . .

—The same as you are warning me now, my dear?

—If that was meant to be a joke, I don't think now is the time. And if you were being serious, then don't worry: I don't have the gift of prophecy. Mother, on the other hand, was a real Cassandra. When we went with Father to the station, Mother took ill before we even left the house. She told him that he would never be coming back, and that was indeed the last time we ever saw him. We received a single letter from him . . .

Do you see the motionless faces of the policemen, the informers, the black-market profiteers? The bloated faces of the ones who just two years ago ate nothing but potatoes, who went down into the shelters daily? Do you see our faces light up, our faces thrown together pell-mell, one on top of the other, do you see our eyes glittering with fanaticism, with indifference, with hatred, do you hear the throbbing of the blood in our dry palms, palms ready to clap together deafeningly? Do you feel the trepidation in the air, on the asphalt, do you hear the deafening rumble of the motorcycles, do you see our eyes sliding greedily over the gleam of the helmets, the muzzles of the machine-guns, where is he, where is he, where is the Führer, the Leader? And our mouths opening wide to acclaim him . . .

*

—But it's not easy living with a Cassandra! Given her constant sense of foreboding, Mother was anxious and depressed, she always had a migraine, a heart tremor, she was always tired. My grandparents raised us both. They were methodical, strict, outdoor types, but the same upbringing does not produce the same results. I regained my equilibrium with them, after all the misfortunes, but rather than shaping her, Catholic home education had taught my mother to withdraw into herself. She was frightened by the thrift required of her at home, she was frightened by the rallies. But you should have seen how full of life her girlfriends from childhood were, fervent National Socialists one and all! They all had seven or eight children, but they never complained. The only time they ever wept was when they heard the Führer's voice on the radio amid the cheering of the crowds. You'll probably see the same thing in your own country when you go back, but don't force me to go through the horror of it again!

Although she is just an absentminded schoolgirl, she knows who the guilty man is, she waits for him to pass, she stands on a corner of the crowded street, surrounded by the motionless faces, guarded by the machine-guns, she hates him, she waits for him to pass. She hates herself, the knot of feeling that bobs up in her throat only because the air is throbbing with cheers, with hurrahs, the asphalt is throbbing beneath the heavy wheels, nownownownownownow, there he is! He is standing in the open-topped car. He salutes, motionless, his arm outstretched. The little face, His gaunt face, which she knows from all the billboards, from all the newsreels, is as familiar to her as Walter's, as Klara's, she rejoices to recognize that little, twitching, tic-ridden face, and she tries to glimpse His paralyzed arm. His voice, shouting amid the applause, is as familiar to her as the voices of those she sees every morning around the oval table, sitting in front of the four, in front of the three cups of tea and equal slices of moistened bread.

—The same as happens when somebody close to you dies and you discover that you could have behaved better, but now it is too late to change anything, I later chided myself for my selfishness, for my outbursts of nerves, for my betrayals. When she received no news from Father, Mother abandoned every last restraint regarding both herself and us. It makes me feel genuinely ill to remember how towards the end, after she let herself get fat and completely neglected herself, I used to try to avoid the albeit rare occasions when we could go out together. The mothers of the other girls at school were well kempt, elegant, even though the period of shortages had begun, and I was ashamed to be seen with her. Now I have passed the age she was when she died, but the more I try to understand her the more foreign she is to me . . .

She would not recognize her face, terrified that it might burst into angry tears, if she caught sight of it in the window of the cake shop on Hauptstraße as she watched the open-topped car, with its motorcycle outriders, and she chokes back her hysterical tears, those huge distorting lenses that cloud her sight. The war profiteers, the provocateurs, the fanatics, the orphans, the grieving parents, the merry widows, all of them, all of us watch the armored car move into the distance, followed by our desperate cheers, racing to catch up with it.

*

Her hands clench the steering wheel. In the car it is now cold, because, pretending not to notice the look of dissatisfaction on his face, she has closed the window and turned on the air conditioning.

—When he agreed to act as Dr. Geiger's defense lawyer, Father naïvely placed his hopes in Karl Syck, with whom he had been at university. You know whom I am talking about, don't you? You've heard other people mention his name, haven't you?

—Karl Syck? Yes, it sounds . . .

Christa is the only person he has heard mention the name. He has heard it in her stories so many times! But he always lets her recount the same memories, although he is not at all sure it does her any good to rake them up. Before him, she must have recounted them to Hermann, without ever coming to the end of them, because Hermann probably was quick to console her. Or perhaps she did not even need to recount them to Hermann, because he knew them from when he was engaged to her sister Klara?

This is something Christa has always avoided telling him about, and nor will he ever ask her: how she came to marry Hermann after her sister's death.

*

With her hands clenching the wheel, Christa delays checking to see whether he has dozed off again. As long as she is talking, sleep, which is contagious, like a disease, like fear, will not be able to lay hold of her.

—You don't remember because you never pay any attention to what I say . . . Karl Syck was the head of the military justice system. He didn't risk his skin for Father, but during the Conspiracy he still made a mistake, for which he paid dearly. At least there is no way you cannot know about the Conspiracy: it's in the history books! Clear heads realized the war was lost and thought about saving Germany. Romania and Hungary, not to mention Italy, were doing the same, weren't they? They were all trying to negotiate with the Allies . . .

Inexplicable confused animal, let it go, forget it! You were just an absentminded schoolgirl and one April morning history passed by, an open-topped car carrying an animal sick with cheers and blood, let it go, forget it! Forget that you encountered the armored car on Hauptstraße, escorted by high-ranking SS men, the car in which He saluted, his arm stiffly outstretched, and your eyes filled with tears.

It is your little humiliation, ours, a shame that will be borne by the descendants of our descendants: how many generations will pass before they forgive, before they understand? Better you forget it and stop wondering why you went from school to the old house, you went to forget all the years when we did not exist, when we did not live our lives . . .

*

He looks out of the window without saying a word.

Does Christa really remember what happened forty years ago or does she remember merely the order in which she has to retell the same episodes in the same words? And the emotion that is automatically released by those words, like saliva released by trained animals.

The endless motorway cut in two by the little hedge of oleanders, laden with white, pink, red flowers. The forested hills climbing into the sky, the white splotches of the villages, perched for thousands, for hundreds of years next to their wells. A blindingly white village, through which advance two solemn black figures, a man and a woman in black.

Does she see them?

Does she remember them?

What was I doing then? Where was I? Was I here? On the Other Side?

The light rises above the white, gnarled, petrified tree trunks, growing from the red earth. Stunted olive trees with knotty trunks, five hundred years old: Dante's forest. The field parceled into rhombuses, the same as in the time of the Gracchi. And receding into the distance, the silhouette of a man riding a donkey, with two huge wicker baskets on either side: to him it is so familiar, because it comes from his past here. In his adopted country.

What was he doing in the years she is recounting? How did he, a man without citizenship, a man without a country, come to be the respected, award-winning professor of today? What is Christa saying? Why, after the disaster suffered by Germany, is she talking about him yet again?

—I don't deny the hardships you must have endured in coming here, although you have never told me about them . . . But I can imagine it wasn't easy for you without your parents, without your siblings, unlike for me. Although at least you had the consolation they were still alive, even if they were far away and your letters didn't reach them . . . And I'm sorry, but even if your parents had been with you, you wouldn't have been able to save them from old age, from the inevitable end. On the other hand, here you have lived in a much more civilized setting than your own country could have given you, you have been able to go much farther in your career . . .

Had it been easy for him? Captive in a foreign land, terrified by the war and summoned to return home so he could be sent to the front, determined not to obey the conscription order, his scholarship cancelled, spending every day from morning till evening in the library, spreading his only suit, increasingly thin in the elbows, under the mattress to press it, eating once a day if he was lucky, a deserter with an appointment at the Court Martial, at the front line, a refugee . . .

More and more benumbed, he dozes in the passenger seat, catching fleeting glimpses of a blurry photograph that dissolves into befuddlement and sleep when he tries to grasp it. And just the words:

insecurity   *fear*   *loneliness*   *hunger*

Neither she nor anybody else will ever hear his story, either whole, from beginning to end, or fragmented, convoluted, complicated, the way Christa always tells a story. Because after an entire lifetime spent among strangers, he knows something that she will never learn.

He knows how to be silent.

Past the car windows glide frail olive trees and their foliage flashes whitish, the same as the foliage of the willow tree, left behind how many years ago? And ever deeper in slumber, once again he mistakes the trunks of the olive trees for the plum trees of childhood.

CHAPTER SIX
Christa's Letters

—Despite your bookish appearance, you have a hankering for adventure, my dear. I said adventure, but I didn't mean the amatory kind. Yes! I can assure you that you do. Don't deny it! It's not enough for you that you expose yourself to pointless risk, you want to expose me too, because you haven't got a clue what that kind of world means! I'm not saying you've had an easy life, but unlike me, you didn't find yourself violently yanked out of childhood and made head of the family overnight!

Hermann, leaning far out of the window of the train carriage to tell Klara one thing more, his blue eyes that remain fixed on Klara's tearful eyes, *I will wait for you, how can you doubt it?* whispers Klara, Hermann's ruffled hair has reddish glints in the afternoon sunlight, but you no longer hear their whispers, they are drowned out by the soldiers' songs and you have a lump in your throat. You don't even have the right to cry. It is not you who are the fiancée of the man who is going away! You are just a little girl, his scrawny sister-in-law, all you can do is crumple in your sweating palm the handkerchief that you will wave as soon as the train starts to move, maybe when the platform starts to glide beneath his eyes Hermann will notice you at last and divine what you wish to tell him. I will wait for you too, you can be sure of me! Walter's hand on your shoulder, I'm bored, Christa, let's go home already, why do you keep waving that handkerchief, can't you see he's not even looking at you?

*

Traian sits up straight in the passenger seat, he unbuckles his seatbelt, he leans forward awkwardly, gropes for the bottle of *té freddo* at his feet, takes a few gulps, refastens his seatbelt, swivels his stiff neck from side to side, and remains silent. Christa too

remains silent for a while: she has tumbled inside the barrel of
memories again or else she is baffled by the lack of any reaction
on his part. When she starts talking again, Christa's voice has
grown smaller.

—I even had to take care of the letter writing! I was the only
one who continued to write to Father, even though it had been
ten months since any letter from him had arrived. Naturally, I
didn't write to him all I would have liked. When he left, Father
himself told us that in wartime letters are read and censored . . .

*Dear Father, the news of the week is that Walter has joined the
Hitlerjugend.*

That was all! Even if the letter had not been addressed
to Obersturmführer Ralf Döring, lost in the snowdrifts of
Stalingrad, whence our army sent triumphant bulletins, but to
lawyer Ralf Döring, away on some court case or other, she would
not have told him how she had rummaged through the entire
attic looking for Walter's diary! Nor is she going to tell Traian
that she was dying of curiosity to find out why Walter used to
get up an hour before she did and tiptoe up into the attic. She
is not going to tell what she found there, under the piles of her
father's treatises on criminal law: badges and pamphlets about
the Hitlerjugend, portraits of the Führer and a leather-bound
diary, which Walter had been given for his fifteenth birthday.
How was it that it fell open at the very page on which he wrote
about her?

*

*If somebody were to take a closer look at Christa's nose and freckles,
she would be sent to a KL for sure, Christa is also hypocritical by
nature, grasping, like a Jewess, but in any case I am going to escape
from this shameful matriarchal regime, because Horst and I are
going to go and defend Germany from Bolshevism and world Jewry.
And Klara, who is of the Aryan physical type, ought to be interned
in a Lebensborn to free her from the unwholesome atmosphere in
our house.*

A pity that she straightaway went and told on him:

—Look, Granma, look at what Walter has written about me! And look what he says about Klara!

Even now, forty years later, she still regrets not having seen all the things smoldering in Walter's head after he ganged up with Horst, the eldest son of the Gauleiter.

—What nonsense!

Her grandmother took the notebook, which was written in different hands and different colored inks (how many different personalities did Walter harbor?) and threw it in the stove. Then she put on her woodcutting gloves, poured paraffin on the notebook, covered it with coals, and lit the match. She squatted in front of the stove until the blaze dwindled into smaller and smaller tongues of flame, which, with a final crackle, like a hiccough, then vanished beneath the heap of blackened pages. The leather binding and cheap coal left a flatulent stench in the salon, since it was too frosty outside to leave the window open for long.

If her father had come back then, she would have accused Walter of being insufferable and of always starting the nasty arguments they had evening after evening:

—Tell me what you have done with my diary! You took it! Admit it! You went up into the attic, when Horst called me outside to go to the campfire!

Never would she have confessed to him that she too, red in the face with fury, used to screech:

—Do you think I'd waste my time on your stupidities, you buffoon! Why not take a good look at yourself? Can't you see how ridiculous you are, with your spotty face? I'd like to see what girl will agree to dance with you at the end-of-school ball!

*

—Go after Walter, Mother would whine, lying in bed, when Walter fastened his shiny silver belt buckle, on which was inscribed *God is with us* . . . Don't go, Walter! Tell him not to go, because he will never come back! You're brother and sister, stop bickering with each other like hounds, go after him, make your peace!

Was it just to escape from Mother's shrieks that you raced down the stairs after Walter, who had slammed the door behind him?

—I hate all of you women, yelled Walter, stamping down the stairs, and then he ran all the way to the train packed with Hitlerjugend singing "Heidemarie."

And there you were, hidden behind the tall billboards with the Führer's portrait and the flags with the crooked crosses, whimpering:

—Walter, come back! You heard what Mother said! Come back home!

But you did not dare to be seen, because he had forbidden you to go with him to the station and who knows what nonsense he would have been capable of shouting about your freckled face.

*

—It was spring, Easter fell quite late that year, almost at the summer solstice, which they celebrated with bonfires, with songs . . . I think that was the atmosphere that captivated Walter, and so he joined the Hitlerjugend as soon as Father left for the front and after that it was harder and harder for us to get on with him. Gradually, all the burdens of the household fell on my shoulders. The neighbors were whispering that the front had collapsed, that the Russians were advancing into the Ukraine, that the English and Americans were landing in France, I was in charge of finding food, electricity had begun to be rationed.

Dear Hermann, I am doing the rounds of all the queues in Karstadt, because Klara's pregnancy is not going well, the baby is due in a month and the doctor has advised her not to make any effort. After the first air raid, when the Mosquitos came, our little town got off lightly. Klara didn't want to go down into the shelter, and Mother is depressed, because in our family, who have always been lawyers and whose history is documented all the way back to 1561, Klara is the first unwed mother.

In vain did Mother have the gifts of a Cassandra, because she could not foresee that our family archives were to burn three weeks later, in the next air raid, and you were to spend the rest of your life wondering what would have happened if Mother and Klara had gone down into the shelter. Maybe they would have died all the same, but of asphyxiation, because the rubble blocked the entrance to the shelter.

Turn your head! Don't look! What do you see there? I see myself, wandering, exhausted, my legs are trembling, my hands are bleeding, I am pushing a buckled bicycle wheel, with crooked spokes. I see myself falling to my knees, I retch, I vomit, the bitter metallic taste, the smell of burning in my nostrils, of burnt, decaying flesh, the dusty air, which turns blacker and blacker, the red hills that grow darker and darker, the leaden sky up into which fly scraps of paper, tattered rags, purple magnolia flowers. Better hide behind the mounds of rubble and wait, don't turn your head, don't look! What do you see there? A truck carrying rotting, liquefying remains, the grief-stricken parents, who else, the prostitutes, the informers, the orphans, the racketeers, the widows, the cripples who sacrificed themselves for the Greater Germany. They were waiting, disciplined, trusting, in the shelter, their torches turned off, breath next to breath, but the rubble blocked the entrance. They all died, burnt, suffocated, burnt, suffocated, burnt, suffocated, and the false civilians would from time to time turn on their torches to see who had spoken, who had not been able to suppress a scream.

*

What would have happened if she had not posted a letter to Hermann the day before the air raids, which found her in the shelter in Karstadt, which she entered when she heard the sirens? *Don't be sad for Klara's child, I love you,* perhaps if she hadn't written what she did at the end of the letter, Hermann would not have kept it inside the lining of his coat, even when they amputated his leg in the hospital train.

Christa takes a deep breath and tries to stretch her tensed back. The pain has made its nest above her buttocks, a triangular animal that gnaws at her without surcease. But she continues to grip the steering wheel with a hand whose skin is dry and speck-led with brown blotches and she looks in the rear-view mirror at the car coming up from behind.

—I don't deny my spirit of adventure, my dear. But if I thought there were any real risk in my taking this trip to Romania, you can be sure that I wouldn't have invited you to join me.

Ah, so Traian has finally deigned to answer her. Defensively, cautiously, lest he annoy the driver! Which means that he ought to be able to control himself on other occasions. Her voice sud-denly becomes sharp.

—Let's not talk any more about the way in which you invited me, my dear! In any case, you did so after you had given your answer to the German Cultural Center, and even to that man you were at university with, I forget his name, the Romanian academician! As soon as he telephoned you, you promised to make the trip. You didn't come to me to ask my advice before making your decision. You never do! You're a lone wolf, you make all your decisions all on your own, and then, very politely, you invite me to submit to your decision . . . I'm sorry, my dear, but I really can't be bothered to see yet again all the things I was forced to see as a child . . .

Do you think that nobody is watching us through binoculars from the stands, from the balconies? That nobody is dividing us into groups, that nobody is marshaling us from the end of the rows of benches? That there are no loudspeakers to augment our cheers, no machine-guns pointing at us from the surrounding windows? That we are the only ones here, we who day after day go down into the shelters, disciplined, smiling at the patrols? That we alone, the orphans, the widows, the grieving parents, the ladies of the night, the informers, the war profiteers, the cripples bare our bowed heads and acclaim Him with voices that never grow hoarse?

*

The sentence does not come out; it is unable to break through from behind her clenched lips. She smudged her lipstick when she drank an espresso at the tourist market, and Traian drank a decaf and looked at the teenage girls with narrow shoulders, with unripe breasts showing from under their low-cut t-shirts, with long, scrawny legs, like she used to have.

And it has been a long time since she could be bothered to explain to anybody what she has been trying to forget for so many decades. The yellow light, the red light that thickens over the leaden Rhine, until it touches the red hills, until it touches the dusty red sky, while she races along on her bicycle, she races along. Who said a bomb fell on Bergstraße? Her throat is clogged with the grey dust, a taste of burning, of ash, on her tongue, she retches, the bicycle hits a soft body and hurls her among the immense mounds of rubble that are smoking against the red sky. She lifts herself onto her hands and knees, of course she is dreaming that she trips over the black, scorching wires that poke from the rubble, from the dusty boards bristling with nails, from the broken legs of the furniture. She falls, gets up, splinters, scorching shards, sharp stones jab her elbows, her knees, her lacerated thighs, look, an inexplicable dirty purple rag, a branch of blossoming magnolia, wilted, whitish-red, suffocated, poking from the mound of rubble along with the last tongues of flame, and she scrabbles with her torn, bloody fingernails, screaming: Klara, Mother, why, why, why? You begged them time after time to go down into the shelter when the sirens sounded, they were slow, depressed, sick, why, why? So that she would be the only one left, to wander choking on the dusty, burning air, amid the mounds of rubble, amid the sound of scraping shovels, the French, American, Russian, Polish prisoners of war searching for unexploded bombs, pulling the dead, the asphyxiated, the mangled from beneath the ruins.

*

Every time she returns to the stories from her past, Christa becomes irascible. She long ago got past the stage of crying in bed after they made love, although this is something they do more and more seldom, her body is withering and is more and more unwelcoming, only the secretions of the past have remained intact. She will apologize for this irascibility in an hour or two, the depression leaves scars, you must understand, he understands, he does not lose his temper, he does not react in any way, better let her get it off her chest, let her say what she likes rather than be angry at the wheel.

—You were angry when I said it's a country at the ends of the earth and strictly speaking you are right . . . But things aren't quite like that. It takes two hours to get there, but you don't count the days it takes to get to Rome, the round trip to the airport . . .

—You know very well, my dear, that I don't want you to tire yourself out with . . .

—We're not talking about me, I'm used to managing if need be . . . But you're the one who complains about not having any impetus, about always having to interrupt your work just when you . . . In a month you'll be complaining that you won't be able to meet the deadline for your book. I know your habit of avoiding any unpleasant discussion or at least putting it off until it doesn't matter anymore, and that's why I insist that we should talk at least now, at the thirteenth hour. There is still time for you to change your mind, like I told you, at our age health problems are a good excuse, or else you could claim something urgent has come up at the Ministry . . . Why should you expose yourself to danger of your own free will?

The endless motorway, sliced in two by the little hedge of oleanders, laden with white, pink, red flowers. The wooded hills climbing into the sky, with the white splotches of mediaeval villages, perched by their wells for hundreds of years.

*

—There were dangers, I don't deny it, but now the situation is radically different. I mean to say that it is different in relation to me . . . I'm a foreign citizen, I enjoy the protection of my adopted country, and what's more, my former colleague,

Alexandru Stan, whom I mentioned, has a good deal of influence. And I can vouch for him, after all, we've known each other since the age of twenty, since we went abroad to study . . . We lost contact then, when he decided to return to Romania and I decided to stay here. He's intelligent, brilliant, my dear, even if he hasn't bothered much with research since he was appointed to important positions . . . But what a joy it was to see him again, unchanged after all these years, apart from his hair, which is grey now, and a few extra kilograms, which is what happens . . . The joy was like that of finding a long lost brother and although the time was short, he gave proof of his friendship . . . Sufficient proof . . .

—And I appreciate him for it, it's obvious he's a man of education, well-travelled . . . There's a big difference between him and those friends of his from the embassy, whom he kept complaining he couldn't get rid of, but whom he kept insisting we invite to our house. And I'm sorry, but I'm still adamant on that point. I don't know how much proof of his friendship the man has given you, but I do know that up to now you have given him plenty of proof as to yours. He needed an invitation to the congress in Berlin and he got it, he wanted to go to the conference in Basel and you recommended him, he wanted scholarships for his students, including his daughter, and you went out of your way to get them for him . . . If not all the people invited got there on time or if not all of them received passports, it was you, my dear, who lost his temper more than he did . . . The canny Alexandru was satisfied because his daughter had been able to get a scholarship . . . a young woman who, I have no doubt, fully deserved one.

The blinding sun. The heat. His eye, rejoicing in the postcard beauty of the landscape and the emotional vibration, when it recognizes something that comes from as far back in his life as his memories of childhood in a faraway land. Like the lines from Homer, which flow, mechanically, oblivious to the frightened void within him. *Stony and harsh is Ithaca, / But like a good mother brave sons does she rear / And nothing sweeter than her land can they see in this world.*

*

She knows it is too late to turn back. But she cannot stop herself from trying.

—And if you are determined to endure the unpleasantness of this journey, then it should at least have been a series of talks, not just a lecture! Which, let it be said in passing, if I have understood well, you are not even going to be paid for, as you normally would be. Shall I ask you how much you will be getting for it or is it best that I don't? Not to mention my reservations about those letters you have started getting! At least the one letter you deigned to translate for me was downright unctuous. How can an academician, the director of an institute, grovel to you like that? And as for what that Victor wrote, the cousin you can barely remember! For years and years you received not one letter, you didn't know anything about your parents, your brothers, and now you're besieged with letters. Your silence just confirms I'm right . . .

—Not at all, my dear . . . I'm silent because I can't see any point in my saying anything . . . Why prolong this pointless argument when the dice have been cast? Whether I'm doing a good or a bad thing by going there we shall see when I get back . . . In a situation like this, no civilized man can turn back . . . But it's not all like you think. Alexandru Stan, for example, doesn't need me to invite him if he wants to travel around the world; he represents his country at the highest scientific level. I don't know what the others are like who keep writing to me now, unfortunately, all of them close relatives, as you yourself said, as they have life only in my mind . . . I can thank God that I have made a life and a career for myself here, whereas if I had stayed there I would have died at the front or rotted in prison . . .

The city begins to loom in the distance, through a milky, translucent mist beneath a bluish sky.

CHAPTER SEVEN
A Generation Past Its Sell-by Date

—THE PLAN OF ACTION! What are you boggling your eyes at me like that for?

For the time being he refrains from shouting at him, although every time he sees that pocked nose of his, striated with violaceous capillaries, he feels like throwing him out of his office with a kick in the ass.

But he can't kick him out of his office, because he was the one who summoned him there to report: Nuţi, send in Captain Gherghina with the current dossier and the plan of action, he knows which plan I mean, let him come straightaway, not when he comes round from his hangover!

And he can't kick him out, because he has yet to ferret out who the saints were who saddled him with the bastard in his section. But he'll see to it that he breaks his own neck, today, with the Defector dossier: he'll just need to keep a close eye on him, to make sure he doesn't compromise the operation.

—The plan of action should have been on my desk last week! Right here! (*He bangs his fist on the desk*) Where is it?

He loosens his necktie and undoes the top buttons of his shirt.

*

At the routine checkup last week, the department doctor, *The Quack*, as he calls him to his face, warned him to slow down, because his blood pressure, his cholesterol, plus his osteoarthritis . . .

—The next time, if your test results come out the same, I'm going to have to file a report on you! Do you want me to force you to take early retirement?

But *The Quack's* face lit up when he slowly slid him the half bottle of Ballantine's and he merely murmured:

—It's for your own good that I'm telling you! With most of you the occupational illnesses come from self-indulgence, from an unhealthy lifestyle, but with you it's just stress and sedentariness. You looked different when you used to go out into the field, but you can't complain, because you've been promoted . . .

And *The Quack* kept prattling and blathering on in the same vein. He talks just so they can hear how principled he is! The coward has been shitting himself ever since they gave him a rank and a pistol and made him part of the system. True, the whole building is bugged, from top to bottom, but who would waste time with the likes of him and the bottles he receives? He's mad for *veeskee*, *The Quack* is, but he'll never get to travel to the *Other Side*, not even in a coffin, given how much he knows; he might as well be entombed here at headquarters. He's shitting himself in case we drop him out of a window, like we did his colleague, Abraham Schechter: we filled up seven fat dossiers on him before we shoved him from the tenth floor of the Emergency Hospital. The CIA and Mossad couldn't even salvage so much as a toe bone! But comparing a drunkard like *The Quack* with the doctor to the Chief is like comparing a raw recruit with General Doicaru! From *The Quack* you won't hear so much as a thank-you, but he's got a deft hand when it comes to taking these bottles; he prefers the little plastic ones, because he can hide them in his first-aid bag.

—To the gym with you! he finally says, in a louder voice. Get rid of that big belly! And remember, above all, whatever happens, don't lose your temper!

*

He does not lose his temper, rather he moves his chair back, he thinks he can smell, or else he really does smell, the whiff of stale plum brandy mingled with Tarr shaving lotion. The alcoholic stench of that bastard Gherghina; the only thing he ever learned in the whole of his military career is how to stand at attention . . .

—Yes, comrade colonel! The action plan for surveillance of defector Manu Traian, yes, we're working on it! I've brought

the file, yes . . . (*He reads from a sheet of paper, stumbling over certain words*) *Manu Traian, born 3 April 1922, in Cărbuneşti commune, Dolj county, director of the European Environmental Research Institute* . . .
    —Didn't you take compulsory literacy classes in '56? Why do you have such trouble reading? You didn't take the classes, did you? You can't shove culture and an ideological education down somebody's throat. You didn't want to, and look how you've ended up! But as for chirruping behind people's backs about not getting promoted, you're good at that, aren't you, you fucker! You think I don't know the stuff that spouts from that trap of yours? You're incapable of even reading what's written on the paper in front of you!
    —I need to change my glasses, comrade colonel!
    —When are you going to have time to change your glasses if you spend all day in the tavern, you moron? Get on with it!

*

    —I've reactivated agent Emilian, who because of his position of responsibility makes trips abroad . . .
    —You reactivated him my ass! Not "because of" but "because he has"! And it was me who reactivated Emilian! Look at me! I've brought the reports from the 4th of March and the last one, which I annotated on the 9th of May: have you got them in the file or did you lose them in some tavern? Let me see them, because I don't believe a word you say! In fact, give me the whole file! What, comrade Gherghina, do you expect me to do your job for you? The "Scientist" dossier has twenty pages and more than half of them are Professor Stan's reports, and I was and still am his liaison officer and all correspondence with the Defector is under my supervision.
    —There'd also be the application for verification from the Files Department, comrade colonel, this is it here . . .
    —Which was written by Matei: a dog's dinner! It takes them three weeks to reply that they don't have any records on him! A bunch of idlers!

—You're right there, comrade colonel. I told that slacker Matei it was pointless him doing it. 'Cause that one I didn't do. —Right! You didn't do that one, but what did you do? What did I sign that expenses claim for? What did you fritter your daily allowances on? What have you been working on these last three months? Go on, tell me, before I lose patience! What have you done to inveigle this Defector, apart from what I've got from Emilian?

—I've brought two reports, comrade colonel, sir!

*

Sheet no. 12

I the undersigned FODOR PAVEL, son of Nicolae and Elena, born on 1 November 1917 in Calafat, domiciled in Bucharest, Strada Caragiale no. 18, Sector 2, hereby declare the following:

I met MANU around the year 1944. He was studying for a doctorate at the Sorbonne, I was working for the Romanian legation.

I had no relations with him of any kind.

I know nothing about his political activities.

I do not know the persons with whom he was in contact in Romania or abroad apart from his colleague Stan Alexandru, with whom he came to the legation to extend his visa.

He said he wanted to go to America.

It is thereby evident that he was engaging in actions hostile to our people's democratic government.

He was middling in height, had blond hair, prematurely greying, bluish-green eyes, he spoke fluent French, Italian, German, and English.

I have no relations of any kind with him at present and I do not know anything about his current situation.

I have made the foregoing declaration of my own
free will and without having been forced to do so
by anybody.

                    The undersigned FODOR PAVEL

                            *

—Do you know what you can do with that? You can wipe your
ass with it, that's what! That Fodor is one of that American spy
ring that stood trial, isn't he? You interrogated him and when he
sets eyes on you he remembers how you bludgeoned him and put
him away for sixteen years. What was it you did to him? Crush
his fingers in the door so that he would write you those three
paragraphs? You call that intelligence work? Is that how we wage
our secret war? What the hell, comrade, you've been working in
our institution for donkey's years and you still don't know the
meaning of a secret file or a plan of action? I've told you time
and time again that you need to improve your professional level!
  —Yes, comrade colonel, like comrade Nicolae Ceaușescu said,
improvement in level is the duty of the entire nation and look,
here's the other intelligence report, supplied by agent "Ene."

                            *

Sheets nos. 14—15

                    INTELLIGENCE REPORT

Professor MANU TRAIAN I met via a recommendation
from Victor Georgescu. I made his acquaintance in
the month of May 1981. Based on the recommendation given by Victor Georgescu he obtained for me
a soggiorno of residence in Italy, as a Romanian
refugee, after that he took us to the Comitato per
profughi rumeni in Rome, Via Babuino 149, to get
the documents for emigrating to Canada. I found

out the following at the time:

He left the country in 1941 on a Romanian student passport. At home he left a fiancée who didn't want to come with him or else he didn't take her.

In 1947 he was summoned back to Romania. He refused to go and they took away his citizenship and he was very upset about it.

He's in right-wing politics because he's in the committee for Romanian refugees in Rome which he is the head of. One evening in the month of June 1984 I had occasion to dine with him and with the Canadian consul in Rome on which occasion they talked about getting me my Canadian entry visa.

I also found out that he's very well in with the Italian Ministry and he's got influence there.

Thanks to Victor Georgescu's recommendation and the fact that I had frequent conversations with him, close relations have been established between us and I enjoy his friendship.

Middling in height, he went white when he was young he told me, a beard, blue eyes, married to a woman with grown-up children.

Source "ENE"

*

He takes his packet of Dunhills from the desk, lights a cigarette, blows smoke rings, and remains silent. He looks up at the ceiling, he smokes, and he remains silent, with his easygoing mug, like a collective farm accountant's.

He's captured his prey and he's not going to let him escape from his clutches. He is savoring the execution that is about to follow, he runs his hand through his curly hair, it has thinned on his brow, on which a knobbly lipoma is growing, what's this, a horn? I hope you didn't put it there, he said to his wife, and she went: Me? It's the devil in you, showing his horns!

Gherghina is standing stock-still, to attention. He'd set him ablaze if he could, put the boot into his belly and his testicles! But there's nothing he can do, He has to stand at attention and swallow it. Who's this animal got behind him? Pantiuşa? Doicaru? Nobody and nothing can help him now: he'll be transferred to the stakeouts department until retirement, he'll have to do the rounds of the housing blocks, swilling plum brandy with all the superintendents.

*

```
MINISTRY OF INTERNAL AFFAIRS
Top secret
Sole copy
Sheet no. 25
```

```
REPORT ON THE AFORENAMED MANU TRAIAN
```

In the discussions conducted on 1 August 1985 with "S.A." and "V.G.," official contacts of our organs, it emerged that the aforenamed MANU TRAIAN—head of the European Mediterranean Environmental Research Institute, a department of the Ministry of Research, Italy—will be arriving in our country. He will arrive at the Otopeni frontier crossing on 12 August.

The following things are known about MANU TRAIAN. He was born in Cărbuneşti commune, the son of Ion and Maria, Romanian by nationality and Italian by citizenship.

In the period 1940—1941 Manu Traian betrayed his country, going abroad to study in France and Italy. At present he carries out actions hostile to our state. From the same sources it is known that MANU TRAIAN has contacts with Italian, Dutch, French, and American official and scientific circles.

```
A room has been reserved at the Intercontinental
Hotel for MANU TRAIAN.

                                        Lieutenant
                                  MATEI SILVIU
```

*

—So, he's arriving on August 12th, is he? And what is the date today? August 10th, isn't it? 15:36 hours. And the plan of action is?

—We're working on it, comrade . . . I've contacted the hotel, the airport, I'm waiting . . .

—Waiting for what, you animal? Colonel Ispas abruptly roars. What is there to wait for? You still don't know what a plan of action is, not even now? A plan of action, don't you understand, you pinhead? A plan of action! He's about to enter the country, he's about to arrive at the airport, and you, you animal, haven't made any preparations! Digging ditches, that's where you belong, not here with us! Get the fuck out of my office, now! The file stays here with me! And don't leave the building until further orders!

Through the open door comes the noise of the typewriter, the creak of the floorboards beneath the soles of the retreating boots. He closes the door after telling Nuți to put him through.

Now that he is talking on the telephone, he can put his feet up on the desk, like an American.

—Who the hell saddled me with that idiot? Where did he work before? It shows! Let him go back to the fucking Canal where he belongs! Eh, not right now! He's been assigned to do some surveillance work, using technical-operational equipment, because he's not capable of anything more than that. I'll send you the report today, put his retirement papers through already, 'cause I've been watching him for a long time! What's needed here is a fine touch, comrade colonel, give me an educated man, what do you call that finicky lieutenant in Department 1, Unit 0744, who made the referral to Files? Yes, yes, I know who his stepfather is, I know the comrade colonel, I know his mother works in the apparatus, I believe you, she's still attractive, but you know my opinion when it comes to women! Women spoil easy, they grow double, triple the size, it's their nature, they should stick to the kitchen, if you ask me, excepting only Comrade Elena Ceauşescu! I can't begin to tell you what a mess that drunkard Gherghina has got me into, draw up the documents for Matei as quick as you can, it's an urgent job! The Chief is right, comrade colonel, we need thoroughgoing institutional reforms! We need real professionals, young men with an education! Our Institution is crawling with the Traitor's men,* with all those shitheads in the pay of the Americans, the ones I forced to take literacy classes in '56! What kind of literacy can you expect from them if Drăghici** signed the order but he refused point blank to attend the classes himself! The past-its-sell-by-date generation that the Traitor Pacepa nurtured in his bosom! There's nothing you can do with that bunch, comrade colonel! To the elephants' graveyard with them! But we're the exceptions! You've seen for yourself that they never go on a hunting trip without us. I'll see you on Saturday at the guesthouse in Brădet, shall I, colonel?

* Ion Mihai Pacepa (1928–), three-star general in the Securitate, who defected to the United States in 1978, thereafter becoming an object of almost hysterical hatred for the Romanian Communist regime. He was the highest-ranking defector from any Eastern Bloc country in the Cold War period.

** Alexandru Drăghici (1913–1993), Minister of the Interior and Minister of State Security during the brutal hard-line Stalinist period up to 1965.

Part Two
The Home

CHAPTER EIGHT
Daniel at the Airport

DANIEL SAYS:

I don't have anything else to look at except the tips of the poplars, the television antennas, the clothes hung out to dry in the balconies opposite, etc., in other words, the usual view from the window of the seventh floor of a housing block the same as any other in the new and wonderful residential districts of our glorious homeland. Taking advantage of the fact that the others have gone out, I am lying sprawled on the fold-out couch, which is spread with a scratchy red homespun rug, the latest shitty example of snobbery on the part of my poor parents, who keep trying without success to fall in step with the tawdry fashions of the communist middle class. But I'm restless and I start pacing up and down the dining room, as Father inappropriately calls it, since we have always eaten in our cramped kitchen. Or the living room, as Mother would like us to call it, but failing as always, an indefatigable Cassandra, unheeded by all. Or the best room, as peasant folk would call it. I have jumbled up the collection of Universal Classics of Literature, arranged in alphabetical order by engineering-minded Father, who, loyal to the traditions of his profession, has no use for literature, but merely lines up the books on the shelf like gravestones in a cemetery. But in the universal Dana-brand bookcase there is nothing worth reading: Faulkner and Alexei Tolstoy and Hermann Hesse. I should have told Gimmi that I had lost *The Spy Who Came in from the Cold* when he asked for it back, as I was only halfway through it. And what a stupid reason he gave! He asked for it out of pure spite! Who would believe that his dad wanted to read John le Carré? The comrade colonel wanted to find inspiration in plump agent Smith! Now there's an ace character! If our secret agents were like that, there'd be an even bigger queue to get into the Băneasa

School,* which is where four of the prizewinning pupils from the Șincai Lyceum went. I've filled the ashtray with cigarette butts, I've even made a contribution to the decoration of Cassandra's living room, in the form of a postcard from Prague and one from East Berlin, sent by Father's workmates during a lucky work trip, gluing them to the wall, which is flaking because of the latest inundation by the neighbor on the floor above. And liking my handiwork, I then added a photo of Maradona, a quite crappy one from *The Bucharest News*, and another one, of the Rolling Stones, which I found in the stack of *Nouvel Observateur*, *L'Express*, and *Paris Match* that uncle Victor tossed at me the last time he came round to our flat.

—Take them, snot-nose, what am I supposed to do with them if they're in English?

Where did Victor get them? Who knows what shady business Victor gets up to, the king of the hard-currency shops, the veteran hard-currency dealer?

*

At the commemorative service three months after Nana died I thought of Uncle Traian for the first time. I knew from uncle Victor that he would be coming in the summer and I thought that in any case for Nana he was coming too late. Once I heard him on Radio Free Europe. Mother says that it wasn't Uncle Traian, but Virgil Ierunca.** Then I thought that if he had married Nana and stayed here, I would have been called Daniel Manu. But in fact I wouldn't have been called that, because Mother was adopted by Nana and ever since she got married to Father, she's been called Izvoranu. And then I decided not to think in advance about how it will turn out, so as not to spoil it.

But I was sure that even if I didn't plan it in advance, the two of us would somehow get a chance to talk together privately.

* The Securitate college in Băneasa, just outside Bucharest.
** Virgil Ierunca (1920–2006), Romanian writer and opponent of the Communist regime, who lived in Paris after 1947.

"You're Daniel, Ana Maria's grandson, come here and tell me whether she ever told you about me," he would have said.

I thought about all this at the airport, in that annoying light that doesn't let you hide your pimples and blackheads and your unruly hair that won't lie flat: if only I had some hair gel like the stuff Gimmi's dad the colonel brought him, I'd smooth it in a flash!

But as for the light, it's the glass walls of the airport that are to blame, although you probably couldn't build an old-fashioned airport nowadays; it's the end of the second millennium. And Gimmi himself, whose parents have got a VCR and two cars, and Gimmi's got loads of genuine tracksuits and pairs of sneakers, Gimmi himself told me on the sly that our airport is a copy of the one in Frankfurt, which in any case is the biggest in Europe. That would have been a world record, for Gimmi not to tell a lie when he was showing off!

*

And as I was looking left and right, excellent, the business, this airport! I didn't realize that Mother was keeping her beady eye on me and, unbelievable! for the first time ever that Nagging Cassandra cottoned on to what I was thinking, and as a result, out of place, as usual, the way she is, footnote: Nana would have used the word *inopportune*, and so Mother, inopportunely, as usual, straightaway informed everybody as to what was going on in my mind:

—Do you like the airport, Daniel? Mother shouted. There, you see, wasn't it a good job you listened to me in the end and agreed to come with us to meet your uncle? Grandfather! Great-grandson! Our Great-grandfather! There, you see, wasn't it a good job that you listened to me for once in your life? You see how big, how beautiful, how new our airport is?

And of course, they weren't shy and reserved enough to miss out on the opportunity not to set the conveyor belt in motion, and so they all pounced on me:

—So, you've never been to the airport? How come? How come? How come?

—Did you hear what Clementina said? It's Daniel's first time in an airport!

—Make a wish!

—You'll have to come again!

—How come? How come?

—Really? Is this the first time you've been to the airport? How about that! How about that! Howaboutthat!

And what was I supposed to say except: *how funny!* And I had to endure it for a while until they forgot about me and started swapping recipes again, totting up their fortnightly bills, their sick pay, their installments. Reeling from the commotion, after the obstacle race that began at a quarter past six in the morning, when they went out of their front doors, their stockings crooked, very late, and right up until the moment when they collapsed on the blue vinyl bench seat, three hours before the airplane was due to arrive, they had managed to escape with their lives, unscathed by all the cars, trams, trolleybuses, and buses, which had come off the rails, got bogged down, stuck in the snow, caught fire, they had managed to add to their not too distant pensions the percentage accruing from tense hours of labor full of achievements, responsibilities, successes. And so, having got rid of one stress only to succumb to another, they had removed their swollen heels from their shoes and covertly unfastened zippers, buttons, belts above swollen stomachs seared by hyperacidity nurtured for decades on end in workplace canteens and labor analysis meetings, they had adjusted their best frocks, from which were steaming Jubileu cologne and Femina underarm spray, and they had once more turned their attention to the exciting, sacrosanct person of the guest: the world-famous Traian Manu.

*

—They say he was the most intelligent in the family.

—The most cultivated, in fact.

—The most ambitious, more like.

—The hardest working.

—The most virile, I expect.

—The most eager to succeed!

—He's hardworking, ambitious, intelligent, if you like, but he's never had a soul.

—The only thing he was ever interested in was leaving! He didn't care under what circumstances, he didn't care about the sacrifices . . .

—Whoever can't adapt here should go ahead and leave!

—He was determined to compete in a foreign world. Here, everybody knew he was an illegitimate child! His mother, a former washerwoman, worked hard to raise him, singlehanded, doing needlework . . .

—He left so that he could be free of his family's influence, free of his father, a rich landowner.

—A merchant!

—A dentist!

—His father gave him money from an early age, his brothers got into card games, casinos, the stock market, whores, nightlife, but all he was interested in was books . . .

—He abandoned his brothers back here, they were babes in arms, his father was old, sick, and he never came to visit them!

*

—He worshipped his mother! She was delicate, a young lady of good family, raised by nuns, she played the piano, knew foreign languages! When she died, he couldn't bear it here anymore, he went off into the wide world.

—His mother died of a broken heart when he told her he was thinking of leaving.

—His mother developed a paralysis, waiting and waiting for him to return. Twenty years she waited for him, all alone, old, insane, without anybody going to visit her.

—And all the while, he never sent her so much as a parcel, an invitation—he didn't put any hard currency in the bank for her!

—Not one letter . . .

—All the same, it strikes me as a lack of character . . .

—A lack of feeling, even!

—Everybody who succeeds in life has to pay that price. Just see if I'm wrong!

—Because of his mother he remained a bachelor. He adored her. He made a fortune, he made connections and a career for himself over there. But he didn't manage to have a family!

—That's the fate of celebrities! That's how they pay for their arrogance, their selfishness, their lifelong cynicism . . .

—That's how they end up dying in squalor! Alcoholics, bohemians, madmen, infected with syphilis and AIDS . . . abandoned by everyone, dumped in an unmarked grave!

—Victor, who's the same age as Traian, remembers that Traian's mother ran off with a baritone, his father died in a duel and his grandparents raised him in straitened circumstances . . .

—His father went to America, his mother remarried, he had stepbrothers, another family.

—His father died at the front before he was born. His mother raised him singlehanded, on a paltry teacher's wage, which didn't stretch to school fees and luxuries.

—His mother's mistake was that she refused to rebuild her life. He abandoned her at the first opportunity.

—His mother died in childbirth.

—His mother died before he was born. His father raised him, blind, deaf, a war hero, a cripple, to whom he had a sickly attachment.

—Ah! That's why Traian was determined to be rich and influential. To be somebody!

—A worthy son! He was dead set on making something of himself!

—A noble soul! What a strong character!

—But still, his ambition is over the top. Don't you find?

—He was determined to get his revenge on the rich members of the family, who humiliated him when he was an impoverished child!

—He was determined to come back rich and powerful, just to spite us!

—He was an orphan, like I told you already! He was raised on the family's charity. They all chipped in to send him to school.

—He might give back what he took, now at least!

—Give whom? They're all dead!

—The last one to go was Nana.

—The second from last, because the last is Victor.

—He should have come back earlier, if he wanted to show his gratitude.

—Why? Any time is a good time to come, we're still here, the descendants . . .

—According to the law, he's in our debt.

—He's in the family's debt!

—He's in our debt! One and all!

CHAPTER NINE
The Awaited Generation

A TWENTY-DOLLAR shirt, always in civvies, you've never seen him in uniform, you couldn't even imagine how he'd look in uniform, with that girly face of his, if you put a headscarf on him, you could take him to the Maids' Market on Mount Găina. Maybe he's an ass bandit, like they say? His nose, his mouth, it's his mother's face, and he has his mother's way of looking you in the eye when he speaks, and he speaks softly, to force you to listen to him. That's a real woman's touch, that is. Prize-winning pupil? Get stuffed! Think you're a prince or something? Tell it to the morons that you're better than all the rest, 'cause with my own two eyes I saw your dad dressed like a peasant, mingling with the lowest of the low in the market, a bodger from Stakeouts, that's what I call having connections! Smile at him, invite him in nicely, care for a cup of coffee? Does he drink anything except green tea?

—Order yourself some tea, lieutenant, and a coffee with sugar and a small brandy for me. And let's get down to business, 'cause the Defector will be infiltrating the airport any minute . . .

I doubt we've got green tea, or blue tea for that matter!

He's brought his own tea from home? What a bloody dick!

—From discussions with source "Ene," our organs' contact, it emerges that the aforementioned fugitive Manu Traian will arrive in our country via the Otopeni frontier crossing on 12 August.

—Today, in other words! He's at the airport right now, you chucklehead! Read the plan of action more carefully, lieutenant, 'cause we're in the shit bucket and I only hope that you'll do a better job than Captain Gherghina!

*

—Action plan: Bearing in mind that this year defector MANU TRAIAN will arrive in the country for the first time between 12 and 25 August for a conference at the German Cultural Center and intends to stay for ten days, we propose to open an individual action file comprising the following tasks: 1) determination of the methods employed by Manu Traian in the actions he carries out against our country; 2) discovery of the elements in this country that Manu Traian exploits to this end; 3) counteraction of the hostile actions carried out by Manu Traian against the Socialist Republic of Romania and the effectuation of missions to act upon him.

—Never mind all that. You're not at the Băneasa School here! What intelligence and operational measures have you come up with?

—Comrade colonel, having carried out checks, up to now I have made contact with the agency that oversees informers. Agent "Emilian" will be permanently in the company of Manu Traian, he will gather his impressions over the course of his visit to this country and will discreetly supervise his contacts. He will be absent at the end of the visit, as he will be on a working trip to Moscow, but agent Bădescu will stand in for him. I have arranged that agent "Emilian" will check whether Manu Traian asks the agent to undertake any commissions for him.

—Go on!

—With the aim of determining his behavior, his connections and the nature thereof a telephone message has been sent to the Surveillance and Investigations Department whereby it is requested that he be made subject to an operation. Via Service F we shall keep Traian Manu's letters and telephone calls under surveillance, primarily those to and from his wife, Christa, but also anybody else who attempts to contact him. Via his cousin, our source, we shall identify Traian Manu's friends and relatives in this country and subsequently we shall organize intelligence surveillance of some of them and their recruitment as agents. Checks will be made to see whether Traian Manu intends to make contact with any of the Free Europe correspondents controlled by us in Bucharest.

—Anything else?

—Since we have information that the target will be staying at the Intercontinental Hotel, Department III will be contacted with a view to putting him in a room where special equipment has been installed. During the course of his travels around the country, the informers will be given instructions in the field. In the event that he stays in a private home, we shall see to it that the room is fitted with technical-operational equipment.

—Anything else?

—The Romanian Institute for Cultural Relations with Foreign Countries will also endeavor to draw up an itinerary for Manu Traian.

—What are we getting mixed up with those idlers for?

—It's to the benefit of our country's image, comrade colonel! It gives us opportunities for a *follow-up*! As soon as we have verified the information about the target's trip to the provinces, we shall send a telephone message to the Craiova Regional Department requesting that he be made the subject of an operation.

—Give me the action plan to sign and get the secretariat to stamp it! And keep your eyes peeled at the airport! Even if you've got men on the ground there, it's your business to be there in person, incognito! You're good when it comes to the theory, but when it comes to the practice you're a monumental cock-up! And if you mess it up, you know what you can expect!

CHAPTER TEN
The Death of Penelope

DANIEL SAYS:

I stuck a poster of Belodedici on the stained door, I put on a cassette of The Scorpions, I emptied the ashtray down the toilet bowl, that was a mistake, no matter how many times I flushed, the butts kept floating there stubbornly, I opened all the windows, because the time was fast approaching when Nagging Cassandra would get back home, and how about I put on Sandra's "Stop For A Minute"? I searched the kitchen and found a slice of *cozonac** left over from breakfast, dry, crumbly *cozonac* without walnuts, without bits of Turkish delight, without sugar, without rhyme or reason, as Father says, but I forced myself to chomp it down anyway, since I'll have to get used to the thought that Nana is gone and she's taken the secret of *cozonac* with her.

Sweet, sticky dough, bulging and pouring over the lip of the basin, imbued with the scented heat of the kitchen, hey, Daniel, would you like a bit of dough?

And the wads of cotton wool stuffed up the yellow, stiffened nostrils from which trickles black blood . . . no, not that, not that, not that, think of something else, but what? Of the damp black cement, covered with a grubby jute carpet, on top of which there are raggedy mats of a motley, dubious grey. Of the deep blue of the vaulted ceiling, on which is clumsily painted a black cross and two angels with huge, stiff, stork's wings, leaning on the arms of the cross. And the ladder, propped against the blackened walls next to the scaffolding erected last summer, when they started painting the church murals, when Nana and Mihnea were still alive . . .

Oh, how the soul struggles when it parts with the body, towards

* Traditional Romanian sweet bread, filled with ground walnuts, cocoa butter, or Turkish delight, and eaten at Easter and Christmas.

people then it turns . . . And the wads of cotton wool, stuffed up the yellow, stiffened nostrils from which trickles, ceaselessly, dead, blood, ceaselessly, dead, blood, ceaselessly, dead, blood.

No! Remember something else, something else, something else! *Lord, remember Ion, Constantin, Rozalia, Ivana, Alexandru, Neacşu, Corneliu, Gheorghiţă, Petre, Mănăilă, Ana Maria, Mihnea.*

Remember them, O Lord, in the kingdom of the righteous.

*

The heads covered with black scarves, the aged bony knees crushed against the damp black cement covered with a grubby jute carpet, on top of which there are raggedy mats of a motley, dubious whitish grey, the kneelers' rubber boots from which poke thick woolen stockings, the sheepskin coats bowing in supplication. My uncovered head has long since frozen in the smoky flicker of the candles and their eyes keep turning towards me, flickering smokily beneath the black scarves.

—Whose son are you?
—Whose son are you?
—Whose son are you?
—Whose?
—Who?
—*I am the lost sheep* . . .

And I look at the three tables of different heights, placed end to end, covered with waxcloth, and the waxcloth is covered with none too clean cloths. The only things that are clean are the baskets in which the candles are flickering, inserted into the consecrated bread, among the woody biscuits, the immortelles tied with red thread, the wine in Cico* bottles, the bronzed plaited loaf from the commemorative service and the small red-and-green strawberry candies placed against the white sugar frosting of the *kollyva*. Their eyes, flickering smokily beneath the black scarves.

* Substandard Romanian soft drink of the Communist period; the socialist alternative to decadent capitalist beverages such as Coca-Cola.

—What are you doing? Are you crying?

—Aren't you crying?

—Whose son are you?

—Whose son are you? Whosesonareyou?

—*Ana Maria, Mihnea, the untended, candleless dead.*

*

At the memorial service I tried to remember Nana. *Remember them, O Lord! Ah, how the soul struggles to part with the body! Towards the angels it lifts its eyes, but the angels . . .*

I tried to remember Nana again, as she was, when she was still with us, but in that instant I was too cold and I couldn't remember anything.

In fact, it was at Nana's three-month requiem that I thought about him for the first time, about our Traian, and it was then that I began to wait for him. Although it would be more accurate to say that I had been waiting for him ever since I was little and I heard the stories about him and Nana. I thought that I ought to tell him this from the outset, at the airport, as soon as I saw him, I wasn't at all sure I would be capable of doing it, but I was sure that in the end we would still talk together, the two of us, without my being pushy about it, which is something I hate.

And then, at the airport, when I was waiting for him, half of the time my relatives, both the men and the women, talked about him and about Nana. The women were slumped in a heap on the blue vinyl bench and as they sat there, waiting, the flesh of their meaty legs kept swelling, a phenomenon that became evident under the straps of their high-heeled sandals in particular, sandals from their distant youth, theirs and Elvis Presley's.

Beneath the unrelenting pressure of the sandal straps, the whitish flesh kept swelling, it was rising softly, spilling over, like dough.

And the women had loosened their belts.

*

—What a pity Nana didn't live at least till this month. The two of them could have talked.

—What would have been the point of them seeing each other at their age if they separated in their youth?

—Who was it that said that there was something between them in their youth? Was it Victor?

—From what Victor told me, they were close relatives.

—They were cousins.

—Second cousins.

—Look, Nana's dead and it's still not clear to me: were they or weren't they engaged?

—They had to get a dispensation from the Patriarchate.

—He asked for her hand, but she rejected him, because he was too young . . .

—It was she who was too young compared with him!

—They were both still at school . . .

—They wouldn't even have had the time, the place, or the opportunity to see each other.

—Yes they would have! Do the sums and you'll see that they'd have had plenty of time before he left!

*

—The truth is that Nana turned him down. He was a failure, he didn't have any prospects.

—Nana refused to leave with him. She ought to have been a student but she didn't like to study.

—She was too close to the family.

—She was too independent, she didn't want to get tied down.

—Nana was very domestic. She took the secret of *cozonac* to the grave with her. Ever since she died, I've been buying *cozonac* from the bread shop . . .

—Nana kept other secrets, too! She never talked about her first marriage, when she was called Mrs. Manu.

—What are you talking about? Her first husband was an

aviator and he died at Stalingrad. Traian was just trying to console her, but you know what Nana was like, very loyal . . .

—Not at all, as far as I know, Nana was partial to German officers.

—Americans!

—Frenchmen!

—Russians!

—Even Romanians! She used to go to dances at the Military Club every night!

—True, in her youth Nana was a bit fast . . .

—He could have made a career for himself here, but Nana, to whom he had a sickly attachment, he truly worshipped her, Nana dumped him and after that what else could he do but leave?

—It seems that Nana was engaged three times.

—I know from Victor that he only agreed to come because it was Nana's requiem.

—Who was it said that Nana was four months pregnant when he left her?

—Six months. But she had a miscarriage, fell down the stairs!

—Now Traian is paying the price because he left Nana to bring up the child on her own while he roamed the world . . .

—You're talking nonsense, Clementina was fathered by another man (*in a low voice, the final two words in a whisper*) who died in Sighet Prison.*

—Clementina was adopted. Look, there she is! If you don't believe me, call her over and she'll tell you herself.

—Victor told me that in his youth, in this country, Traian was a big philanderer, he left a lot of broken hearts behind him when he left.

—The only broken heart was Nana's, she was dying to make him her husband.

---

* Prison in north-western Romania, near the border with the Ukraine, where, during the Dej period, Romania's inter-war elite (ministers, politicians, high-ranking army officers, bishops, intellectuals) were imprisoned. Many perished and were buried in unmarked graves. The prison is now a museum, dedicated to the victims of Communism.

—All Traian wanted to do was leave! He made her have an abortion and then he scarpered!

—He didn't even write to her, he didn't tell her to come after him! He never even sent her anything, a Wiener Kaffee, chocolates, nothing!

—What are you talking about! I know from Victor that he was desperate, he sent her letters, money to follow him, that there wasn't any way he could come back.

—They'd have sent him to the front . . .

—They'd have sent him to prison . . .

—They'd have sentenced him to death . . .

—He was sentenced to death! I'm amazed he's got the brass-faced nerve to come back!

—He came back to see Nana before she died, to beg her forgiveness for not wanting to take her with him.

—Nana would have had an easy life!

—An easy death! . . .

*

—What ridiculous stuff you come out with! Don't you stop to think: two elderly people! Don't you have any respect for the elderly?

—Why? She herself used to talk about him all the time!

—When it came to Traian, Nana was very discreet. She never so much as uttered his name!

—Nana used to speak very nicely about him, because they were relatives.

—Nana used to speak nicely about everybody.

—Leave it out! Nana had her moments! If she didn't like a person, you should have heard her then!

—Whatever you might say, Nana was a real lady!

—The last lady in the family, unfortunately.

—If I tell you she was the only one, I hope nobody will take it amiss.

—It would shock you the things I've heard about her from people outside the family who knew her well.

—Stop it, stop it! Don't speak ill of the dead.

*

I was standing there, panting like a shaggy dog, because Bucharest had been stifling since six that morning. I wonder what it must be like at Frankfurt, if Otopeni Airport is so muggy under its glass dome? Except that on the *Other Side* they probably have air conditioning everywhere, but Gimmi, whose parents go *Abroad* all the time, Gimmi says that on the *Other Side* it's even worse, because the air conditioning makes your tonsils or one of your eyes swell up. Then tell your folks to stay at home, I advised Gimmi.

Anyway, here in this country, the women were puffy-faced from crying, from laughing, from the heat, with both eyes swollen, they were moaning and they were tearing Traian and Nana to shreds.

—Do you think that poor Traian came all this way just for Nana if he wouldn't get to see her?

—In my opinion, there's no point in your coming to see an elderly, knackered ex-fiancée.

—It's ridiculous . . .

—It's sacrilegious . . .

—It's sacrilege to say that Nana's knackered!

—If Nana had been in his shoes, she'd have known how to behave.

—Women, take it from me, are different than men.

—More sentimental!

—More sensitive!

—More concerned!

—Victor wanted us to hold a requiem for Nana now because Traian is coming, but he didn't get permission from Professor Stan.

—Let's see whether Traian asks after Nana! Whether he goes to the church, whether he tries to find out who paid for her requiems.

—Let's see if he gets his wallet out!

—Over there, on the other side, they don't have requiems! They burn you and keep you in an urn on the mantelpiece.

—God forbid!

—If Nana talked about him so often, it means that she was waiting for him to come back.

—Why would she have been waiting for him? What could they have done together at their age?

*

If Nana were still alive, she would have come with us to meet him at the airport. She would have found a seat in the middle of the bench and she would have fidgeted with her hat, nudging the others, tittering shrilly, cooing. The very next moment the others would have started going on about her shoes, they're really nice, where did she get them, they really must get themselves a pair, sniggering and nudging each other.

And Nana, little by little losing the ground under her feet and travelling through a denser and denser mist, would have given a detailed and highly confused explanation of a convoluted journey, with landmarks from a hundred years ago, the King Ferdinand Boulevard, the Queen Maria Boulevard, the Flower Market, Strada Bateriilor, the Brătianu monument, Strada Sabinelor, the Mihai-Vodă Church, the Brîncoveanu Hospital and suchlike, since demolished, having perished in clouds of dust beneath our very eyes, our eyes that brim so full of wisdom.

Nana would have kept interrupting her own explanation and blinking her sparse eyelashes, screwing up eyes misted by *pride and prejudice*, she would have confessed that she could only wear soft shoes, which didn't squeeze her toes. And with her innate courtesy, footnote:

Courtesy—the word that best describes Nana.

E.g., *Please have the courtesy, Miss.*

E.g., *He was a courteous gentleman/shop assistant/policeman.*

And so, out of courtesy, Nana would have got up from the bench, with the intention of giving a sports demonstration, that is, look how easy it is to walk in these shoes and I think I have explained quite clearly where it was I bought them, my dears.

Advertising break: I put on Madonna's "Live To Tell," the song that Diana likes, *my dear, my dirty Diana.*

*

And so Nana sprints to the middle of the pitch, takes a few short steps, intercepts the ball, dribbles it, she runs, runs, runs, and . . . with her soft new shoes she shoots straight at the net and . . . goaaal! Listeners, it's a goaaal! Goaaaaal!

The goal has been recorded for you with the highest fidelity, the equipment was working at full capacity, the maximum rpms, engines roaring, photoelectric cells blinking, and in just a few hours the customary press conference will take place!

For the time being, every smiling face will have turned to Nana, every sense will be on the alert, ready to weigh her up, to measure her. Above the five dry curls of her perm, her dyed perm, gleaming like bronze in a serene September sunset, the ultrasonic bat signals are crisscrossing, the meaningful glances. Attention! Slow motion! Nana stands up, the round shoulders rise first, then the hunched little back, which bends the neck forward, then the trembling knees, are you looking? look look look look look look look look look look look look how many degrees her knees are flexed, her shoulders, her neck, her elbows, how much older Nana has grown since the last time she had to bear, even without her noticing it, such public scrutiny, in the banal official setting of a baptism/wedding/wake. We are unable to specify the date/place/reason for the previous family reunion, since the chronicle of our devoted Daniel was destroyed through the negligence or maliciousness of the maternal tutelary authority, Nagging Cassandra.

*

Although chronicler Daniel would have turned his back as usual, doing everything possible to preserve the poor regard in which the others generally held him, to demonstrate by means of his scowls that he was not paying attention, the grandmothers, great-granddaughters, daughters-in-law, nieces, mothers-in-law, mothers et al. would have intensified their whispers and nudges, there being two explanations for their lack of restraint:

1) Daniel is usually their sole viewer/listener, as he is also the sole male scion of the family, albeit not a manly one, and this is incontestable proof of its decline.

2) In regard to Nana, it has been established that she hears/sees/remembers less and less, more and more poorly.

Moreover, practice has shown us that in the extremely rare cases when it dawns on her that she is the butt of the family's jokes and snide remarks, her annoyance lasts no longer than a quarter of an hour, after which she goes on smiling with her wonted courtesy. And that's why we all love Nana, our ridiculous and outmoded plaything, the last, the only lady in the family! Of course, dear listeners, we do not nurture the same feelings towards the moody Daniel, who is the only one who can hear the imagined voices coming from the bench.

*

—What a nice hat you have, Nana!

—A good thing she's finally noticed that Nana always wears comical hats.

—What I admire most in Nana is that she's brave enough to wear light colors.

—I like the pink and white dress.

—Turn around, Nana, let me have a look at your dress from the back.

—Do you still have that red dress, Nana?

—Do you still have that orange dress, Nana?

—The loud green one? The sky-blue one?

—Don't apologize, Nana! It's your style! You're the only one it looks good on! If other women want to go around all in black and wearing headscarves, looking like old women, then that's their business!

—What's it like being an old woman, when you feel like the youngest in the family?

—Enough of your tomfoolery, because I want to ask Nana a serious question. Listen, Nana, when you were young, before Traian left, did you know him or not? Did you know him well, if you catch my meaning?

—Ah, so you really were engaged!

—Ah, so you really were relatives! Close? Distant?

—But tell us, Nana, is it true what they say about him now, that he was the most intelligent member of the family?

—The most handsome?

—The most virile, the most manly?

—Aren't you ashamed of yourself asking Nana questions like that?

—What, Nana, are you excited? Look at her, the dear, Nana's excited!

—Is it true that you were five years older than him?

—Is it true that he was ten years younger than you and that was why you broke off the engagement?

—Can you see him, Nana? Look over there, the man just coming through customs! A tall man, with a white suit, with white hair, with a beard . . .

—Can't you see that far even with your glasses? Can you see him or not?

—Yes or no? Tell us, Nana!

—What, are you crying? Don't cry, Nana!

—You never miss a chance to put your foot in it! She's not crying, her eyes are watering because of her cataracts!

—I almost forgot to ask you, Nana, how are you feeling? How are your eyes? your heart? your illness?

*

—What I admire Nana for more than her shoes, her dresses, her hats, is the way she plays Chopin's sonata on the piano!

—Beethoven's!

—Brahms's, more like!

—But now, what with your illness, now, what with your death, can you still play the piano, Nana?

—Stop it! Cut it out! You know full well that it's been years since anybody heard her play the piano! How stupid you are! Don't you know when she sold her piano? When she didn't have any money to eat, her husband had died in prison and they'd sacked her from her job!

—What is it you have? Glaucoma or cataracts? What is it you have, Nana?

And Nana would have nodded her head, a smile frozen on her face, continually agreeing, her sole concern being to give the impression that she can hear everything, see everything, nothing is lost, nothing is gained, my dears, don't worry! The blue/pink hairclips framing her made-up little face, her wrinkled little face, with her aforementioned five dry curls, and her eyes, once green, now watery, childishly delighted. Nana smiling nonstop, content to be the center of attention, the center of the family and in fact she has long since been somewhere else, where no pain can reach, no humiliation at being an old crock.

That's something I'll never, ever, ever, accept! I'll never accept to become an old crock! Since the night when Mihnea fell off the balcony, I've seen that you can travel from one world to the next in five hours in thirty minutes . . .

—We'd have had *cozonac* this year too, if we'd been able to get hold of the ingredients and Nana were still alive. She knew the secret. But as it is, I've been keeping three eggs in the fridge for ten days and I can't bear to use them.

—Never mind, the *cozonac* from the Scala is good too!

—Never mind, the *cozonac* from the bread shop is good too!

And who knows if life is in fact death and if what we call death does not in some deeper way mean life.

CHAPTER ELEVEN
The Life of the Unknown Traian Manu, Part One

DANIEL SAYS:

I could put on "We Still Have Dreams" and "Don't Be So Shy," Mihnea didn't like The Scorpions, not like I do, but I don't want to think about Mihnea again, or about Nana's requiem, instead let's get back to our folks, who, if they'd had any nose at all, would have sniffed out our Traian while he was still groping his way through customs, along with the people coming back from jobs *Abroad*, from Libya/Syria. And the cops were swooping on the packets of Lux and Kent in their suitcases. It was only when they scented *the distinctive fragrance of Tabac Original* that they decided to unglue their fat bottoms from the blue vinyl benches on which said bottoms had been growing numb for three hours, as they goggled at those boards saying NEW YORK MOSCOW BERLIN PRAGUE which go clickclickclickchirrchirrchirr, which flip over and . . .

—What do you see now, Daniel?

—Now I see BUDAPEST ISTANBUL LENINGRAD MADRID . . .

Then perhaps the suspicion will cross their hairspray-clogged minds that those strange names, LONDON BRUSSELS COPENHAGEN ROME, are cities that really exist, and so, if you could get past the sliding door and another few such doors, you would probably end up in an airplane fuselage, in the prow or the poop of a ship.

—Crew, hoist sails! Raise anchor! The winds are favorable! Westward ho! PARIS MADRID BERLIN ROME *to the heart of Europe and the world*, passengers, please fasten your seatbelt, we wish you a pleasant journey!

But even the infinite must come to an end, and so too would this voyage, and after you have paid your obol to seasickness, to vertigo, you would descend whistling towards a glass dome even fancier than ours and probably similar looking buses would take you to somewhere in the center of town.

And so you really would arrive in PARIS LONDON MADRID ROME and can you really imagine the like?

*

I'm the only one who thought of anything like that, certainly not them, the women who were staring at stray Africans, Japanese, Malayans, Chinese. And when they moved out of their field of vision, they went back to their earrings, hairdos, dogs and cats in birdcages, almost forgetting to exchange recipes, miscarriages, black-market purchases:

—You do it quick, you do it in five minutes . . .

—The chore of those five minutes I could do without!

—With mine it takes twenty minutes!

—With mine half an hour!

—Forty minutes! Two hours! I don't know how to get rid of him, I tell him I need to go to the bathroom and still he won't let up!

—I know somebody who works at the Cocor department store . . .

—I know somebody at the Bucur department store . . .

—I know somebody who owes me a favor . . .

And although *respirer c'est juger*, for once in their lives they set eyes on Milena and forget to ask her:

—How are you, Milena, dear? Are you ever going to get married? You can see the years are passing, you can see that . . .

And you won't believe it but they forgot to ask me:

—What about you, Daniel? Have you decided where you're going to go to university? Are they going to enlist you in the army?

—Give yourself plenty of time to think about it! Don't give your mother yet more grief!

—But isn't there any hope of them giving you another place at university?

—You should have gone and said everything! You should have said everything! Saideverything!
—And your poor mother! One misfortune after another! First Nana died, and then your trouble at the university . . .
—But think about it in plenty of time, don't give her . . .
—Think about it!
—Think about it!

*

And looking at them, I kept saying to myself: *les camps d'esclaves sous la bannière de la liberté.*

I got the quotation from that book by Camus, which Letitia Arcan left at our house the last time she came, and how frightened she was when she came back for it! Her husband had brought it back with him after his latest trip *Abroad.* He's an ass, that Petru Arcan, the great professor, but at least if he brought back *L'Homme révolté,* you can be sure he doesn't do like Gimmi's dad does with John le Carré. Arcan devours everything. He reads everything. The book was full of underlined sentences. Otherwise, how would I have hit on the aforementioned quotation? I was hardly daft enough to wear my eyes out reading a story without any plot or dialogue, was I?

Proof of how good I am is that I was the only one who recognized Traian from that photograph from a hundred years ago, in which he had the same crooked teeth and gullible eyes as me, but even so I was the first to recognize him.

—Look, I said to Milena, as an aside, see that man? That's got to be him!

Honestly, it wasn't all that difficult to spot it was him. From the very beginning I thought that, unless they'd been telling fibs in all those fairy stories of theirs about what an important figure he had been even in his distant childhood, when he was still wasting his time around here, he would have to be the last or next to last man to come through customs.

And that was exactly what happened! There was only one person who came out after him: she looked like some character from

The Visit of the Old Lady, Letitia's favorite play, wearing gloves and a hat. She looked sternly left and right. She was devastated that the municipal brass band wasn't there to greet her. And then some shady guy holding a crumpled, stained, handwritten piece of cardboard leapt out and whisked the old dame away!

And right in front of her, there he was! With his cool glasses and his trench coat flung over one shoulder and his immaculately trimmed beard.

How much do you bet that's him? I said to Milena.

*

I couldn't understand why my folks weren't able to spot him from the very first moment, despite the fact that their eyes were wandering groggily all around the glass-domed airport. Probably even after the three hours they had spent languishing there, they had still not worked out where the people came out and where they went in. Or else they had worked it out but then it had all got mixed up in their scalded brains. Otherwise, it was a no-brainer that he was the only one who could possibly come out last, that only He could be the last man to enter our country from the world at large!

But my folks must have been expecting him to be decked out in a black or navy-blue pinstriped suit, with a polka-dot tie, a cane, a crutch, a briefcase, a bowler hat. Who knows what crappy notion of classic old-fashioned elegance they've got in their heads? But nor could you expect him to be dressed up like a rocker!

And so no matter how hard they boggled, they still didn't manage to spot him, and even when there could no longer be any doubt, even when they started smiling at each other, bowing stiffly like undertakers, wringing their hands, their eyes were popping out of their skulls in amazement, they couldn't believe it: is that what he looks like? Is that him? What if it's not him? With his cool glasses and white clothes and pockets and zippers on his sleeves, but *le charme n'attend pas le nombre des années!*

*

But what really blew the women away was that trail of Tabac Original, *the successful range for men of the world all over the world aftershave lotion*, mingled with yet another manly cologne that to this day hasn't been picked up by or passed on to our press agencies over here. In this respect we shall be cautious in our suppositions, dear listeners, we shall now go over to our studios, where at this very moment the family spokesman to official circles is now waiting, the much talked-about Victor.

—We were certainly not expecting to find any bog-standard rexonagreen or eighttimesfourherbfresh bars of soap in cousin Traian's luggage, 'cause you can get them any time you like on the black market, and cheap too! Maybe there'll be some pacoraban or ugoboss cologne in there. Call us if you're interested!

Live from our studio, that was cousin Victor, salesman and veteran hard-currency racketeer.

But please bear with us and as soon as we have further information, we shall be broadcasting it. After the news, we shall be returning to the airport.

*

In any event, the women were on the ball, because from where they were dozing all in a heap on the blue vinyl couch, as soon as they caught a whiff of Tabac Original they gave each other looks and started fidgeting.

But Victor was ahead of them, brandishing a bunch of flowers.

—Out of the way! Out of the way! Out of the way, please!

And the women started conferring with each other in voices loud enough to drown out the exciting, ultramodern hum of our airport, where planes land/take off every two to three hours.

—Get out of the way, will you, I want to see him!

—So that's what he looks like!

—Which of them did you say is him?

—The one with the sporty clothes and glasses!

—With the contact lenses and a sports bag slung over his shoulder!

—And a beard!

—Amazing! I was sure he was younger!

—Older!

—Shorter!

—Fatter!

—Balder!

—I'd pictured him completely different! With a straw hat, a trench coat, a cane.

—A frock coat, a bowler hat, a monocle, a black umbrella . . . A smoking jacket! A bowtie!

CHAPTER TWELVE
Progress Report

WHAT A REEK! Captain Gherghina is not much of a one for washing! It's no wonder his wife went and left him, even if she blemished her file by doing it and they kicked her out of the apparatus! But that beast Ispas didn't send Gherghina to stand in the corner because he was stinking up his office, rather it was because his friend from the Cadres department passed the denunciation on to him. That was all it took; he blew his top! Apart from that, they're around the same age, one is past his sell-by date, but the other's on the crest of the wave. Ispas, the king of the Comrade's hunting trips, he doesn't have any problems, what with his peasant cunning, and his apprentice-school education, and his night-school degree, which he took when he was in charge of national education—as mommy says, he's the man of this, our golden age! When he saw that the Russians were losing the match, he stepped aside and you'll always find him on the winning side! How are you getting along with the beast, *son*? mommy asks every evening. All right for the time being, but his foul mouth puts me out of sorts! I tell her, reassuringly. I can't even repeat to you the names he calls me! Don't even think of repeating his vulgarities, honey, after all, it was with the likes of him I've wasted my life!

*

—Comrade captain! Comrade captain Gherghina! You were on the stakeout team and you yourself were in charge of the operation to keep Traian Manu under surveillance. Would you care to list the conclusions of your investigation and the elements on which you base them? I have to draw up the report for the comrade colonel . . .

—List what, you swine? List my hard work, eh? Two men

to do the digging and another five to look at the plans! This institution is going down the drain if I, decorated five times, by everyone from Teohari Georgescu to the Comrade himself,* if I've been reduced to reporting to a brainwashed snot-nose like you! Why didn't you go out and do the fieldwork yourself, you swine? Like when the target landed and you showed off, using my files! Have you forgotten that when you first started you used to eat from my hand? You all think I don't have friends in high places anymore and you can kick me in the ass whenever you feel like it! You'll come crawling to me not to give you the sack, mark my words! Take the papers, don't say I didn't give you them, I've got witnesses, and wipe your ass with them!

*

—What an oaf! What friends in high places has that alcoholic got, comrade lieutenant Matei, that he can allow himself to talk to you like that?
     —His pension, Nuţi! He'll drink away his pension and swear at his colleagues, unless somebody steps in and puts him in his place! He's a dangerous individual, who from the very start had no business being in the apparatus. I hope you won't mind if I open the window a little. I'll dictate it to you, because he has dreadful handwriting, he makes logical errors, spelling mistakes, but don't alter anything. His texts ought to have been immaculate when he submitted them! *Surveillance report, yes. At 10:30 hours, the target came out the hotel, carrying on him a large beige briefcase. Outside, official car no. B 31255 was waiting for him in the hotel lobby was the driver and the target shook his hand.* Transcribe it exactly like that, Nuţi! Let the comrade colonel see how the past-its-sell-by-date generation writes. That's what

* Teohari Georgescu (1908–1976), Minister of the Interior under Gheorghe Gheorghiu-Dej, in which post he oversaw the most brutal phase of the Stalinist repression in Romania. Purged and arrested in 1953, he was released in 1956 and assigned work as a proofreader at a publishing house (despite his only ever having completed four years of schooling—like many of Romania's high-ranking Communists, Georgescu was semi-literate). He was rehabilitated in 1968, after Ceauşescu came to power (in 1965). The Comrade with a capital C is Ceauşescu.

he calls that lot from the 1950s. *They journeyed to the Gorjului stop*, journeyed, listen to that (laughs), *after which they parked, the target got out with the driver, they crossed Fraternity Between Nations Boulevard, went to tenement block 16, entrance C, in front of the block an individual came up to him who was waiting in front of block 16, entrance A . . .* Which entrance, A or C? Captain Gherghina must have had a skin full when he wrote this report! Type it up exactly the same as he wrote it! *He entered the building with the target but as the apartment was not equipped with listening equipment, it is not known what was discussed. In discussions with the superintendent, a contact person, she said that he is the son-in-law of the target's first wife, who died 8 months ago, domiciled in a house in the courtyard, now demolished. The individual's distinguishing features, age 48–50 years, tall, bodily build full, oval face, fat, chestnut-brown, rectilinear nose, mouth average! In conformity with regulations etc. etc.* That's all! Eyewash! And muddled! When he goes back out into the field, and he'll be going for sure, as he still comes to claim expenses, you give him a copy to sign and keep another for my files.

*

Let's hope I get that transfer to the World Economic Institute and then the scholarship to the States so I can escape from this toilet! Unless that beast Ispas finds something to clamp onto, unless he puts spokes in my wheels! The uproar he made over each discrepancy between the action plan and the timetable! The running around he made me do! I'd arranged with the drunkard Petrea from Department III to have the target put in a room covered by special measures, but if they informed me later that it couldn't be effectuated, that they didn't have the rooms available, why did he have to yell at me about the Court Martial, and in front of Nuți too! When the Defector is under constant surveillance anyway! I talked to Department III personally, you'll see when the reports come in, the target was covered twenty-four hours a day by our agents, the intelligence reports are thorough, the reports made by the hotel auxiliary personnel, the manager, the waiters, the porter, all of them! That's what I told him. Not to mention source Bădescu, the target's cousin, and source Emilian, who travelled with the target to his home village, Cărbuneşti, and when the conversation came round to family matters, source Bădescu gave him the information that had been authorized in advance, about how his parents and brothers died. I told him all that and I also told him I would append the intelligence briefings and the recording to the progress report, because when he returned from Cărbuneşti the Defector had a room fitted with special equipment at the Nord Hotel. And that beast Ispas didn't even listen to what I was saying, he kept yelling: Be careful how you write that report, 'cause it'll be going all the way to the Top! I won't let you get away with it this time! It's not the first time that Department III has seen fit to ignore our demands!

*

—Comrade lieutenant! That oaf left behind another two pages: shall I type them up?

—How should I know? Read them to me quickly and let me see what they're about.

Nuţi (reads, sometimes stumbling): *The intelligence report on the aforenamed Izvoranu Cornel, born in Cărbuneşti, in 1940, the son of Ilie and Rodica, of Romanian nationality and citizenship, a forestry engineer by profession, married, one child, domiciled at Fraternity Between Nations, no. 16, entrance C, apt. 313. From the investigations effectuated at the domicile of the person in question it emerges that the man under investigation has unwholesome attitudes towards his neighbors, being arrogant and holding in contempt both his neighbors and the working class, he has hostile outbursts against the Party, being dissatisfied with the reforms made by the Party and the Government and listening to Radio Free Europe, constantly listening to this radio station on the landing. At his domicile the person in question is visited by various persons who have not been able to be identified due to the fact that they do not introduce themselves. The circle of friends is made up of engineers and various well-to-do people from within the environs of the city of Bucharest and elsewhere who visit him and he visits them, he receives letters from various towns, from Bucharest in particular, and from our investigations it emerges that he has a relative in the USA, but it has not been possible to establish how close a relative. From the political standpoint, prior to 23 August 1944 it does not emerge that he was a member of any of the bourgeois political parties. Married to Izvoranu Clementina, born in 1939, 13 August, in Bucharest, the adopted daughter of Ana Maria Bădulescu and Șerban Bădulescu, of Romanian nationality and citizenship, a teacher, they have one child. The woman in question is notorious at her domicile for being a non-communicative element, arrogant towards her neighbors, friendly only with elements such as doctors' wives and various persons who were members of the bourgeoisie, who she visits, she looks down on the working class, having as a source of income two salaries together with her husband's. She receives letters from various towns around the country, being a refined element, she does not have hostile outbursts against the Party, and from our investigations it emerges that she has a close relative in the USA, a brother or nephew it wasn't possible to specify because she does not want to have relations with the neighbors or whether she has written to him. From the political standpoint, prior to 23 August 1944 it does not emerge that she was a member of any of the bourgeois parties, at present she is politically unaffiliated.*

—It's written in a clumsy manner, but there are a few things of interest in it. Type it up and put a copy in my file, Nuți.

CHAPTER THIRTEEN
The Life of the Unknown Traian Manu, Part Two

DANIEL SAYS:

—The last one out, that old dame, with the gloves and the hat, is it or isn't it his wife, what do you say?

—Presentable!

—Horrible, you mean . . .

—For her age, she's not bad.

—At her age, beautiful, ugly, it no longer matters! The main thing is that she's old!

—I'd have gone to talk to his wife, if Traian hadn't come alone . . .

—Victor, who writes to him, told me he's an incorrigible bachelor . . .

—On the contrary! I know from Victor that his wife's under-age, an alcoholic, she takes drugs, she's an embarrassment to him, that's why he can't take her anywhere.

—I'd never for the life of me believed that I'd live to see the day when Victor looked after the family's most important correspondence.

—From what I've heard, his wife's a martyr, she stays at home all the time to look after the child.

—The grandchild, you mean.

—The great-grandchild!

—That means Nana knew a thing or two when she broke off the engagement.

—She tore up the plane tickets and her passport!

—And how she regretted it afterwards!

—Victor told me that our Traian managed to get where he is today thanks solely to his wife, it was she who had the connections, the wealth, the inheritance, the businesses . . .

—His wife's up the spout and the doctor wouldn't let her travel!

—It's not easy to keep a pregnancy when your husband's that old!

—I know from Victor that they celebrated their silver wedding anniversary recently. His wife is thirteen years older than him, she's rich, she has a coat of arms, castles, they get on perfectly, he adores her.

—For him it's a problem being seen in public with his wife, she has a tendency to shock.

—Ah, yes, I've heard she's a cripple.

—Quite the opposite! She's too young, too healthy, and anybody who sees them together can't help but ask: what is she, his granddaughter? His great-granddaughter? His daughter?

—Famous people have got a mania for marrying late and unsuitably. Remember that film about Goethe, how many princesses and duchesses he had and how he went and married his housekeeper?

*

So, made to feel guilty by the authoritarian voice that mercilessly reminded them that not even at their age were they au fait with foreign languages, their heads reeling from the nasty gossip, swept back and forth across the deck of the huge glass liner known as Otopeni Airport, the women were all talking simultaneously. It was as if they swallowed aphrodisiacs, AIDS and all, it was as if they had taken ecstasy, hash, belladonna, cocaine, superglue, menoctyl, that was how loudly they were buzzing.

—Just think, he's been married five times!

—Five wives would be too expensive, even with his money!

—Victor says he's not married, but living with somebody and he gets on with her in every possible way . . .

—At his age, I don't really understand why you'd need to get on with somebody in every possible way.

—At his age, over there, please believe me, you can live very comfortably alone, as long as there are boarding houses . . .

—As long as there are sex shops, bistros, babysitters, escorts, brothels, drugs . . .

—At his age and with his money and position over there, you just push a button, open the catalogue, make your order, and she comes directly to your bed, without your lifting a finger.

—You have everything you want over there, but you don't have family feeling!

—You don't have feelings in general! Over there, it's every man for himself. Even in the family, competition is the rule.

—You're mistaken! At weekends, for example, when the cities empty, where do you think they all go? To see their families!

—But in their films as well, haven't you seen how you get attacked by terrorists, by muggers in the metro, and nobody comes to your defense?

—But at his age, with his money and his position over there, he's hardly going to take the metro!

—But if they've got their own families, why would they come over here to find wives?

—Over there, it's hard to find the kind of women that are ten a penny over here, I mean a solid-gold wife, to keep your house spick and span, to give you children, to wash and iron!

—Over there, your life is just beginning when you reach his age . . . You've got money in the bank, you can travel the world at last, you have hobbies, you do sport, you get married, test tube kids . . .

—The Pope ought to ban that kind of thing!

*

—He confessed to Victor that he had a mongoloid child, which he keeps upstairs.

—In the attic!

—In a separate wing of the castle!

—In a Benedictine monastery.

—In a special sanatorium, very expensive, fifty dollars a minute . . .

—He was lumbered with it, because his wife died in a plane crash.

—In a car crash!

—It destroyed him! He's been in a state of lethargy ever since, he just can't get over it . . .

—That's why Professor Stan invited him over here, so that he could relax, unwind.

—The professor cares about his country! About the collective, about us! About the family!

—Professor Stan cares about arranging things to his own best advantage!

—But Traian came from over here: at his age, it must be hard for him over there.

—If it weren't hard for him over there, he wouldn't have bothered to answer all those letters from Victor.

—He answers him straightaway, on the very same day he receives the letter, I had occasion to see for myself.

—Out of politeness, that's the only reason he replies, they're all polite, they're all punctual over there.

—They don't have feelings like we do, instead they've got rules of behavior that nobody breaks.

—But he hasn't got a wife, he hasn't got any children!

—He hasn't got a dog, he hasn't got a pig!

—Just think, he doesn't have any other relatives anywhere else!

—Just think, at his age, with his money, with his position, just think, he's all alone in the world!

*

A poor orphan of sixty-seven, seventy-seven, eighty-seven, one hundred and seven, besieged by women hell bent on adopting him, women capable of incest, forged wills, delation, murder, fits of hysteria for his sake. No matter how hard you tried, you wouldn't have found one under the age of forty, but as I told you before, *le charme n'attend pas le nombre des années*! And so it was that he, in his sporty clothes, with his travel bag slung over his shoulder and his greying beard, was their final chance in life to feel like young girls again, with short skirts and rosy cheeks. Libidinous old biddies, who, from all their cooing and excitement, had swallowed their lipstick for the tenth consecutive time that day.

And all the while, cousin Victor, the regular customer at the hard currency shops, the king of the black market, who has been buying and selling information for half a century, was swimming forward through the throng, flowers in hand.

—Make way! Make way, please!

Victor, sowing panic around him. All of them terrified that somebody else might turn up and kidnap our guest or that Traian himself, unaccustomed to wasting his time without any intellectual gain, will turn on his heel and get on the next plane, regardless of its destination, and vanish in a puff of smoke, taking with him all the deodorant sprays, coffee, chewing gum and video cassettes he is presumed to be carrying.

I was the only one who thought of anything like that. They certainly didn't, as they were still straining to identify him.

—Which one did you say he was?

—Look, him with the sporty clothes, the bag over his shoulder, the jacket.

—He doesn't look bad for his age!

—Open your eyes! Where are you looking, that's not him! That's Stan, you've seen him on the television, on *Tele-Encyclopedia*!

—At the Grand National Assembly!

—At the Eleventh Congress, he was next to you know who . . .

—I can't help but be surprised when I see Professor Stan and his sidekicks . . .

—I can't understand why Victor wants to have anything to do with them . . .

—Victor and the professor persuaded Traian to come here to this country!

—But what was in it for them when they invited him?

—You're hardly going to be standing next to Traian when he opens his suitcases and gets out the Wiener Kaffee and cartons of Kent!*

* In Communist Romania Kent cigarettes were an unofficial currency, essential whenever it was necessary to give bribes to petty officials or doctors.

—Hardly! That's where Victor will be standing!

—Can't you see how Victor's fighting with Stan's chauffeur to see which of them gets to carry the suitcases?

—All the same, it's a mystery to me how Victor of all people managed to get in with him.

—How hard it must have been for poor Victor to write all those letters: at school he was never much of a one for writing!

—Look at Professor Stan, he's dancing round him like a spinning top!

—If you're bothered about the professor being top dog, push your way to the front, introduce yourself, crack a few jokes!

—What, and have him think I'm out for what I can get? And have you all say afterwards that I went to butter him up?

*

But now there was no longer any shadow of a doubt. The last person to come through, the old woman with the gloves and the hat, was surrounded by a large group of young children, and in front of them, there he was, standing solitary, an angelic, reformed disco man, with his cool glasses and white clothes, covered with pockets and zippers, his travel bag slung over his shoulder, and that was all. And then the penny dropped and I realized why the others hadn't been able to spot him from the first, like I had. They were focused on other things.

—That woman from the union saw me.

—From Labor and Wages.

—From accounts.

—What's he doing over there by the gate? He doesn't have any relatives abroad!

—He's looking for you, you know!

—For me!

—Who can I tell him I was waiting for at the airport when I see him tomorrow?

—Who? Who? Who?

CHAPTER FOURTEEN
The Accident

DANIEL SAYS:

I drew the tatted curtain across the view of the poplars, television antennas, balconies full of shabby laundry and barrels of pickled cabbage, all the things usually visible from the seventh floor of an apartment block. I made a trip down to the letterbox. Nothing had arrived from the Rector's office, although Nagging Cassandra had delivered the bars of Fa soap and the Nivea deodorant to the secretary, who had assured her that the order to re-matriculate Gimmi and me had already been signed. Gimmi's dad, the colonel, had summoned the Rector and I had taken advantage of it.

On the stairs it reeked of carrion. Yesterday, the superintendent had put poison down the rubbish chute, Paris green, he alone knows what he used, and the dead rats were still there in the uncollected rubbish. I held my nose until I was safely back in my room and I then opened the window.

I cut out the poster from *Paris Match* and pasted it to the door of my room: the bodies of two bronzed girls, toned muscles, white smiles, no tooth decay. *Imagine you're in Spain. After a delicious breakfast served in your hotel room you're deciding how to spend the morning.*

I turned off the cassette player and lay down on the bed. I was restless. From the Dana-brand bookcase I took Traian's favorite book, *The Odyssey*. He had recited from it in the house at Cărbuneşti. What's this? The book opened at exactly the quotation he used to repeat, I recognized it straightaway, what a sharp memory I have! *A task even harder you must perform, poor man! / How were you, a living man, able to come hither to the realm of Pluto, / Where the insensate dead make their abode, / The wretched shades of the departed?* And then I dozed off, I was asleep, I was awake, I can't say which. And who can even say whether or not

I'm dreaming now? But maybe I wasn't dreaming, maybe I was just thinking about what the Realm of Hades would look like, if I descended after Mihnea, after Nana, thither . . .

*

I wanted to hold each of them back; I wanted to hold back Mihnea and Nana. I wanted to go there with each of them, not to lose one another. I wanted them not to remain there forever, in the cold, in the darkness.

—Whose son are you? Whose son are you? Whose son are you? Whose son are you? Who? Charon would ask me, slapping the water of the Acheron with his cold, slippery oars, water so dark that it reflects no shade.

In the darkness I would hear nothing but the rippling of the smoky river under the heavy, lowering, leaden sky of the underworld. I would blink dumbly, blinded by the pitch darkness; I would not be able to see either the hideous bearded face or the cold hands clenching the oars. Nothing around me but the invisible roiling of the black water, all but tearing the bark away from the bank just as I step forward hesitating, trembling, so that I tumble into the icy bottomless depths, which, oily, silent, close above me, engulfing me in cold and darkness. *Whose son are you? Whose son are you? Who? I am the lost sheep* . . .

In fact, I wouldn't like to go there really, but when things are shitty and I think they're only going to get worse, then I remember Mihnea and I say to myself: never mind, grin and bear it, you can go to the *Other Side* any time you want, in five hours and thirty minutes, like what happened to Mihnea when he fell off the balcony.

I haven't told anybody about it, not even Diana, and at the enquiry in the Rector's office I answered the questions and that was all. But so many times have I tried to imagine what would have been, if I had been in Mihnea's place.

So . . .

*

To be Mihnea, to be tipsy and to hear Gimmi talking big, saying what hot stuff Lumi is and how she and her friend really get it on during the three hours when their square roommate Gabi goes out on Wednesdays, which is when, without fail, she goes to the Cinematheque. She's got a season ticket. Let there be noise all around, let nobody except you, Mihnea, listen to Gimmi as he carries on talking big, going into details of what Luminiţa and her friend are supposed to be good at. And then let Mihnea come up with the moronic idea of walking along the balustrade from your room to Lumi's balcony, let him be the invisible man, "The Invisible Man" by Michael Cretu, your favorite song, Mihnea. And then let him start bragging about how he's going to go all the way to Lumi's room, walking along the balustrade, so that he can see what's going on there today, because it's a Wednesday and Gabi's at the Cinematheque.

*

So, you're Mihnea, you're drunk and you're in a hurry, and slurring, you ask:

—How many rooms are there . . . from here . . . to the girls'?

The separate sounds clog up together and so you have to repeat it:

—How many rooms are there from here . . . to the girls'?

I, your best friend, I, Daniel, having come from town to fetch some course notes, was the only one who heard you and I answered:

—Two.

I still haven't fathomed the mystery of how I knew the answer, not being very knowledgeable about the topography of the Student Complex. And after that it was also I who turned to the others there with us, I turned to the tragic chorus and said:

—Don't give Mihnea any more to drink! Can't you see he's drunk?

But unfortunately it was too late, Mihnea was already

opening the door to the balcony, and so Cătălin rang the bell
on the first round:

—Shut that damned door! Can't you get enough of the cold?
he said and promptly hauled him back to his corner of the bed,
as he was to do a number of times over the course of the evening, until eventually he was lulled by Mihnea's cunning docility,
forgetting that the cunning docility of the drunkard conceals a
mind just as murky as the madman's and a perseverance just as
great.

*

Footnote:

This is just a fragment from the chronicle of the morose
Daniel, in which are recorded the most important moments of
the evening, when in room 325D friends and non-friends gathered there accidentally and non-accidentally. Mihnea, who had
received a care package from home, Daniel the chronicler who
had come to fetch some lecture notes, Gimmi, who had turned
up from who knows where and who knows how, bringing with
him the booze, Cătălin, who was to keep slamming the door to
the balcony every time Mihnea opened it, and a few others, who
were to make up the tragic chorus.

—Who's going to fetch Lumi and her friend? What's her
name? They're both inseparable.

Nobody knew what her friend was called, but they all knew
they were inseparable. If, as I had suggested, somebody had gone
two rooms down and fetched them, then without a doubt the
intrepid Mihnea would not have clambered up onto the balcony
half an hour later. But Gimmi pulled that grin of his:

—It wouldn't do to disturb them right now, when that square
Gabi is off at the cinema watching Antonioni's *L'Avventura*! Just
imagine the frenzied action that will be going down in their
room as we speak!

*

Not even in the immediate aftermath, when the sole occupation of those present, albeit differentiated according to how influential their fathers were, consisted of grueling interrogations and declarations, prompted by desperate parents and by competent bodies, severely criticized by higher and more competent, more indignant bodies, was it possible to establish whether Gimmi, the insinuator, was or was not cognizant of the relationship between Mihnea and Lumi.

The next significant phase, the second round, commenced after the final cigarette had been passed around and its butt had been stubbed out on the lid of a mustard jar, thereby giving rise to the crucial question:

—Who's got the balls to go and scrounge a couple of cigarettes from another room?

Or:

—Are there any dives still open at this time of night where we can get some cigarettes?

It was a lot of fuss over nothing, since all the indications were that the task of tobacco envoy would fall on me, Daniel the chronicler, since I was the only one who wasn't wearing student dorm uniform, that is, flip-flops and an inside-out ragged shirt, but rather normal outdoor clothes.

—I'll go to Lumi's room to see whether or not she's got any cigarettes . . .

As you will have realized, listeners, we are now in the middle of the second bout and he who mumbled the foregoing words was the intrepid Mihnea.

Rewind.

—I'll go to Lumi's room to see whether or not she's got any cigarettes . . .

—Better you go to bed, if the porter sees you in that state, we're done for!

—What do I care about the porter? I'll go from balcony to balcony: haven't you seen how wide the balustrade is?

Lacuna in the text.

*

In the next round, Mihnea looks with infinite regret at the empty cardboard box that formerly contained the food sent by his solicitous parents: various rinds and peelings, plastic wrapping, salami skins, eggshells, crusts from the day-before-yesterday's loaf. He must be peeved at having been such a sucker to open the food parcel from back home, which contained rations for a whole month.

Starting tomorrow, *ragazzi di oggi*, you'll all be back to tea with bread and margarine, if you were so clever as to sell your ration cards!

Maybe Mihnea was in the same depressed mood as he had been at the start of the evening, as the mood he had been in when he sent out random invitations, as the mood he had been in when he donated the parcel to the collective, all because of the midterm exam he had flunked. Maybe he was feeling stressed because of the coming term and the memory of last term, which he had wasted. Maybe he was unable to reconcile in a single image the kind of girl he had thought Luminţia to be and the things Gimmi had said about her an hour previously.

*

But in vain did I remember his sadness as he looked at the empty box during the many nights that followed, when an unbearable feeling of guilt woke me at exactly three o'clock every morning, as if some unrelenting clock had chimed. And only when I ceased to hear the chime of my inner clock in the middle of the night, thanks to your inane chatter, my irresistible Diana, rather than the sedatives administered by my solicitous mother, only then did I say to myself that the feelings of guilt, which arise when you can no longer do anything for a person close to you, a person carried away in the ghostly boat on the smoky river beneath the lowering leaden sky of the underworld, would no longer arise to torture us if we always treated each other with the same patience as we treat the people we definitely know are going to die in a day or two.

*

In any event, all the declarations made by those present were to attest that Mihnea was upset at the beginning of the evening, when it came to the food, he barely ate, but when it came to the drink, he started directly on the hard stuff, he got drunk very quickly, which is why he was talking mostly nonsense, for example, he kept repeating what somebody had told him about some video or other. Mihnea kept asking how many rooms away the girls were, although he was the one who should have known, but he didn't explain his intentions, except by opening the door to the balcony over and over again, for which reason his roommate Cătălin chided him for letting the cold in when the room was barely heated as it was. And since very few of those that lived there had attempted to go from one balcony to another walking along the balustrade, none of us in the room imagined that Mihnea could have come up with such an insane plan.

In fact, after he sadly looked at the remnants of the feast, like any other greenhorn drinker Mihnea started to feel nauseous, the stale reek of cigarettes, the warmth of the bodies gathered in a close space drove him to the door, but as often happens in our lives, he went the wrong way and instead of going towards to the bathroom, he headed to the balcony. But he was turned back by Cătă, he of the keen eye and swift reactions.

After that, Daniel the conscientious chronicler, on whom had fallen the fate of having to go out to buy cigarettes, exits the scene, not before giving repeated assurances that he would not be long, that he would go only as far as the first dive bar, that he had enough money, enough even for a pack of Golf. And the last words he heard, as he was closing the door, were uttered by Cătă:

—Hey, Mihnea, cut it out, will you? Can't you see that Daniel has gone to buy cigarettes? Why don't you go and put your head under the cold tap?

*

The last part of this chronicle will be based not on my own impressions, but on the accounts of the tragic chorus, each more discontinuous, syncopated and confused than the next. From what I have heard, imagined, deduced, I the chronicler will compose *ad usum Delphini* the following highly objective narrative, which at a given point I am afraid I shall interrupt either with my own silence or my own tearful voice.

Soon after Daniel's departure, an observer, Cătălin, according to some, is supposed to have drawn the attention of the collective to the danger that Mihnea posed to them all, given his confused pacing up and down and his constant temptation to open the door to the balcony.

—Someone take him and put him in a diaper before he lands us in the shit!

—If any of you think I'm wasted after drinking so little, cried Mihnea, then come outside with me and I'll prove I can go from balcony to balcony, as far as the second room down, just walking along the balustrade. Is anybody coming outside to watch me? Does anyone want to make a bet that I can get from here to Lumi's room just walking along the balustrade?

*

It may be supposed that even Cătălin grew weary of hauling the greenhorn drinker back to his corner of the bed and this is why, amid the din of talking voices in the room, Mihnea's mumbling went unheard. And the stale cigarette smoke and the late hour made the final opening of the door to the balcony seem a welcome breath of fresh air. In the given conditions, cigarettes: zilch, booze: nada, the assembly seemed to be dispersing, and so nobody cared about the others' reactions, about doors opening and shutting, and so I imagine that you, Mihnea, went out onto the balcony, convinced that Cătălin's voice would eventually fetch you back, the same as thitherto:

—Come on, Mihnea, cut it out! You can show us what a

daredevil you are tomorrow and how you can fly all the way to the beauties' room! Give it a rest now, will you, sword-swallower! It's time for beddy-bye, you fool! You haven't given me a minute's peace all night! The next time I'll make sure to feed you your Calypso brandy by the pipette!

*

I was on my way back, triumphantly clutching the cigarettes in my clammy palm, while you, dear Mihnea, were still waiting for Cătă to come and grab you by the scruff of the neck and toss you back onto the safety of your bed, but all you heard was the laughter of Gimmi, who was acting the big wise guy yet again:

—Let him freeze for a little outside, because the state he's in, it's hardly going to do him any harm!

And so, perhaps less and less eager to see what Luminiţa was up to in her room, tottering, barely holding down the contents of your stomach, you, dear Mihnea, climbed up onto the balustrade and when after a few steps you came to your senses, you discovered that it was much narrower than you had imagined and that the distance to the ground was much greater. "Strangers by Night" by C. C. Catch was going round and round in your mind, and, of course, "Like a Hero" by Modern Talking . . .

No matter how much I thought about it later, no matter how much I will think about it, I'll never be able to know whether you were sober, whether you were drunk, whether you were dreaming, gazing blindly into the darkness surrounding the Complex and further still, into the darkness where you could sense the city, "In the Heat of the Night" by Sandra, of course. You were cold, you felt sick, you had lost all patience, all curiosity, and you had no urge, absolutely none, to watch, like the invisible man, what was going on in Lumi's room at that moment.

*

And so within let there be smoke, a din of voices, sour smells, laughter, jokes, let them stop laughing and may you tread more and more fearfully, outside, on your narrow balustrade, *in the cold, in the darkness.* May you hear their laughter, their voices, more and more distantly and let the last words that reach you, repeated distinctly, over and over again, be those uttered by the big wise guy Gimmi:

—Let him freeze for a little outside, because the state he's in, it's hardly going to do him any harm!

May you be cold, may you freeze, and, nonetheless, may you keep going, stubbornly, lest you lose the bet against yourself, the bet nobody else wanted to make. May you not go back inside the room, defeated, risking that nobody will notice, just as almost nobody noticed when you went outside. May you be cold, may you be sleepy, may you no longer feel any urge to watch, like the invisible man, what is going on in Lumi's room. And in any case, nothing is going on in there, Luminiţa is out visiting an aunt, and as for her inseparable friend, whose name nobody seems to know, where else can she be except nattering with the girls in the room next door? And nonetheless, may you keep going, tottering, ever more sober, ever more frozen, because after you have taken a few steps along the so narrow balustrade it becomes just as difficult to go back as it is to go on. May you be ever more sober, ever more alone, in the hallucinatory darkness, illumined by a few streetlights. May you tread onward, taking sparse, deep breaths to delay vomiting for a second, may you keep tottering as you go, but may you tread onward, one more step, and yet another. More and more frozen, more and more terrified, tottering, thinking what? Feeling what? However much I might try, for the rest of my life I will never find out.

And may you make your misstep just before you step onto the balcony of Luminiţa's room . . .

*

I would have been able to cry out to him, to drag him off the balustrade, down onto the balcony, and if we had started tussling, the others would have jumped in to separate us. Why did I have to listen to them? Why did I have to go out to buy cigarettes, why do I always do that, why do I rush to do the things that nobody else wants to do? And when I pushed my way through the people standing around him, with candles, with torches, there was nothing else I could do but look. The ambulance still hadn't arrived, naturally.

—Does it hurt? I wanted to ask him, but I did nothing but look.

I couldn't understand why that inhuman whistling was coming from his open mouth and the trails of blood trickling from the corners of his lips, from his nostrils, from his eyes, which were still staring from his frozen face.

—Does it hurt? Does it hurt? Does it hurt?

And somewhere there still flickered a light of understanding, as big as a pinprick. Still flickering, smokily, the contracted, concentrated pupil, like a pinprick.

—Does it hurt? Does it hurt? let me cry out.

And the light, as big as a pinprick, suddenly flaring, what else can it answer me but:

—*I will go my way beneath the earth and you will go your way beneath the sun . . .*

And there will be nothing else for me to do but bend down and cry out:

—Whose son are you? Whose son are you? Whose son are you? Does it hurt?

—*J'irai sous la terre et toi, tu marcheras dans le soleil.*

And after that nothing but the wads of cotton which we stuck in the stiff yellow nostrils, from which trickled ceaselessly, dead, blood, ceaselessly, dead, blood, ceaselessly, dead . . .

*

That's enough! Nagging Cassandra has been ringing the doorbell for the last five minutes. She's forgotten to take her key again:

—Daniel! Open the door, Daniel! Open the door! I've got the letter! The letter from the Rector's office! I bumped into the postman downstairs!

Imagine you're in Spain. After a delicious breakfast served in your hotel room you're deciding how to spend the morning.

On sand or grass?

It's so hard to choose.

And who knows whether life is in fact death and if what we call death does not in some deeper way mean life?

CHAPTER FIFTEEN
The "Scientist" Dossier (1)

Source: BALACCIU
26 August 1985

At the meeting on 25 August 1985 informer "Balacciu" recounted the following to me:
In the last week of July he received a postcard from the Izvoranu family in Călămăneşti, where they were at the spa and hot springs, from which he found out that MANU TRAIAN would be arriving from France to see his relatives for the first time since he left the country.

After receiving this postcard, the informant's wife met with Daniel Izvoranu at a food shop in the Militari district, who, on his own initiative, told her that MANU TRAIAN had arrived from Rome, that he had stayed in his hometown of Cărbuneşti for a few days, after which he had arrived in Bucharest, where he was going to give a lecture.

The informant's wife invited Izvoranu Daniel to pay them a visit along with MANU TRAIAN, but he was evasive, claiming that MANU TRAIAN was too busy and such a visit wouldn't be to his liking.

The informant supposes that this refusal was due to the fact that he had not kept the promise he made to Izvoranu family to intervene on behalf of Izvoranu Daniel so that he could be readmitted to university after having been ex-matriculated together with his friends who threw a party in the hall of residence and one of them fell off the balcony and died.

I indicated that the informant should try to

keep his promise and reestablish relations with the Izvoranu family, to make such relations permanent so as not to miss any other opportunities to come into contact with MANU TRAIAN when he comes to this country.

Material to be delivered to lieutenant Matei Silviu who is working on this case.

Col. N. ISPAS

Part Three
The Return

CHAPTER SIXTEEN
The "Scientist" Dossier (2)

Sheet no. 73

Informant "Emilian"

"Sandu" house

23 August 1986

On 12 August year in progress Prof. MANU TRAIAN arrived in Bucharest on a family visit and to give a lecture. At the airport he was met by his family and by a number of biologists and biochemists. He very quickly left to go to Cărbunești commune, Dolj county, and stayed for a few days at the family home of the Party secretary. In Bucharest he stayed at the Hotel Intercontinental and the source handled relations with the auxiliary people. The source also accompanied him to Cărbunești, but because of a foreign trip was unable to stay there for the whole length of his stay. In Bucharest, MANU TRAIAN made contact with a series of individuals, including Cristian Dobrotă, who requested that he intervene on his behalf with the Izvoranu family, which by adoption had become the family of Ana Maria Bădulescu, his lover from his youth. On 19 August, MANU TRAIAN paid a visit to the Italian ambassador, Giuseppe Palumbo. From what he recounted to the source, they talked about the opening of the Romanian School in Rome, which is undergoing restoration. MANU'S comment was that given its lofty cultural traditions it is a pity that the Romanian School has ended up being a boarding house for Securitate agents.

The rest of the conversation centered on issues of scientific interest and issues of a family nature, with MANU wanting to find out exactly how his parents and brothers died, and with the source providing the information that had been agreed on beforehand.

MANU then went back to Rome on 22 August year in progress.

"EMILIAN"

CHAPTER SEVENTEEN
"Always a Fiancée, Never a Wife"

THE GROUND FLOOR of a house in the style of the '30s South, built using money earned by emigrants who had come back from America and rebuilt ten years ago. A rooftop terrace, small windows with different-colored laundry hanging on lines stretched between them. Through the open door the old trees can be seen rustling in the courtyard: a warm, thin wind is blowing; here it is still summer. A huge living room, floor tiles in muted colors, at the back a kitchen with ageing wall tiles, posters and calendars pasted on the fridge and the sink unit.

The young newlyweds join two tables together and lay a tablecloth of red-and-white checked paper. Professor Manu is inspecting the books on the unpainted wooden shelves. His wife, Christa, is looking at the photographs of the church wedding and smiling.

—Forgive me, my dear colleagues, for not having come to your wedding! Yes, yes, colleagues, what else? Hardly subalterns! Up until a year ago, my eminent students, and now my colleagues!

The young couple protest, but the professor insists. He knows that to him they will remain the children he never had; but he does not know how long they will want to continue investing attention and energy in their relationship with him.

—Believe me, I regret my absence all the more given that lately my travels have brought me ever fewer pleasant surprises and ever more health problems. There is no better medicine for it than to give it up and lately I have turned down plenty of invitations . . .

Christa's ironic smile and the fine lines at the corners of her thin lips float above her *chemisier* blouse, buttoned right to the top. But he prefers to ignore her and goes on:

—What are you doing, in fact, except going from one place

to another? All you do is exchange cheaper and cheaper copies of the same decor! Tokyo looks like New York, which looks like Los Angeles, which looks like Rio de Janeiro, which looks like San Francisco. Tomorrow, maybe even Beijing will end up looking the same! Our world is becoming uniform, the peripheries are copying the center as best they can. Maybe it is old age that makes me see nothing but deterioration and monotony everywhere. But to you, even the most ordinary journey must look different . . .

*

—You mean to say, Professor, that it was an ordinary journey?

The young man's voice sounds insinuating, but he does not lift his eyes, he goes on carefully pouring Chianti from the small raffia-encased demijohn into the plastic cups.

—Not at all! There is any number of things I might say, my dear Antonio, but not that it was an ordinary journey! It was there that my life began, after all. It was there that my parents and brothers remained, and the girl I was in love with. *Stony and harsh is Ithaca, / But like a good mother she rears brave sons / And to their eyes no land is sweeter . . .*

The professor recites, gesticulates, he is in his element in front of his young listener, his second family. Or is he his first family, as Christa reproaches him?

—Of course, you know where the quotation is from, don't you, my dear?

Silence has fallen, like in a classroom. Their scientific careers have required mathematics, chemistry and a lot of biology, but not the bizarre sounds of a dead language.

—*The Odyssey*! Your favorite book, Professor!

Naturally, she was the only one who could answer. Giulia caught it all in passing, as she was making return trips to the end of the dining room, bringing platters of pasta, vegetables and pieces of grilled meat twisted and skewered on toothpicks. Although she knows no more ancient Greek than Antonio, she has been attentive enough to pick up on the professor's obsessions.

—*The Odyssey* is indeed my favorite book, as you have well observed with that keen eye of yours!

Ulysses enchanted by the grace of Nausicaa: this is what Christa would recite right now, if she had not hated ancient Greek at lycée and if the exchange of pleasantries between Giulia and her husband had not irritated her.

Blushing at having given the right answer, Giulia now asks in the coddled, childish voice of a shy young girl discovering the power she has over an older man:

—But why did you like *The Odyssey* so much? You must have been forced to read it at school, like we were!

—I read *The Odyssey* so many times that I knew it by heart from an early age and as you can see, I know it still! Why did I like it? Perhaps I preferred it to *The Iliad* because it had what you would nowadays call a happy ending. And naturally, like any other adolescent, I dreamed of travelling to faraway lands. But there was also another, more prosaic reason: I was very good, brilliant even, at Greek and Latin, because in them I saw my only salvation. My father had forced me to enroll at the Theological Seminary, where you didn't have to pay fees, but I knew I didn't have any vocation to be a priest and around the age of sixteen or seventeen I started dreaming of sitting the examination to enter a classics lycée and of becoming a teacher.

*

Christa is listening with an air of superiority and boredom. She knows the story that is about to follow and it is only from politeness that she does not lose her patience. She will keep a lookout for the moment when they make the toasts and the hour when they will be able to get up and leave, because tomorrow, before the long journey home, she has a matinée in store: at the castle a remarkable violinist from Russia or Poland will be giving a concert, one of those strange talents that crop up from time to

time in Europe's wild East. Like the final man in her life, Traian
Manu: look at him, giving away his memories, memories hidden
away from her for so long. And the young woman, to encourage him, does not take her eyes off him, although she ought to
be inviting the others, if only silently, to take a plastic plate and
help themselves to the food. That is what she, Christa, would
do, but what can you expect from the younger generation, with
their lack of a proper upbringing?

—Ancient Greek and Latin were of great help to me. In the
first place, I began to earn pocket money thanks to them. Unlike
my fellow students, I didn't receive any money from home, and
adolescence is a difficult age in itself, but it's even harder if you're
poor. I gained notoriety at the seminary thanks to my interlinear
cribs, thanks to which some of the students in the years above
me passed their exams without knowing a jot of Greek. After
that I started giving private lessons and that was how I made a
friend: Anton. And so there it is, he had the same name as you,
my dear Antonio!

*

He is facing the young man as he talks, but he is sooner addressing Giulia, who, as ever, listens to him, her eyes glinting with
discreet intelligence. It was probably at similar such moments
that the erotic charge of her silence, her transparency, captivated her young husband, because the rest of the time she is
anodyne, sometimes even quite ugly. But Traian Manu has lived
long enough to learn that erotic charge has nothing to do with
physical appearance.

—Anton Dobrotă had also ended up at the school for priests
against his will, but for different reasons than mine. I might say
opposite reasons. I was there because of my parents' poverty,
whereas he had been expelled from a select lycée, without the
right to re-enroll, for the kind of high jinks that spoiled children from wealthy families usually get up to. Despite his father's
numerous connections—he was an influential politician and
county prefect—he was unable to find another school prepared

to take his son. Or else who knows? Maybe he hoped that seminary discipline would temper his favorite son . . .

He is so caught up in his memories that he is oblivious that
the others do not dare to start eating. But thank God Christa
is here. Tactfully, she intervenes, raising her glass. Traian will
have to continue his story after she makes a toast to the young
newlyweds on behalf of them both, wishing them happiness
and a long life.

—I used to go twice a week to the Dobrotă house, which was
sumptuous to me, and there I gave Anton private tuition in Latin
and ancient Greek. Gradually, we became friends. Or at least so
it seemed to me. It may be that he was a member of that category
of people who are incapable of having real friends, because they
are too self-obsessed. To me Anton seemed endowed with what
I believed at the time were the qualities of the mature man, and
in fact this was indeed the case.

*

But you, can you really make friends? Feeling a pang in your
heart, you look at Anton's suntanned arm as he bounces the
white tennis ball on the dark floor. Do you envy him? Admire
him? You don't know what to say, but you would like to laugh in
the same carefree way as him, baring broad, healthy teeth, and
you would like your shock of curly blond hair to be thick and
black like his, tamed by fine brilliantine and slicked back obedi-
ently. What wouldn't you give to be the most applauded stunt
pilot on Aviation Day, the man who in the tennis club changing
room mislays perfumed pink letters from Riri, the little ballerina
who adores chocolate and refinement in bed, as none other than
the famous aviator himself recounts, filling the other seminary
students with desire and venom, their uniforms impregnated
with the reek of dormitory living! You would even agree to suffer
Anton's bad luck at all-night poker games, on the condition that
at the end of classes a carriage with its top up would be waiting
for you opposite the school, inside which would be waiting the
petite Riri, wearing a fluffy white fur over nothing but black

stockings with flowered garter belts, patiently nibbling peanuts coated in the finest chocolate.

You do his homework, you prepare the cribs for his ancient Greek translation, envenomed by a mixture of adoration and envy. And every time you close behind you the solid wooden door of the Dobrotă house, you wish you could be him, but you remain you.

You have no way of knowing that the Maenads will give him long years in prison, humiliation and torture.

*

—It was thanks to Anton that I decided to take my life in my hands and give up seminary school. When, via his father's connections, naturally, his old sins were forgiven and he obtained the right to sit the lycée examinations, I gave him private tuition and we both passed the examinations for the same lycée on the same day. I came top, he near the bottom of the list. I received a scholarship, then I studied for two different degrees at university simultaneously, I received another scholarship to continue my studies abroad—as you can see, a standard academic career. It wasn't easy, but in the end I got where I am today, where we all are today. And if I had stayed there, I would have had problems as a priest in a declaredly atheist regime, and as a university professor I would have died of starvation, because immediately after the war they abolished not only the Classics departments, but also the English and French ones, and children were forced to learn only Russian, the language of the occupier. That is why I shall remain eternally grateful to Anton . . .

—The end of his story is so sad that it would be a real pity to tell it to you on such a festive occasion. During my trip I found out from his brother, Cristian Dobrotă, that Anton had paid the price for his fame as a pilot in the war: he was sentenced to long years of humiliation and torture in prison. He was the only one who ever managed to escape, but they caught him quite quickly. As a punishment, he was held barefoot in a cell full of freezing water. He got gangrene in his leg, they amputated it without anesthetic, in short, a terrible end to his life . . . From what I understand, his family paid for what the people over there call, using a theological term, Anton's political "sins."

*

Giulia gathers the disposable plates, with their remnants of sauce and streaks of grease, and stacks them in a plastic bag, which Antonio will throw away after the guests depart. She is scrawny, even quite ugly, sometimes she is attractive in her fragile femininity, of which she is unconscious, because her mind is more intense than her senses. She fetches fresh plates, the salad, the cheeses, fruit, ice cream, she moves swiftly and signals Antonio not to get up, as she will manage by herself. In fact they all know that she is the best, she has a phenomenal memory, an associative mind, he, the groom, knows it, but he is in a rush to get ahead of her and that is what he will always do. And the others, in a few years, will forget that she was the most gifted, because she chose to deprecate herself of her own free will. Because she wants to be an ordinary woman and in the end that is what she will become. Because of her passionate hope that if she denies her intelligence she will be able to live the long-dreamed-of life of an ordinary woman, they will all forget that Giulia was the best among many successive graduating classes of students.

They will all forget, apart from her teacher, whose trained eye, albeit clouded by a cataract, foresees the future development of each.

Traian Manu looks sadly at Giulia Mazzoni, his favorite student, who has chosen of her own free will to carry back and forth plastic plates and whom he will have no way of helping. He foresees even now the moment when, too late, she will come to regret that she hid the brilliance of her mind for the sake of the deceptive joys of a mediocre life.

There is a pang in his heart because he is thinking of Ana Maria, who probably had no choice when she gave up her concerts.

*

—Anton was the cousin of the girl I was in love with, a distant relative of the Dobrotă family, who had adopted her. My visits to their house were a longed-for torture, awaited fearfully. In the hour's break between lessons with Anton, who got bored quickly, and dinner, for which I used to be invited to stay, I would tiptoe into the salon where Ana Maria practiced on the piano. She had just begun her career as a pianist . . .

The little black veil with elegant beads that would prevent you from seeing how many wrinkles she had developed since then, but perhaps her musical voice would be the same. After so long a separation, you would have preferred to sit and talk, just the two of you, however, you had no choice but to go there in Professor Stan's car, down the street with hideous apartment blocks, where, up until a few months before, she had waited for hours and hours in the queue for bluish-grey frozen chickens.

—When I left to go to Montpellier, we agreed to meet in Paris, where she wanted to study. But Paris was occupied, it was increasingly difficult to travel because of the war, and Romania was occupied by the Russians soon after. Ana Maria was kicked out of the Philharmonic and devoted herself to her family. And for decades I received no news of her or of any of my relatives over there. On my trip I found out that she had died not long before I arrived there. And the saddest thing is that from what they told me, she could have been saved, but over there, people of my age and her age don't receive medical care. The hospitals are in a deplorable state anyway; it takes hours for an ambulance to arrive. It seems that she applied countless times for an exit visa to travel to the West, but . . .

You love her because she never made it to Paris, but instead traipsed all over town giving private piano lessons, at five lei an hour, instead she looked after the adopted daughter of her neighbors, who were both arrested the same night. You love her because her fingers, swollen with rheumatism, but with carefully clipped cuticles, were timidly to push the wrongly counted money over the greasy counter towards the contemptuous shop assistant, and because her successful application for a passport to travel to Bulgaria, her first trip abroad, was to arrive a week after the hospital refused to admit her, leaving her to die at home.

*

—When you depart from your loved ones in youth, my dears, you end up struggling with nostalgia for the rest of your life. Ever since I left, all these years I have dreamed every night that I am in that old city with its mulberry trees this thick. Mulberry trees are not very common here, but over there when you walk down the street, the pavement is covered with fallen mulberries, a fruit very popular when I was a boy. They used to fall on the hats of the smart gentlemen as they alighted from their motorcars. I used to dream I was in the comfortable rooms of those days, furnished in different styles, like the different styles of the houses and the different languages of conversation. As time went by, my parents and brothers used to appear more and more clearly in my dreams. I had no news of them except, after a time, that they had passed away, but I was unable to understand it or believe it. I always used to dream I was with the people who had meant so much to me, and until that trip I refused to believe they were gone. Only now, in the last two weeks, have the faces I preserved intact in my mind for almost half a century dissolved once and for all. If I had thought about it rationally, there were few chances of my meeting my loved ones again, simple arithmetic would have told me: measuring the time that has elapsed since I left, I would have seen that the poor things had little chance of survival, given how hard life is over there. Work it out for yourself . . .

*

—To work it out, we would need to know the year when you left, Professor . . .

It was a good job the young man interrupted him, like a

cold knife blade severing the confession in which Traian had lost himself. Christa seizes the moment to steer the conversation to a lighter topic. The indiscreet curiosity in the eyes of the young people sitting at the table irritates her greatly: idle curiosity, idle interest, because they are incapable of conceiving that anybody other than them has ever experienced the blind, happy arrogance of youth.

—I hope your disciples won't discover that you, who has such a prodigious memory, don't know how many years you celebrated on your last birthday, with speeches and Festschriften to mark the occasion!

—Of course I don't know how old I am off hand, because I don't even want to know! When I saw that too many years had accumulated, I refrained from counting them . . .

A provocative gleam has rejuvenated Traian Manu's eyes. Beneath the weary gentleness of his gaze there is expectation, disquiet. His pupils flicker for an instant, uncertainly, and then his face relaxes: he hastens to laugh.

—I am afraid that half a century may have passed since I left there to begin my life here! And when you go back, it is always as if in a dream: the same houses, the same streets, except they are smaller, shrunken. They have deteriorated in time, just as your own body has deteriorated. In childhood, all the people around me were, if not young, then at least full of life, strong . . . The whole world was new, fresh, because the eye of the child projects his need for protection onto those around him . . . But you, my dears, you are too young to understand what I am saying . . . You have nowhere to go back to and you know perfectly all there is to know, but only from books!

*

—Am I to understand that you are reproaching us for our youth, Professor?

He is the same. The newlywed man. His latest, his most ambitious assistant. The future head of laboratory. The future director. His constant urge to come top. To advance faster than his peers.

—Me, reproach you? Good God, not a bit of it! I'm not reproaching you, on the contrary, I envy you, because there is nowhere and no way you can come up against your past! I told you that I envy you, although if I had to start all over again, if I were given the chance to go back, to the beginning, I don't know whether . . . Too tiring . . . and sometimes so boring!

—Were you bored on your trip, Professor?

—Well, I'm bored even over here! How could it be otherwise? And besides, nothing out of the ordinary happened to me there, unlike what you had been expecting, my dear . . .

—I had been expecting it, you say!

Christa's expression of outraged dignity makes him do an about turn.

—I was rather uneasy, she says, and I still believe I had good reason to be . . . You know very well the circumstances in which you returned . . .

—The return, true . . . The way things unfolded when I returned, true . . .

There is nothing else he can do except begin with his return.

CHAPTER EIGHTEEN
The "Scientist" Dossier (3)

Sheet no. 103
Source "Bădescu"
24 September 1986

Intelligence report

The source reports that on 12 August 1986 biologist MANU TRAIAN, an Italian citizen, came to Bucharest from Italy. The reason for his coming to our country was a lecture in Bucharest. From Bucharest he went to Cărbuneşti commune and on the way the source's car broke down and was towed by two tractors that happened to be passing. The source was with MANU TRAIAN constantly at restaurants and hotels and will later submit a list of the names and addresses of those with whom MANU TRAIAN came into contact as well as an expenses claim for a suitcase and restaurant bills.

MANU TRAIAN did not say whether he would be coming to our country again but he promised to invite the source to his house where he lives with his wife, Christina.

"BĂDESCU"

COMMENTS
The source has been given the task of maintaining relations with the aforementioned and trying to bring about the visit to him in Italy. A copy of this report will be forwarded to Section III.

Lt. MATEI SILVIU

In agreement with the planned measures.

                              Col. N. ISPAS

CHAPTER NINETEEN
Gifts on Parting

GIULIA SERVES THE ice cream and fruit, she fetches the tray of
Rémy Martin and Amaro Lucano, the professor's favorite cognac
and digestif, and she sits down to listen, with her hands in her
lap, like a well-behaved little girl.

—You're not going to believe it, but whenever the head of
state leaves on an official visit, whenever he comes back, all the
other flights, including international ones, are grounded without
warning for hours! I've no idea whether the airport staff know
anything, but they don't tell the travelers anything. You may well
ask me why the delays aren't included in the timetable and the
answer can only be that the head of state doesn't feel loved by
his people and takes the most extravagant measures to protect
himself from them.

—But the international airlines must lose a great deal of
money because of such disruptions! Why do they agree to have
relations with that country! cries Antonio.

—How come such a ridiculous figure is invited to England
and America with great pomp and ceremony?

Christa shakes her head in perplexity, reaches for her handbag, and with feverish motions extracts from therein her cigarette
case and lighter. She lights a cigarette, ignoring the reproving
looks her husband is giving her. As she inhales the cigarette
smoke, rapidly at first and then at longer intervals and more
deeply, Antonio gets up to fetch an ashtray. With a sigh of relief,
he pulls out his own packet of cigarettes and triumphantly tosses
it on the table.

*

—Can you imagine, my dears, what it means to wait in an airport
for hours, without having any idea why? The most extravagant

explanations were passing through my mind: that a third world war had begun, that there had been an earthquake, without my knowing it, that I was about to be arrested, sentenced to death and executed. I started to panic, but there was nothing I could do except look at the frozen departures board and gulp lemonade, which had an irritating chemical taste, and eat sandwiches made with damp bread and rubbery ham. And the heat was suffocating, like an oven! The air conditioning wasn't working or else there wasn't any, and the windows didn't open. I was like a mouse, like a rat, caught in a trap. And you know full well, my dears, from the simplest experiments, that a rat develops an ulcer after twenty-four hours of captivity! As for me, wracked by my chronic illnesses and having reached the age the Almighty has granted me to reach, what could I expect! At one point, I glimpsed myself in a mirror and it gave me a fright when I saw how I looked: scarlet and sweating, my hair plastered to my forehead, my shirt soaked, my coat and pants rumpled. And I was gasping like a fish out of water, my mouth was open and my eyes were bulging from their sockets! And the constant buzzing noise that accompanied me the whole journey! Could it have been the water in the bathrooms, which were in such a deplorable state? Could it have been fluctuations in my blood pressure? What do you think, my dear? Or was it the bugs that record absolutely everything, as the people over there believe? And there wasn't even any way I could phone an embassy, Amnesty International, Helsinki Watch, some association to rescue people in danger, so that somebody would come and get me out of there!

A didactic habit: the pause to relax. He turns his gentle, encouraging smile to each of the smiling faces around him. He will not continue talking until the laughter has died down, until the last vibration fades from the air. A thrifty hand will carefully gather up the crumbs of the others' attention: beneath the generous bonhomie there still throbs the longstanding lack of self-confidence that Giulia recognizes within herself.

*

—Just think of the tension I felt, my dear, knowing that you were travelling hundreds of kilometers to meet me at the airport and I had no means of telling you I would be late . . . I remembered all your warnings and I regretted not having heeded them!

His penitent face makes the young couple laugh, but Christa waves her hand impatiently, stop clowning, I know you far too well, and she reaches for the ashtray, so as not to tap her ash in her fruit dish like that ill-educated Antonio, it can't be easy for Giulia living with him.

—No, I'm not one to be scared, but I hope you will never experience what it is like all of a sudden to be catapulted outside every rule of our civilized world! And knowing my reactions, I was perfectly aware that every passing second increased the danger of something fatal happening to me. When I finally boarded the plane, my first concern was to look for my blood pressure pills and to ask the airhostess for a glass of water.

A Vittel, miss, a Period, even tap water, anything, I have to take my medicine straightaway!

*

Noble son of Laertes, Ulysses, / Cunning one, why have you left behind / The light of the sun and come hither / To see the dead and their mournful land? You place the pill on your tongue, you slowly swallow, hiccoughing, the water that scorches your dry mouth, below you the maquette of a toy city, whither you swear you will never return. In the seat next to you, a motionless young woman, she is swarthy, well fed, the sadness of the motionless faces that conceal their contentment/discontent.

But nor did you cry out: open the windows already, let the air in, why should I suffocate with the rest of you in this hermetically sealed container?

With an unsteady hand you tuck the box of pills in the top pocket of your jacket, no, thanks, I don't need anything, miss, you look at her suspiciously as she stands there stiffly, obligingly, wasn't she the same one who kept coming to the door of your room at the hotel in the evening, asking you for a lighter, a match? It can't be the same one, it's a different woman and they're all the same, it's been half a century since I touched a woman from my native land, but it would be pure madness to let you come into my room! The thick green eye shadow, annoyingly green, below the mercilessly plucked eyebrows, on the withered eyelids, above the sticky black, annoyingly black eyelashes. It's always the colors that first reveal the difference between your world and theirs!

By the porthole, the thin, yellowish face of the woman who is masticating tenaciously, quickly, the glint of metal teeth in the greedy, wide-open maw, the pink plastic plate is empty already. On the other side of the porthole, the velvety white glare. Down below, has the minuscule maquette of a plaything city glided away behind the airplane's wing? Did you close your eyes so as not to see it?

I don't know who you are and I don't care, you want to shout, I've got a lot of work to do and I want to arrive home as quickly as possible, I don't want to waste any more time, and I can't waste any more time trying to understand that which can't be understood, *then why did you come hither, stranger, to the mist and darkness?*

*

His opaque, absent gaze, turned inward to his memories, has remained fixed on the colorful poster on the fridge. He has even forgotten about Christa's protective, ironic gaze, her eyes that say she understands him better than he understands himself.

—The return was indeed a nightmare, my dears. True, I was tired and irritated even when I set out for the airport, because I had had to pack my bags in the midst of an insufferable commotion! Around me there was a constant to-ing and fro-ing, like in a station waiting room! People kept appearing, each of them carrying something, and very soon my hotel room started looking like the altar to some idol, heaped with offerings. When I gauged the items with my eyes, I worried about how much all those wooden, metal, leather items would weigh down my suitcase. Not to mention the books, as thick as they were hideous! You know very well how carefully we need to ration the time we have for reading anything outside our strict area of specialist interest!

"Are you trying to kill me, my dears?" I told them at one point. "Are you really trying to get rid of me? I'm not young anymore, you know, and I don't have the strength to carry heavy luggage. Consult among yourselves nicely and see what you can do about it!"

Consult among themselves nicely! From the very start they had been bickering in a whisper, and then more and more loudly, and they kept coming to me to complain about each other. That was what they had been doing all along, and a more disagreeable spectacle there could not have been. And they were all standing in a throng around my suitcase, which by now had become a real battleground: each was trying to eject the other's parcels to make room for his own. I caught one of them trying to remove my toiletry bag. And what do you think he wanted to cram in its place? Some wooden spoons! That was when I lost my temper and shouted at the wretch, but do you know what he said to me? Astounding! "Dear cousin," he said, that man whom I'd never even seen before I went back, neither him nor his garrulous wife, nor his son, a lad who kept hanging around me, but who never said a word. Let me open a parenthesis on the word "cousin," which drove me out of my wits: the social relationship it denotes is one of tribal complicity; the cousin is neither a brother nor a stranger. "Dear cousin, Mr. Traian," he added, probably realizing that I was annoyed, "don't get upset, Mr. Traian! I was sure that your toothbrush and sprays, your soap and your shaving kit—like you were a woman, not a man, the amount of time you take grooming yourself in the morning—I was sure you'd find somewhere to put all that stuff in your suitcase! You're not going to leave without them! But what I've brought you, this set of wooden spoons, made by a real craftsman, when you see them there in your kitchen, you'll realize how handy they'll come in!" And then he went off on a long tale about his long journeys around the country, I think he said he was a forestry engineer, an awkward, horny-handed man, always tired, who sweated when he spoke, it was obvious that he wasn't in the habit of stringing more than two words together . . .

*

Christa's ironic laughter.
—Awkward, awkward, but stubborn! Because those wooden spoons of his, in the heavy suitcase you crammed shut there, are going to end up in our kitchen tomorrow evening! And the poor forestry engineer was right, his set of kitchen utensils is a museum piece, of an archaic design that you only find at special fairs. The last generation of folk craftsmen, with nobody to hand their craft down to!

Is Christa laughing at the "cousin" or at him, her husband, when he speaks sarcastically of the archaic world whence he has just returned? But he never even had time to belong to that primitive world! Is the annoying voice in which he answers Christa due to the unpleasant memories of his trip or to his dissatisfaction with the way in which he senses she views him, even if he pretends not to notice?

—Maybe the spoons do have a museum value, but because of them my blood pressure kit had to be left behind in the hotel room! Instead, I found myself weighed down with perishable and spicy foodstuffs and local liquors that the doctor banned me from drinking years ago. "Better you keep them for yourselves, my dears!" I told them. "You'll have much better use for them than me, I assure you!" Because, believe it or not, in that country, the people have to queue for food like in wartime! But all my appeals were in vain and I was unable to find any diplomatic solution to the whole situation. To have given back just a few of the things and to have kept the others would have meant creating even more enmity between them. To have given everything back would have meant insulting them en masse. But at least I warned them: "Pay attention! It will be an utter disaster if you end up breaking the zipper on my suitcase!" I must have put a jinx on it. Not ten minutes later, I hear furious whispering. When I turned my head, there was a sudden silence: each of them tried to sidle away from my suitcase. They had indeed broken the zipper and God alone knows what they had managed to stuff inside and what had been left strewn around the room: on the chairs, the bed, the nightstand, even the carpet, there were parcels piled one on top of the other. And little by little they regained their voices and started to lay the blame on each other, in a whisper.

—You ought to have demanded that they all leave the room and taken all the alien parcels out of the suitcase! cried Antonio harshly.

—But what was I to do about the broken zipper? In any case, I have to admit that I had lost my sangfroid, especially given that the official car was late. If Professor Stan had been there, I wouldn't have had any practical problems to deal with, but he had had to go away on some urgent trip to Moscow or East Berlin. I asked them to call me a taxi, but the number was engaged all the time. There aren't very many customers, they told me, because taxis are a luxury, given the average wage, but on the other hand, there is only a single taxi company, which is state-owned. The same as everything else is state-owned over there . . .

—Who would like some tea? What kind of tea? Coffee? Decaffeinated or regular? whispers Giula.

Shh, her newlywed husband scolds her, but the professor waits patiently while she reels off her list and sets the water to boil for the tea and the coffee. And not until the steaming cups are on the table and Giulia has resumed her wonted position, with her hands tightly clasped in her lap, like a little girl from the country, does he continue.

*

—To be honest, my dear, I don't know what I would have done if my cousin Victor had not come up to me then. I chide myself now for having taken my irritation out on him. "Why are you so upset?" he said and patted me on the shoulder. "I imagine that it's the way you've learned to be over there, that you can't afford to waste a single minute, because where you come from time means money. But if you lose your temper, what do you gain? Calm down! Get a grip on yourself! We'll all lend a hand and in a few minutes your luggage will be ready! What won't fit in the suitcases, we'll pack nicely in carrier bags. We've brought carrier bags, don't you worry on that score! Then we'll tie up the suitcase with the broken zipper as elegantly as can be! You'll see: it won't even be noticeable and in any case, you're not going to want to take anything out before you get home, are you? And hey presto! Anything else? The car? It'll come, you'll see, it'll be here at the last minute! Or if not, just when you think all is lost, we'll get through on the phone and order a taxi. Or if not, we'll go outside and we'll find some private car which will take us there just as quickly and not necessarily for very much money." "I don't think you will find anybody in this country prepared to do such a thing!" I yelled back. "We'll find somebody, we'll find somebody, we can hardly be that unlucky! You know, there's always a solution! If you keep calm and wait, in the end things have a way of sorting themselves out. The truth is that there is a thing or two you can learn from us! In the first place: don't get upset over nothing!" "All very well, my dear," I yelled in exasperation, "you're not telling me anything new! I was born here and all my life I have been trying with all my might to forget that way of thinking! It's not just a question of me, but I represent an institution! An entire province! A country! I can't be seen in public laden with plastic bags and a suitcase tied up with string!" "Never mind," he answered. "What's the big fuss! We'll sort things out one way or another. We'll get hold of a nice suitcase! A smart one! Better than yours!" He went out straightaway and in five minutes he came back with a new suitcase. The design was horrible, but it was bigger and fastened very well. It's impossible for me to work out how he found it so quickly and how the car arrived immediately after that . . . I know, my dear, that you don't like the sound of Victor, but you're wrong about him, you know, after all he did for me. He's a man of action, not words.

CHAPTER TWENTY
Cassandra's Speech

DANIEL SAYS:

Then there was all the bother over the broken zipper . . . When I heard the moans and the whispers, I was certain catastrophe had struck, precisely the catastrophe that he, with the cool eye of a Westerner, having landed in his high-tech UFO, and with his caustic futurologist's mind, had predicted when he told them:

—Be careful, my dears! Don't stuff all your presents in the suitcase, because we won't be able to close it! It would be a real catastrophe if the zipper broke!

And so, even without looking at the unraveling black knot of guilty people vociferating: "I told you not to!" "But I told you, I begged you!" "You had to go and . . ." "Now what?" "Always the same!" "I'd have given you a piece of my mind if Traian hadn't been here!" I knew that the perfect jinx had to be Father, the same as ever.

And likewise without looking, I saw him quickly gulp down the Rudotel pill that Victor gave him, which he got from Professor Stan, who always takes one when he has a meeting at the Central Committee, at the Grand National Assembly, so that he can be photogenic when we see him on the television:

—Look, there's Professor Alexandru standing next to . . .

—Isn't he embarrassed to stand there next to . . .

—Look at him standing there next to that awful . . .

—Why should he be embarrassed? He's there for one day and reaps the rewards a whole lifetime! Are we any better off here, trying to scrape a living?

And as if that weren't enough, after he gulped down the precious Rudotel, I saw poor old dad going straight up to the lofty Guest and—unbelievable, unbelievable, unbelievable—say to him:

—Cousin Traian . . .

And then, horrified at what he saw on the Guest's face and remembering Cassandra's advice too late as always, he corrected himself:

—Dear Mr. Traian . . .

And the rest I didn't wish to hear, I didn't wish to see any more, I went out and I knocked back a short and smoked a fag.

*

And so we come to the moment when Traian was ready to go through customs with the suitcase that Victor had, with unbelievable promptitude, conjured up out of thin air, and, no matter how hard it was for me to believe it, the lofty Guest was about to depart, even though we hadn't managed to talk to each other so much as once, no matter how hard I had tried to get close to him.

The biggest failure was when he came to our house and I was at the university secretariat. They were repeating the inquiry into Mihnea's death yet again, Gimmi's folks had come back from abroad and were putting on pressure to have us readmitted to university, because it wasn't our fault that Mihnea had gotten drunk and fallen off the balcony. How embarrassing to end up being glad that Gimmi's old man, the colonel, was turning the screws, but I have to admit it, I'm a pygmy, a nobody, a nothing, I sat there in the rector's office and my heart had shrunk to the size of a flea as I waited to hear whether we would be readmitted in the autumn and not have to miss a year.

But if I had been at home, I could have walked with Traian to the car, the two of us could have talked together! What possessed him to come right then I don't know, Mother said he just wanted to see where Nana lived for twenty-seven years, after they arrested her husband and evicted her from her house, banishing her to the Militari district at the edge of town.

In any case, after that, the whole of the time until he left, Traian was unapproachable yet again, flanked by Professor Stan and the whole gang of spongers, of bodgers, plus the ever-present

Victor, foreign banknotes sticking to his fingers, his eyes swiveling in his head like the lights on top of an ambulance.

The apogee of the madness was that because of the zipper, it was Father of all people who got to talk to Traian the longest, although it would have been better if the opportunity had not arisen! Traian wouldn't be lugging around that monster suitcase and Father wouldn't be gulping down Rudotel, Extraveral, Valium, and Distonocalm every time he remembers.

*

And so I kept one eye on Traian, who was about to go through customs, and one eye on the huge electronic clock. And I listened to the male voices of the tragic chorus, and they kept repeating their mutual wishes, accompanied by friendly slaps on the shoulder, by little dirty jokes, for which they lowered their voices, joining their bellies of various sizes, their bald patches, their warts, their hypocritical, obsequious, cowardly smiles, their acrylate teeth, their metal molars, their briefcases, their scuffed portfolios, the wisdom of their maturity.

And once the joke had been told, there would be the same worried glance all around, who might have heard, who might have seen, that guy by the gate, the Party secretary, that girl from accounts, our Securitate man?

You could have taken them away en masse in an ambulance, blood pressure of twenty-seven by twenty, but they were still alive, they kept automatically turning their heads left and right to see who could see them, who couldn't see them.

And in the end, the danger having passed, barely able to breathe they would repeat to each other the wishes, the pieces of advice accompanied by a friendly slap on the shoulder:

—Let's all stand here!

—Let's not lose each other!

—Don't let anybody get ahead of the rest!

—Let's get ahead of him now, before he enters customs!

—It wouldn't do for us to get ahead of him!

—Maybe the toilet's down in the basement!

—Maybe the canteen's down in the basement!

—Maybe there's a shop in the basement selling cigarettes, blended coffee, *nechezol*!*

—Genuine instant coffee!

—Maybe . . .

—Maybe . . .

*

And Mother was picking up on Father's panic and at the same time putting together her strategy for facilitating a confidential top-level meeting with the Guest, who was by then moving towards customs. With a gift for improvisation worthy of Miles Davis, Mother was packing together the outlines of failed scenarios about how she would go up to the Guest at the very last moment and tell him what nobody else was of a mind to tell him.

I am Nana's daughter, Cassandra would have cried out, so loudly that the customs officers, who were rummaging through the multiple pockets of Traian's jacket, in search of letters to Radio Free Europe, and passing Father's wooden spoons through the Roentgen machine, would have immediately hooked up their recording equipment. And he himself, the famous professor, the eternal fiancé of the unforgotten Nana, would all of a sudden have pricked up his ears and listened piously, one foot already resting on the steps of the UFO, his eyes on Victor's suitcase.

I am Ana Maria's daughter, her only daughter, Mother would have liked to shout, in tears, Nana raised me, but I let her die and I reproach myself for it every morning as soon as I open my eyes.

---

* Slang word for the coffee substitute that replaced the real thing in the shops during the severe shortages in 1980s Communist Romania. Nechezol (pronounced neh-keh-zol with the stress on the last syllable) was made from oats, chickpeas, chestnuts, acorns and the like. The word is derived from the verb a necheza (to whinny, neigh), given the coffee was made from horse fodder and also perhaps with reference to an involuntary effect of drinking it. The suffix -ol, used to form the names of organic compounds, is possibly an ironic allusion to the fact that the semi-illiterate Elena Ceaușescu was praised as a "world-renowned chemist" in regime propaganda.

My husband, who is a good man, although he broke the zipper of your suitcase, tries to console me, saying it had to be, such was her fate, never mind, Clementina, because not even we will inherit the earth, we will all meet on the *Other Side*, he tells me. When I took her to the hospital, she was only in a semi-coma, but they didn't want to take her because she was over the age of sixty-five and they didn't have any vacant beds, or any medicine, or any cotton wool . . .

I am Ana Maria's daughter, Mother is about to shout at the top of her voice, for all the airport to hear, but I am adopted, I keep the certificate in a bundle of old photographs, you were there, Mr. Traian Manu, or the other one was there, the one who died at the front, in Stalingrad, or in Sighet prison, I can't remember where.

That is what Mother would shout, and taking advantage of the Lofty Guest's discombobulation, she would quickly ask of him some trifle, something for me, a pair of Adidas sneakers at least, or some stonewashed jeans, or medicine for Father, but nothing for her, nothing, nothing, except the sacred duty of washing, sweeping, cleaning, ironing, darning, and grumbling after us.

*

So, Mother would be torn between these exciting plans and the fear that Father might notice her desperate last-ditch attempts, which would cause him instantly to become that alien and unlikeable man whom she constantly encounters in her worst hallucinations and she would hear his intolerable voice shouting at her:

—I forbade you to ask him for anything! I forbade you to humiliate us by begging from him! I forbade you to ask him for anything, anything at all!

Father might instantly become one of those people who when angry are all the more intolerable the more they are shouted at, pushed around, snapped at by all and sundry, most of the time they smile, they quip, they apologize when they have the least cause to, but then all of a sudden they will start yelling in a hoarse, squeaky voice, their hands trembling, their faces turning scarlet:

—How could you do something so stupid? When you told me that you were thinking of speaking to him and asking him for something, did I or did I not forbid it?

So, in that imagined instant, the impassioned soul of Mother/ Cassandra will have been wavering between her natural desire as a female soldier ant to carry back to the ant hill whatever fate cast before her and her habit, ossified over five millennia of cohabitation, of taking Father's every interdiction as being subject to martial law, the breaking of which could only be named GUILT.

*

It's so hard to choose.

So, my first instinct would have been to go to him at the very last moment, to talk to him, to ask when he would be coming back, if he was coming back.

My heart was thudding, my hands were sweating, I was Nana, who had waited for him without a letter, without news, for half a century, and now she saw him leaving before they had had a chance to meet.

I was Father, an implacable serpent was biting my stomach and I was bent double with pain, smiling happily, any minute now redemption was going to arrive, the requital for my own successes/failures.

I was Mother, this is the easiest role, it's not hard at all to imagine what Mother, Nagging Cassandra, would tell the Guest.

*

Mother would straightaway get down to business, her eyes would blanch from the panic and grimly clutching the handle of her handbag, in her mind she would recite, with the passion of a zealot repeating a prayer, those worthy words whose hidden purpose was, as I have already said, to scrounge a pair of jeans or a jacket or some authentic Adidas sneakers for the boy, without my husband knowing, please. As hard as we have tried, and we have always tried, it hasn't been possible before now, although that doesn't mean we're complaining. Praise be to God, we get by like everybody else, we get by as best we can. Except that we can't afford what people like you can afford. But you're an adult, you can understand that we can't do any more than that, we'll be able to afford more when we'll be able. I'm saying all this so you won't get a bad impression of us, especially since my husband forbade me to ask you for some small token. But in my opinion, he's over the top, because not even at his age does he know what kind of world he's living in! It's as if he does it on purpose, just to cause trouble for himself, my husband I mean, who, apart from that, is an upstanding, hardworking man and with reference to you he always tells me:

—Don't put us in a humiliating situation by asking him for something! Better we give him something!

We'll give him something, but what? With what's available here, what are we supposed to give him? And that set of wooden spoons he wants to give him, how stupid is that? I told him, forget it, what would he want with something like that? I'll swear on my life that Traian's missus, whoever she might be, whatever she might be like, doesn't spend her life in the kitchen, unlike me . . .

Other than that, I don't know what the appropriate way to address him would be: Traian? Mr. Manu? There's not that much of an age difference, because we're not young anymore either, but you are an important man and we're nobody. I've been writing to the cadres department for years and years to tell them we don't have any relatives abroad, we don't write letters to anybody, we've put it all in the past! And as for in-laws, what's that supposed to mean?

And so if it was to do with kinship, I wouldn't have created the extra bother for myself trying desperately to catch a moment when we could be alone together. I would just like you to know what you meant to my mother, to my son, he'll never be capable of telling you himself, and she, as you know, is dead. My good parents did something stupid and I paid the price for years and years, and they paid a heavy price, too. They sheltered some resistance fighters from the mountains and both of them, mother and father, went to prison and nobody ever saw them again.

And so it was that Nana took me from the orphanage and adopted me, I call her Nana because that's what everybody calls her, but she was like a mother to me. Nana sent me to night school, because they wouldn't take me at the day school, she looked after my child when I had to attend political instruction, when I had to do patriotic labor, picking potatoes and maize, when I had to go to meetings and rallies. I think she was thinking of you in her hardest moments, of which there were plenty. If Traian can succeed in a foreign land, why not you here? Nana used to say to Daniel.

But I'm afraid that if I don't manage to tell you all these things before you leave, then there will be nobody else to tell you them . . .

Daniel laughs at me and says I'm a nagging Cassandra and it's true, I know some things even before they happen. For example, I know that you are going to continue to put your faith in Victor. You're going to be too harsh with us sometimes, but with him you're going to be too indulgent. And in any case my husband wouldn't open his mouth, it's always irked me how easily he gives up, it's a way of going about things that leads to great inconvenience. He's not one to stick his oar in like Victor, he doesn't go round making connections with people left and right, he doesn't have money to go drinking in bars, he hates to have problems at work like Victor does with his gifts, his money, his one hand washing the other, his getting off scot-free thanks to his connections, his people in high places . . .

Because I'm in a hurry, I'm afraid of repeating myself, Victor might show up any moment and push me aside cracking one of his stupid jokes.

—Clementina doesn't have a sense of humor, he always says.

—How's that my fault, I tell him, if I don't find as many things funny as you do?

I'm not keen on people who are too jolly, like Victor, the way he always turns everything into a joke, as he makes his way from taxi to train restaurant car, arm in arm with some big cheese or black-market racketeer, everywhere he goes he spreads rumors, gossip, stories that are half truth, half lies, but not one of them told at random.

Victor, with his season ticket to the hard currency shops, the king of the black market, buys and sells information that's half a century old, says Daniel.

I'm amazed he hasn't popped up yet, to prevent me from having the opportunity to say what I want except to my in-laws, cousins, nieces, aunts, like what happened at the house in Cărbuneşti, when I had to make do with whispering in the kitchen.

But maybe it's better like this, because if you heard me, you might spill the beans to my folks, who always scold me for being indiscreet as it is, for butting into the conversation uninvited. In our house there are rarely quarrels, but I do admit that there have been discussions. In my youth I was quieter, but later I noticed that if you're quiet, the others have no idea what you're thinking. It's only in novels that people read each other's thoughts, but in real life, the quieter you are the more of a mess you get yourself into, just you remember that.

But don't you go thinking that Daniel sent me to ask you for something, if you give him something, then fine, but if you don't give him anything, it makes no difference. It's just that I would have liked to make him happy, whereas others are given a helping shove, he got into university all by himself and then just a few weeks later they kicked him out! His bad luck was that he'd gone over to the Complex to fetch some course notes and a friend had just received a food parcel from home, another one brought the drinks, I can't say that it was a party or an orgy, just harmless nonsense! And one of them went out onto the balcony and fell off, what he was doing on the balcony I don't know, he was looking to die, obviously. But it seems to me that the Lord punished him too harshly, to be young, to get drunk once and die for as little as that when all around you, you see so many villains thriving!

And after that Daniel didn't say a word for months and months and the doctor told me:

—As much as you can, try to do something to make him happy . . .

And I wrote letter after letter to have them take him back, after all he wasn't guilty of anything, I kept trying, I wrote, I begged, but I never got any reply. I said that no news is good news, it means there's room for hope and I was right, like I always am, except that nobody ever believes me. They made an exception for one of them, Gimmi, the irony being that he was the one who brought the booze, but his dad's a big colonel, one of the blue-eyed boys, as we call them, he's constantly going *Abroad*, and his mother works in the same place. Yes, it's a good thing that Gimmi's folks have managed to get him re-admitted and the others along with him, and now a letter's come from the rector's office, for him to re-enroll . . .

It must be down to Nana, wherever she might be now, dear old Nana, because I'm convinced that there must be people who help us, if not here, then from the next world . . .

*

It's so hard to choose.

And I still hadn't chosen, I was standing with my back to my family, facing the people coming through customs the other way.

On the one hand, I want to rush over to him, at the last moment, and ask him:

—Say, when will you be coming back? Say, when will you be paying another visit? Say, when will you be calling me over there, to the *Other Side*, the other world?

On the other hand, I wanted to walk out of the airport and leave, knowing that I would in any case go on waiting for him, the same as I had been waiting for him for as long as I could remember.

Maybe I had waited for him so long because I had never seen him coming back day after day, dragging his legs, dragging his briefcase, dragging himself home from work, irritable, exhausted, unshaven, rumpled, poisoned with his own desires, powerlessness, envy, and longstanding resentments.

Maybe I had been waiting for him because I had not seen him, had not heard whispering head to head with Mother, evening after evening, totting up how much money they had borrowed and how much they had to pay back. I had not glimpsed the panic in his eyes on the days when he came home in a panic:

—They called me in to the director's office to tell me . . .

—They called me in to work this Sunday . . .

—They called me in to Labor and Wages . . .

—They called me aside to tell me what is being said about me. They told me that a big merger, a big change is on the way.

*

And so, I was keeping an eye on what was happening at check in, they were moving towards customs, with their backs to the family, but amid the laughter coming from the bench I kept hearing a phrase that made me hopping mad:

—I hope Daniel will inherit his father's success with women and young ladies!

And without turning my head, I espied the merry eyes in the sallow face and the body stooped with pain, in the clothes that became rumpled and stained as soon as he put them on, instantly annihilating the afternoon Mother had spent brushing, buffing, darning them, all the while giving him a steady stream of niggling advice.

And still standing apart with my back to them, I saw him take out a fistful of tablets, which Mother had carefully wrapped in little pieces of paper and which he had carelessly got mixed up with dry breadcrumbs, tram tickets, paper clips, and so on. And as he was unwrapping the pills and nonchalantly swallowing them, gulping, he cast an uneasy glance at the huge electronic clock and cracked another tender joke, gallantly teased the cousins, aunts, sisters, sisters-in-law sitting on the eternal blue vinyl sofa, in that inimitable way he has of showing off, making fun of himself, belittling himself.

And straightaway was heard the mezzosoprano voice of Mother, Nagging Cassandra, providing medical tips along with a report on her husband's health, interspersed with revealing little details of our family habits and gloomy predictions.

*

—What are you doing, Cornel? Even a child knows that you're not supposed to take pills without water! It's as if you're dead set on doing yourself a mischief! It's as if you're dead set on departing for the next world, just to spite me! So that you can leave me behind to bear the burden! I'm not saying you shouldn't take them, if your stomach, your kidneys, your liver, your gallbladder are hurting, take them, but don't take them without thinking! Take them at the time you're supposed to, at the right hour and minute. A savage I may be, like you always say, because I hate pills, but you know, there is such a thing as alternative medicine, natural cures, acupuncture, read *The Flame*! Read Păunescu!* Otherwise, you'll see what will happen to you eventually: you'll get blocked kidneys!

And all of a sudden becoming rigid, he goes:
—Shhh!

And she takes fright at the panic in his puffy eyes, but straightaway she understands what he means by that: shhh! Because in the five millennia they have been together, they have broken each other in, they have achieved synchrony, they have learned how best to transmit the alarm: when one of them, always him, complains of hyperacidity, bloody stools, machinations, micturition, maneuvering, hellish itches, backstabbing, colon bacillus infections, never-ending meetings, cabals of malevolent individuals, gangs, terrorist groups, gangsters plotting against him. And so

* Adrian Păunescu (1943–2010), the logorrheic "bard" of the Ceauşescu regime and editor of *Flăcăra* (The Flame), a weekly magazine and mouthpiece of the national-communist ideology.

as a rule there is not even any need for words, sufficient being a *shhh*, a *tsssk*, a *hmmmmm*, a shrug of the shoulders, a twitch of his increasingly sallow, increasingly lined face. And now *shhh!* means WARNING! Somebody has seen them waiting there, accompanying somebody to the airport, whom? Whom might they be waiting for, accompanying, etc.?

This is something I'll never accept: sharing with somebody else my aching liver, colon, teeth, my resentments, constipation, humiliations, diarrhea, old age.

No, never will I accept to become a symbiotic creature, and never will I accept to become an old crock.

CHAPTER TWENTY-ONE
Trustworthy People

—I DO INDEED have reservations about the letters from that cousin of yours, which after a given point began to arrive frequently, after decades in which the postman never brought you anything from your country, said Christa. But I can find Victor, or whatever you say his name is, neither agreeable nor disagreeable, as long as I have never met him . . . And it may well be that I'll have occasion to meet him here. Maybe he'll ask you to send him an invitation . . .

—Why do you have to smile so ironically, my dear? It's precisely because you're so suspicious that I'd like you to meet him. In a lawless world, bogged down in bureaucracy, like it is over there, you have no idea how much good it can do you to have somebody capable of solving the infinite administrative quibbles you come up against at every step. Victor knows how to deal with every bureaucrat, he knows what to give them. And you can believe me when I tell you that he intervened every time I found myself in difficulty . . .

—I expect such gestures weren't free of charge . . .

—Well, there's where you're wrong! I might say that it was I who cost him! Although the standard of living is very low there, he manages to do all right. He runs a small workshop, state-owned, of course, but he is viewed like a genuine owner. And because he knows by instinct how to conduct himself with every kind of person, he gets on well with his bosses. As far as I was able to tell, he has served time in prison for illegalities, but he has always bounced back. His position holds a certain amount of importance in our small town, but I saw that he also felt like a fish in water in the capital. In order to realize that he's not a profiteer, as you imagine him to be, I have to tell you that there were countless occasions when he offered to pay: "Don't worry," I can almost hear him say, "here, my money is better than yours!"

And indeed, whenever he opened his wallet, I saw it was full.

Traian's low voice is sooner trying to persuade his young, confused lady assistant than the suspicious Christa.

—Out of his own pocket Victor bought me the suitcase, when I was leaving. I only remembered when it was already too late. But in any case, knowing that I was leaving, I had spent all the money I had changed and I would have had reservations about giving him hard currency, because the law doesn't allow that sort of thing over there. At one point Victor offered to help me change some money on the black market, if I needed, but I preferred to go to the official exchange, even though the rate was very disadvantageous, rather than get him into trouble. Because they must have been keeping us under surveillance, even if I wasn't aware of it. And so the suitcase hasn't been paid for, and poor Victor, with his customary honesty, warned me: "It's not going to be easy carrying it on the journey. It's heavy even when it's empty, let alone when it's full! I'll keep the suitcase with the broken zipper and repair it for you. I'll be here waiting for you and I'll give it to you when you come back," he told me when I left.

—Don't you even think about going back there!

Irritated, Christa reaches for her cigarette case: another cigarette.

—He's won't be going back unless it's with us! And I'll be the professor's bodyguard! I'm thinking of gradually taking Cousin Victor's place! cries Antonio.

—I don't think you'd be up to it! Especially when the bill arrived at the restaurant! laughs Giulia.

The professor laughs too, Christa smiles, but what about the cake? she asks. When is the cake coming?

*

—The money over there is not worth anything except in their world! And as for poor Victor, from what he told me, he's never been abroad . . .

—But now that he's met you, it's not out of the question that he'll have an opportunity to go abroad, Christa adds, on edge.

—What would be the harm in that? After a lifetime of toil and suffering, because to live over there means to suffer from dawn till dusk, I would like to see him visit a different world. As soon as I met him at the airport I sensed I could place the same full trust in Victor as I could in Professor Stan! Who else do you think would have been capable of doing all the things he did for a foreigner? Because, let's be fair: the people over there must have reacted to me the same way as I reacted to them. In other words, as a foreigner, not a relative!

Why does he become more and more disagreeable the more he praises him? Is it because of Christa's contrariness, which her parents detected in her from an early age? Or is it because she remembers the lame owner of the confectionary shop on Hauptstraße and his attempts, ever renewed, ever failing, to win her goodwill—the younger, unexceptional, but hardworking sister of the brilliant Klara? The parcels of cakes, the invitations to the shop . . .

With a grimace of disgust, Christa pushes away her plate of cake.

*

Savoring the first spoonful with his eyes closed, Traian Manu is still thinking of Cousin Victor: how is he to break down Christa's resistance?

—Given his age, he must have lived under different regimes, but he's not interested in politics. He told me that from the very start and it increased my trust in him, because it is something unusual for someone from a country like that. He's only interested in food, drink and friends, that's what he says, what he always repeats. He was a little boy when I left. Now he is a giant of a man, with a ruddy, fleshy face, a Rabelaisian figure. He always had business to attend to, always a joke on his lips and a glass in his hand. From the very start, he told me straight out: "Call for me whenever you need something doing." Even his unusual physical strength made me feel safe when I was with him . . . A simple man, but you know my opinion: more often than not, a simple man is worth more than an educated one . . .

—More often than not? Don't you mean always? sneered Christa.

—You and your ironies! He's like a character from a Russian novel . . . true, you're not much keen on them . . . I don't like the French style of gardening and the Baroque, you don't like Dostoevsky. But it's not a question of what we like, but of what's useful . . .

It is the role of the host to defuse such moments, when the conversation keeps coming back to the argument between the professor and his wife, which certainly has nothing to do with so uninteresting a character as Victor. And Antonio does so in his usual direct manner: what in fact were the most shocking differences between our world and theirs? he asks Traian Manu.

*

The velvety layer of dust and debris on the faded leaf, the grey walls with their even greyer streaks of rain, the whitish vegetation, the red flag hanging limp, frozen on the wall striated with pollution and rain.

—There is even a different acoustic ambience, different kinds of noise. But the real shock is produced by the colors, there is a flagrant difference in the colors, as soon as you arrive there. And I didn't realize that until after I returned, although probably I registered it at the time. But it was not till I was back here that the impression of a different world became clear to me, of something you sense before you actually manage to see something to provide the colors. And I'm not talking about the clothes of the people over there, of the sad, ridiculous way they were dressed . . . I'm talking about a world of dark and faded colors, like in a black and white film . . . *Arriving at the bourn beyond the waters, where dwell the Cimmerians, ever swathed in mist and darkness, who never see the light of the sun . . .*

The motionless faces of the well-brought-up young couple: it is as if his voice, suddenly pathetic, and the strange sounds of that long-dead language in no way elicit their laughter. He apologizes, laughing:

—*The Odyssey* again! In my end of year dissertation at the Theological Seminary I chose to reconstruct the journey to the underworld based on the information provided in Greek literature . . .

—But why was it that you were drawn to such a topic at that age, Professor?

Traian Manu hesitates, his eyes resting on Giulia's sharp gaze, before abruptly realizing that he has hesitated too long and glances away. His eyes turn toward the other questioning eyes.

—It must have been the morbid curiosity of adolescence, an age haunted by the thought of suicide and all kinds of ultimate questions. But the poverty of the accounts of the underworld was to disappoint me. And how promisingly it begins: *Is there anything harder to do, poor wretch? / How were you able to come hither to the realm of Pluto, / Where the wretched shades of the dead make their abode?* That is how the account of the journey begins, but it continues with the story of Tyro, of Alcmene, of Iphimedia, stories of life, in fact. Not one concrete detail about the realm of Proserpine. The world of the shades, the next world, cannot be understood or recounted . . . But how did we get on to this?

The increasingly panicked gleam in his pupil. Don't leave me here to sink into the shifting sands, stretch out a helping hand to me! Don't you see how I'm sinking up to my knees, up to my waist? Cast me a rope! The water has risen up to my mouth! The sand is about to fill my eyes! I have been wandering through the dark so long and I no longer know how to go back! You, my dear, you can't leave me like this, shine light into the thickets in which I am lost!

—Giulia asked you why as an adolescent you picked such a morbid topic, Christa says calmly. And if she or Antonio has anything else to ask you, they ought to hurry, because we need to be keeping an eye on the time. It promises to be a long day tomorrow and you are obviously exhausted after you journey.

*

—You have told us about your return, Professor, but what about your arrival? Was it just as dramatic?

There is a note of irony in his assistant Giulia's voice, but the professor did not notice it, thinks Christa. Or else he chose to ignore it, thinks Giulia, who, as she has in the past and as she will many times in the future, feels torn between the desire to be faithful to her husband, on the one hand, and the promptings of her lively mind, which tells her differently, on the other.

—My arrival? Although I was obviously expected, or perhaps precisely for that reason, my arrival was also difficult. Just think, from the moment I set foot in the airport, all kinds of faces started parading in front of me, each as much a stranger as the next. But I ought to have recognized somebody in each of those faces. In theory, the sons, daughters, granddaughters, great-granddaughters of people who had been close to me "in the first part of my life." Most of those who were waiting for me there had been born or had grown up after my departure. And so, I had to remember as quickly as possible each name, along with the face and the story that went with it. And my memory has been getting worse and worse lately . . .

—Don't get annoyed if I interrupt, but . . . Even so . . . Why did you use the expression *in theory*, Professor? "In theory, the sons, daughters, grandchildren, great-grandchildren . . ."

Only she could have asked such a question, in such a seemingly hesitant voice. Only her quick mind could catch that which in the mind of her old professor still remained enveloped in mist.

—Maybe it will seem to you mere fantasy, but I know that in that instant, there flashed through my mind a thought that has kept recurring. Who are all these people? I asked myself. Are they really the descendants of the people who were once close to me, as close as you have become? Or are they just strangers, trained to play this role?

His eyes, wandering questioningly over the faces of the young couple. Is it the silence of well-brought-up, polite young people in front of a loved and feared professor in a traditional classroom?

Or is it the silence of adolescents who yearn for the wild earth where adventure sprouts?

*

—Ooh, what a detective novel you've started! And just when we were getting ready to leave!

Christa's voice: gentle, cautionary at first, then evermore shrill, like the supple blade of a high-quality knife, which you flex in your hand and then slowly, slowly release.

—But we won't let you leave until you finish the story of your arrival! Antonio insists, with that note of irony in his voice that makes Giulia feel embarrassed. So, was the hardest moment when you met your relatives . . . or so-called relatives?

—No, definitely not! That was a confusing moment. But the most unpleasant moment was at customs. I was standing there, feeling more and more tired, more and more irritated, waiting for my turn to come. That's what I call an inspection, my dears, because even before they open your suitcase, you can see it in the eyes of the customs officers that they think you are a criminal: the decision has been taken, sentence has been passed, and they will find the evidence! And so I was standing in the queue and it took ages! True, it took so long because the suitcases of the people in front contained fur hats, even though it was the height of summer, blankets, cassette players, packets of coffee and Kent cigarettes. Kent is the only brand well-to-do people seem to smoke in that country, I find it hard to see why . . . Bulging suitcases, sweating people, harsh officials with thuggish faces, swearwords that I can't remember ever having heard in that language . . . Naturally, the swearwords would start after the traveler left customs, his suitcase still open, with bars of soap and sprays and packets of cigarettes tumbling out of the crumpled bunches of underwear. I found out later that they were coming back after being contracted to work in the Arab countries and the aim of the inspection was for them to give as big a bribe as possible to the customs officials. Fortunately, it was then

that Alexandru Stan appeared, like a guardian angel. We were
at university together and now he is the director of an institute,
an academician, among other high-up positions. The customs
officials respectfully lifted their hands to the peaks of their caps
and in an instant my wait was over. Professor Stan uttered only
the conventional pleasantries: that he was happy to see me again,
that he was looking forward to my lecture . . .

*

Christa laughs.
—He is looking forward to seeing you again over here . . . I'm
almost certain that you'll get a phone call before long: he's just
arrived and he would like to see you. Perhaps you can help him
with a letter of recommendation for his daughter, introduce
her . . .
Christa laughs; Traian does not. The young couple smile,
in puzzlement. Is he not laughing because only his own set of
didactic jokes amuses him? Is he not laughing because his sense
of humor has been educated to appreciate a different kind of
joke? To him her jokes will always be jokes in a foreign language.
And after so many years of life together, he still finds that he
cannot tell from her voice whether she is joking or being serious.
—It's true, the last time we saw each other, Professor Stan
hinted that he might visit me here very soon. He insisted that I
pay him a visit at the institute before I left. It was a mere formality, it lasted a quarter of an hour, he left his office and walked
with me to the car that was waiting for me outside. Naturally,
protocol did not demand it, but he made an explicit sign to me
to show that his office was bugged, he pointed at the ceiling,
at the telephone, and by then I had already learned their secret
language. Outside, as I was about to leave, he recited some lines
from *The Odyssey* to me. He had remembered from when we were
young that it was my favorite book. I shall translate the lines for
you, so that you will understand why I felt for him with all my
heart when he whispered them to me: *I would rather be slave to
a lowly master than to be great here in hell* . . .

—Oh-là-là! As if he had been forced to accept all those lofty positions! In fact, if I have understood rightly, he has made an important political career for himself, given that he's a very clever man. And his scientific work is long since out of date. You feel sorry for him for having wasted himself on public life and for not having any serious work to leave behind him, but I doubt that that was his goal in life. You were at university together, you are friends, but you don't resemble each other one bit . . . And don't think I'm saying this because I'm piqued at your making that journey . . .

Christa's voice, brittle at first, becomes more velvety as she continues to speak. When she finishes, she thrusts her lighter and packet of cigarettes into her handbag, she puts on her glasses, she looks at the watch that hangs from her neck by a chain.

But her husband still has something to say:

—When you hold such important positions as he does, in a state like that, of course you pay a certain price. In the first place, you no longer have the time to dedicate yourself to research. In the beginning, I myself was suspicious when I received a telegram from him, informing me that he wanted to visit our European Center, which he had read about in specialist journals. I couldn't turn him down, but I took precautionary measures, which I am embarrassed about now. I even asked Marco, my assistant at the time, who went to America on a scholarship, your predecessor, dear Antonio, not to leave us alone and because Marco was present, we talked in Italian the whole time. As Professor Stan is a consummate polyglot, it didn't bother him. But it was an exaggerated precaution, because during my stay over there, the whole time I felt he was as attentive and devoted as a brother. But enough of these stories! You were saying, Antonio, that you have some Martini champagne? Then, let me propose a toast!

CHAPTER TWENTY-TWO
A Golden Boy

—I've got something to show you, comrade colonel! We've already reaped quite a harvest. Yes, yes, don't be so skeptical, you'll see for yourself right away! The Defector, as you call him, has only just left and I've already compiled a first little correspondence file. I'm optimistic. The omens are good! Allow me to present to you the most significant items . . .

This snot-nosed Silviu Matei really lost his marbles when they sent him on that mission to Păltiniş.* They decided we weren't going to limit ourselves to just technical operations and of all the ones that got an education there that lieutenant Matei of mine ended up the craziest! He's outstripped everybody else in the apparatus, a real golden boy, he'll go far! Shitten boy, more like! It's come to my ears that the brood of his relatives, them undercover Gorbachev agents, want to send him to the States, and not on a job, like us peasants, but on a scholarship! Let's educate him at the highest level, because the future of our institution lies in him and his ilk! Our country's youth, in whom we place our hope, screw that! He'll go far because he's got the folk behind him to propel him, his godfather the general, his ma the major, his stepdad the colonel, his real dad in Army Intelligence! Not like me, who's got farmyard dirt under his nails, I was an activist in the Communist Youth, I joined the army when they reorganized the security services, worked my way up rank by rank till I became head of the Department of Security and Protection! Just let him mess with me, that monkey, who's only ever laid the girls his ma procured for him! Parroting all that fancy talk he overheard around that Noica, it's like he's poking you in the

* Păltiniş is a small hamlet in the Carpathian Mountains, where philosopher Constantin Noica (1909–1987) spent his retirement. Noica, who had been a political prisoner during the Dej period, was visited in Păltiniş by young intellectuals, who also, of course, included Securitate infiltrators.

eye when he spouts off like that, and he'll go on spouting off until he sprains his tongue in the end! If he thinks he's going to sit behind this desk, he's got another thing coming! When pigs fly! My family is the apparatus! Here we are and here we'll stay, we'll go on being what we were and then some! That upstart's not going to budge me . . .

—Give it here and let's see what you're capable of!

*

Sheet no. 90

REPORT

Correspondence service "F" communicated to us the following in communiqué 0025722 of 5 September 1986:

The aforementioned MANU TRAIAN, Istituto Europeo di Ricerche sull'Ambiente Mediterraneo, Neapole, is listed in the records of service "F" as having corresponded between 23 and 28 August 1986 with Dobrotă Cristian, from Bucharest, Strada Cîmpineanca 13, Sector 3, tel. 32145, Izvoranu Cornel, and Izvoranu Daniel, tel. 46071, from Bucharest, Fraternity Between Nations Boulevard, Block 16, Entrance C, Flat 313, Sector 6.

The D.S.B. was informed of the correspondence sent by the abovementioned via communiqué no. 0023836 and Dept. I via communiqué 00143267.

In the period from 12 August 1986 to 25 August 1986, the aforementioned Manu was under surveillance by Service "M," and currently he is target code no. 313.

In compliance
Lt. Maj. CHICUȘ MARIN

*

—But I don't see any letters!

—They're on their way, as you say, comrade colonel!

—On their way my ass! Get down to Service "F," quick march, and tell them cut out the black-marketeering and put their shoulders to the wheel, 'cause their feathers will start flying if I come down on them!

CHAPTER TWENTY-THREE
Family Feeling

HE CLAPS. Once, twice, three times, enough. He casts an impatient glance towards the exit, but the only people standing next to the cherry-red curtains are the usherettes; not one member of the audience has got up from his seat. He looks at Christa from the corner of his eye: her profile is regular, stern even now, when she seems transported by the music. Her hair is cut straight, below her ears, she is not wearing makeup, she has wrinkles at the corners of her eyes and her lips, on which she has hastily smeared pale-colored rouge. The audience continues to applaud, he too starts clapping again, prompted by the enthusiasm of Christa, who follows the general enthusiasm. She has now risen to her feet. He remains sitting, clapping slowly, out of time, and casts sidelong glances at his wristwatch.

—Was it too long? hisses Christa.

He looks up at her from where he is sitting and continues to clap.

—I'm thinking of you, about what a long way you have to drive, he whispers by way of apology.

Christa's motionless face shows no sign of her having heard him. He hears the sound of his faint claps, which fail to synchronize with the rhythmic applause. He does not like displays of enthusiasm, standing ovations, but he has to submit. He stands up, along with the last reluctant concertgoers.

—I was thinking of you . . . that you have a lot of driving to do this evening, he repeats.

Christa replies with an absent smile. She shows no intention of leaving early. They are both enveloped in the decorous enthusiasm of the audience: well-off people, many of them elderly. Not one cry of "bravo" or "encore," not one sound of human unruliness: stamping feet, shouts, scraping chair legs. Nothing but

the grateful vibration of approval dilating to the muted rhythm
clapping, the exhibition of an evanescent sentiment of solidarity
beneath the lights, beneath the gilded arabesques of the ceiling.

—I'm thinking of the long journey ahead of us, Traian stubbornly continues.

The sole sound of scraping chair legs: his.

Christa's smile of satisfaction: she knew in advance that he
would scrape the legs of his chair. She can predict his move-
ments, words, gestures, annoyances; she is waiting for them in
advance. She tries to arrest them, suggest others to him.

The illusion that we know each other, if we are together.

*

He is now looking at the violinist, who is bowing, natural, graceful, distant. Who could have taught her over there, in the cradle
of the revolution, to make a curtsey? Can there have been a sister
of a grandmother or great-grandmother who described to her the
protocol of the Romanov court while the damp climbed another
half a centimeter in the moldering basement, waterlogging the
decaying chairs of the Aubusson salon? Can she have managed to
preserve a violin or cello without selling it, stowing it in a corner
of the hall of the communal apartment that reeks of cabbage and
where the members of the four other families who share it are
always spoiling for another quarrel?

Four, six, eight generations since the cataclysm of the Great
October Revolution—how many more generations must perish
in fear and poverty before you arrive at a Mullova? For here she
is, and how incredibly she played. And how touchingly young
she looks. The eternal age of the eternal Ana Maria . . .

Again the mechanical rhythm of the applause in which he
joins, feeling embarrassed, as if at something childish. Why? He
is not in the habit: he never has time to waste on such things. He
has never been able to afford to waste time. He never willingly
went to concerts, except to Ana Maria's.

*

Christa has stopped clapping. She keeps tugging the chain around her neck: she is trying to read the face of her watch, screwing up her eyes, helplessly. She does not want to put on her glasses, not at such a moment.

—Shall we leave before the encore starts? she asks him.

He is always out of synch with Christa. It would seem that now at last she is willing to leave. Now. Or is it the swiftness of her reaction when his gaze lingers on a young woman?

—Why should we be the first to leave? he says, amazed. She's obviously not going to give an encore.

Goodwill, fair play, selfishness, tenderness towards children, animals and helpless creatures, respect for the truth, tradition and accepted ceremony: these are what each of the forty years he has spent here have inculcated in him. This is what he believes he can recognize in this mature and reserved audience, carried away by decorous enthusiasm.

But what about Mullova, the violinist?

With naturalness, a startlingly simple dress clothes her slender body. Who can have instilled such impeccable taste? Equally austere is the clip that impeccably binds her bronze hair; discreet makeup around her oblique eyes, her wide cheekbones. She has been trained to play impeccably, to run impeccably, to jump impeccably, to thank impeccably. To conquer audience after audience in this part of the world whither the tanks painted with red stars have not yet reached, where the monochrome empire—omnipotent grey—does not yet rule.

Let him not succumb to the charm of Mullova, a soldier trained to relinquish nothing. Anywhere. Ever. And above all not to relinquish those unfortunate territories, that land *which was ours and is no longer anybody's*, which Cioran hated too intensely.

No, that is an ugly thought. Mullova is Ana Maria and that is all. At least not here, at least let us drag art from the path of the tanks and our resentments. Stop . . .

*

The applause has begun to subside, but the same perseverant enthusiasm is visible on every face. Every pair of hands is engaged in the same unending movement. But they all know that these are the final reciprocal acknowledgements: those of the music-loving public, those of the violinist, those of the pianist . . .

—Just a minute ago you were in a hurry, whispers Christa.

His bewildering reaction, although it was one that she was expecting. To scrape your chair legs when there is complete silence. To want to leave at the height of the applause and then not to want to when everybody else is hurrying to leave. Obviously, his mind is still on his pointless journey to that barbarous land, a journey on which she had no mind to accompany him. On the other hand, she did well to persuade him to come to this concert . . .

Sonate für Klavier und Violine No. 1 G-dur op. 78 von Johannes Brahms Vivace ma non troppo Adagio Allegro . . .

You slowly close the lid of the piano and go to the open window, if you stretch out your hand, you can touch the blossoming branches, and their scent of greenness, of melodious freshness, enters your room along with the golden, velvety light of late April.

—What difference can an extra minute make? says Traian with a shrug.

An extra minute can sometimes seem an enormously long time, as it now seems to her. She is suddenly gripped by a desire to breathe the fresh outside air. A park as refined as the castle concert hall, as she told Traian yesterday, trying to persuade him to attend that concert by that exceptional violinist and to unwind with a short walk through the park full of animals and artworks before setting off on the long journey home.

*

The pink, the white, the green flash past the speeding bicycle, the pink and white corollas, magnolias, Japanese cherry trees blossoming above the huge crystalline windows.

And you are pedaling slowly now because it is too lovely outside to hurry, from the bridge you are crossing you can see the green Rhine stretching into the distance, you can see the white foam rising above the sluices, you can see the white trees blossoming on the green hills, you can hear the cathedral bell. In a week it will be Easter, in a week it will be the holidays, you press the invisible doorbell and you wait for Klara or Walter or Father to come and open the door and you look up at the open window of your bedroom. Over Hauptstraße pours the music of our soirée, *Sonate für Klavier und Violine.*

*

Mullova's smile has cooled by another quarter of a degree, but her bow is just as graceful. Wreathed in increasingly anemic applause, she vanishes behind the stage with youthful, springing steps, carrying her violin with harmonious distinction. She has left the stage, but she lingers in his astonished, distant gaze, along with her unseen music teacher and all the other unseen educators and supervisors who propelled her to the concert hall of that rococo castle (the main building dates from the fourteenth century, the new wings from the eighteenth century), a wild young thing with broad cheekbones, with oblique eyes and bronze hair . . .

—You fidgeted all through the concert and now, when half the audience is already at the cloakroom, you're all of a sudden interested and we're the last people to leave the auditorium. If it's just one more minute, then why don't we enjoy it in the park?

—We're leaving at the same time as everybody else, my dear . . . See how you exaggerate? I thought that this is what you wanted, to linger, but I can see I was wrong . . .

His voice is conciliatory, indifferent. His long white fingers fasten the buttons of his navy blue raincoat. Why, when it is so warm outside? It is the beginning of September, but the air in the park is fresh and as warm as in late April.

—When I was giving you signals that I wanted us to leave already, I was thinking of you, because you have to drive for hours, like I said. Maybe we shouldn't have burdened ourselves with this concert, because you look tired already . . . it's as if you're still asleep . . .

*

Ride your bicycle down the middle of the street and don't think about why you are moving as if you were asleep, who can tell you which is your real life, which is your real home? Who can vouch that you are not dreaming even now? Maybe you are only dreaming that you are crossing the castle grounds towards the parking lot where the car is waiting for you, maybe you are actually going down Haupstraße and you can hear the cathedral bell.

Maybe it is just a dream that for eight months no letter came from Father, that Walter joined the Hitlerjugend and later the Waffen-SS and went off to defend Berlin on a train that was singing "Heidemarie." Maybe it is just a dream that you wrote to Hermann, *don't be unhappy, even if it is not your child in Klara's belly, because I love you, I will wait for you, that's why I dutifully go down into the shelters every day when I hear the siren* . . .

*

—When I found out that your plane had such a long delay, I wanted to cancel the visit to Giulia and Antonio, but they insisted so much that we come, no matter how late, I had to accept. We wouldn't have been able to get out of it, we would have had to visit them today and you would have been unhappy about wasting another day in Rome. I think that you were over-wrought yesterday because of your tiredness, you talked more than you usually do and at one point you even started ram-bling . . . Perhaps you still remember what you said, about your so-called dilemma, whether or not your relatives were really family. It was a metaphor, of course, but they didn't take it like that, it was plain from their faces that they didn't know what to believe.

His wide eyes, their blue more faded, more baffled by the thick lenses of his spectacles.

—No, not at all, my dear. It wasn't a metaphor. When I was among them, over there, it's true that I asked myself the question a number of times: are they really my relatives? *Poor me, where I am, what country is this, what barbarous nation?*

—Why wouldn't they be your relatives? They could be your relatives, even if you didn't like them. Even if you didn't get on with them . . .

*

Maybe Walter would not have ended up dying in Pankow, before he managed to throw the grenade he was clenching in his narrow, sweating hand, if you had not thrown his diary on the fire. Maybe Mother was indeed drinking on the sly from early in the morning, as Walter shouted to her face the last time you argued and he left slamming the door.

Maybe Klara did not want to give Germany another soldier, to be a girl-mother, as she put it, but had merely lost patience because Hermann had not come home on leave . . . At the age you are now you could understand how relieved of household worries she felt when the lame confectionary shop owner started filling the house with black-market food and packets of cakes.

Maybe Klara did not want to go down into the shelter on Bergstraße because she was upset, because she had discovered the letter you wrote to Hermann and was afraid that he was going to break off the engagement and that you would take her place.

But as it was, only you remained to bear the shame of the memories, to cry tearlessly in your sleep, to howl voicelessly in your sleep.

And then, were all those years but a dream? A dream. What else would you want them to be?

*

—It's not a question of liking, how could I have liked those poor people who paraded in front of me when I arrived at the airport, each one poorly dressed, each awkward, each as much of a stranger as the next? As for the encounter with them, it was completely devoid of affection! Our conferences are much warmer, they give me an occasion to meet dear friends! The people on the *Other Side* did not convey any family feeling, their faces remained motionless, even when they smiled. I felt it from the very first, although I was besieged by strangers, each of whom was trying to explain something or other to me. Some of them absurdly asked whether I recognized them! Whom could I recognize, tell me, when their age clearly told me that they had been born after I left? And all of them claimed that they had been thinking of me and waiting for me. Why would they have been waiting for me, if they had never even seen me before? And so every time we were together, the suspicion returned: who are all these people in fact? Are they really my relatives or just strangers playing a role? I would ask myself. And by the end I still hadn't worked out which . . .

He does not look at Christa as he speaks; he looks straight ahead. Something has been irritating him since he left the concert hall, there is something he dislikes, but what? And all of a sudden he realizes what it is: the tulip beds, irritatingly straight, irritatingly even. He would like a garden with jumbled plants, with flowerbeds full of last year's leaves, rotting in peace, in the light, with moist spiders' webs and flies buzzing unwittingly above them. Where is this garden in which he would like to lie on a blanket in the sun, his eyes closed? *In the land that was ours and is no longer anybody's*, as friend Cioran says.

*

—Forgive me, but your suspicion is devoid of all logic and verges on paranoia. Why would they have put on a show with strangers playing the role of relatives especially in your honor? Absurd! Not to mention that not even Victor would have been your cousin then, would he?

—Victor is the exception, my dear! That's why I argued his

case in front of you and our young friends, although perhaps I went too far. I literally don't know what I would have done without Victor and his jokes, especially when Alexandru and his daughter Teodora happened not to be there. With them I laughed and joked, but apart from that it was as if I was on stage. You criticize me for being taciturn, but it was I who ended up keeping the conversation going! The others rarely spoke a word. And whenever I was sitting at one of those interminable, dreary dinners, I could sense that all of them, some of them furtively, some of them openly, were looking at me, so as not to let me out of their sight for an instant, so as not to miss a single word I said . . .

*

The moist vivid green of the lawn. The peacock with its festively outspread fan hastens, solemn and ridiculous, towards the groundskeeper surrounded by wild ducks, crowding around him to feed. A ring-necked dove comes up to them, like an overly tame hen.

—Go over there! Go over there and have your dinner! We don't have anything to give you, Christa playfully advises it.

But no, the dove stubbornly continues to follow them.

—Go away when I tell you to! Go away! shouts Traian.

Christa shakes her head in disapproval.

—Poor dove! Why are you yelling at it?

—Dove? That's a dove? Look at the state it's in! It's so fat and clumsy it can't even fly anymore, it just flaps its wings on the gravel! It reminds me of the people *Over There*, although their captivity is infinitely more uncomfortable. But over there, few still have any degree of freedom. In fact, apart from Cousin Victor and my friend Alexandru Stan, I didn't meet anybody who was free . . .

He stops and emphasizes his words with sweeping gestures. He stops and the grey ring-necked dove waits patiently, its head cocked slightly to one side. Traian shoos it away, like a barnyard fowl, but the dove does not move. Christa watches the spectacle with stirrings of indignation: it is plain that in the barbarous world whence he came, the animals from Noah's ark are poorly treated. She says so in a moralizing voice, waving her hand, on which no ring, no bracelet conceals the creases, the puffy veins, the blotches of old age.

—Do you imagine that you can be free in such a world? And your suspicions about your family seem pure fantasy to me. A tawdry television serial. Did you see or hear anything that . . .

—No, I can't say I saw anything, or maybe, I don't know, in fact I have no proof . . . It was sooner the tense atmosphere . . .

—But to them too you were somebody new, a stranger! And your fame might have intimidated them!

—It might have been that, at first, I agree. Afterwards the relationship ought to have become natural, but it didn't. Even when we all went to our small town, they were too silent. They didn't let me out of their sight for one instant, but they were silent. They were like extras in a play. And what set me to thinking even more was the orderliness in the rooms. It was as if they weren't allowed to touch anything. Might the house they took me to have been some kind of official house? It crossed my mind at one point . . .

*

Christa has succeeded (but how?) in persuading the dove to go over to the groundskeeper, who is waiting next to the tray of birdseed. She stands there watching in delight as it heads towards the familiar spot, swaying clumsily, like an overly domesticated hen.

—You turned that poor inoffensive dove into a metaphor for your discontentment with the people in your native land!

—I've told you before it's not my native land. And I'm not annoyed, although I admit that that degenerate dove provoked an unpleasant feeling in me . . . a feeling of slight repulsion.

—Degenerate? Why? Because it followed us all this way?

—Exactly, yes! Because it followed us, although it was in its own interest to go to the groundskeeper who feeds it! It has lost its bearings, its instincts! It no longer knows where to find its food; it can no longer fly. I observe in it what everybody knows: creatures in captivity degenerate.

A tiny wild duckling sits motionless in the middle of the tiny green pond. Near the bank, there is a group of statues: a stag cornered by hounds. The kneeling stag, brought to bay by the barking hounds that mount its haunches, its back, its neck, their stone teeth forever planted in its stone flesh, the twisted foliage of the heavy wreath resting on the plinth drowning in the red of the tulips, the crystalline jet of water spurting from the wounds. How horrible! But no, that's not the way to look at art!

*

—And for that you yell at an innocent bird? Old age is neither wise nor calm, as people think: old people are irritable, depressed, impatient . . .

—Christa knows everything! Now you are an expert in gerontology. Since when?

—By keeping myself under observation! But before that, I had to watch while my grandparents' health gradually deteriorated. And they were long-lived, they had an enviable old age, I would do well to be like them, and it was they who saved me. I was with them in the shelter when the earth quaked, darkness, screams, a horrible smell, the shelter was poorly ventilated and some people vomited from fear or wet themselves . . . We realized that the bomb had not fallen near us, but farther away, and somebody, it was a man's voice, said: they've hit Bergstraße. When the sirens stopped, I ran there like a mad thing, from a distance I saw the ruins of the blackened houses, in flames. My grandparents pulled me out of the mounds of rubble, from the ruins in which I was wandering lost, they took me home with them and they took it in turns to sit with me, day and night, until I recovered from the state of shock. My grandfather had a PhD in psychology, he was awarded his doctorate at the beginning of the century, in Vienna, and he had taught at the university for many years. He undertook a long course of therapy with me, because after I got over the state of shock, I fell into a severe depression, which lasted for months. My grandfather kept telling me that if I wanted to get better, I had to control my emotions and above all I had to stop projecting the painful images in my mind. I had to make an effort to banish them from my memory . . .

Why should you be the only one to keep on wandering among the mounds of rubble from which comes the sound of scraping shovels, in a town of rubble, plunged in pitch blackness illumined only by the flames?

Stop scrabbling with your broken, bloody fingernails among the shards of glass, among the red-hot wire, stop shouting: Klara! Mother! Wait! The French prisoners will come, the Russian prisoners of war will unbury the corpses and the unexploded bombs, can you see their shadows next to the mound of bricks where you once dreamed that it was our house on Bergstraße? Stop digging with your hands in the scorching rubble, stop screaming: Klara, Mother, wait! The prisoners will come, can you hear the sound of their digging, getting closer and closer, Klara, Mother, wait just a little, they are coming to unbury you! They are going to dig carefully, so as not to hurt you, so as not to . . . they are going to unbury what?

Don't scream, wake up! It's just a nightmare, you were dreaming!

Don't lose your head, go forward as best you can, this is your real life.

I'm afraid to go to sleep and to dream, I'm afraid to scrabble, screaming, in the scorching rubble, in the shards of glass, with my bloody fingernails, I'm afraid to go forward, through the dark, groping, in my real life, I'm afraid . . .

CHAPTER TWENTY-FOUR
The "Scientist" Dossier (4)

Sheet no. 86
MINISTRY OF INTERIOR AFFAIRS
BUCHAREST DEPARTMENT
29 AUG. 1986
SECTOR 6 MILITIA

During the course of the month of August year in progress the aforementioned Izvoranu Daniel of Fraternity Among Nations Boulevard Block 16, Entrance C, Apartment 313, Bucharest, sent a postcard to the aforementioned Professor MANU TRAIAN in Italy Istituto Europeo di Ricerche sull'Ambiente Mediterraneo, Neapole, no street or number.

Take measures to identify the aforementioned Izvoranu Daniel to establish when and in what circumstances the aforementioned MANU TRAIAN left the country.

Head of Department
Major EFTIMIE GHEORGHE

CHAPTER TWENTY-FIVE
The Lecture Fiasco

CHRISTA STOPS IN front of the wooden board showing the program of next month's concerts, as if she were looking for something, a certain soloist, a certain concert. She reads words at random, unconnectedly, aware of the pointlessness of it. Traian stops too, but only to look closely at her, because he is surprised at her silence these last few minutes.

—What are you doing, my dear? Are you crying? Are you crying or am I only imagining it?

The smile in his voice comes up against her forced smile.

—It's something mechanical, you know. After forty years, unfortunately, the tears come to my eyes mechanically. At certain words, at certain music. Maybe it's just an allergy . . .

The feeling of humiliation at your body, which is beginning to betray you, the tears welling up at the same time as the emotions, the urine spurting at the same time as the sneeze . . .

—Have you been urinating more often than before and in smaller quantities?

—Why do you ask me that, doctor? What diagnosis do you have in mind?

—Calm yourself, madam! They are common symptoms at your age. There are plenty of other men who have similar problems . . .

Christa pulls out the watch that hangs from a chain at her throat and holds it up to her squinting eyes: here, in the light, she can see the watch face without her glasses. And what she sees persuades her that it is time to quicken her steps. By the time the next concert begins they will be far away from this old castle and the park where fresh tulips will bloom tomorrow.

*

—So, your only cause for suspicion is that the people on the *Other Side* didn't give you a family feeling. It seemed to you like they were bad actors, amateurs, playing the role of relatives . . . They didn't speak naturally . . .

—They spoke barely at all. They sat quietly each holding a book, there was one book in particular that seemed to interest them, which was in fashion and everybody was reading it or talking about it. The rhythm of life is slower there and so what do they do? They read. I noticed one person who read all the way through my lecture . . .

—Now I understand at last why you are unhappy about your trip! Somebody had the audacity not to pay attention while you were talking! I have seen it here, how you get annoyed about certain reactions on the part of your audience that other speakers don't pay any attention to! You try to be indulgent, but in fact you are miming indulgence, and after a given point you don't even bother to mime it any longer . . .

—Not at all! It means that not even after all these years do you know me, my dear! The last thing that would have bothered me would be somebody reading in the lecture hall! It's my fault if I didn't manage to capture his attention. With my students, yes, I'm less indulgent, because I find it unacceptable that some ignorant, unfledged youth, armed with three quotations from Trotsky and two from Marx, should come and take you to task! I find it unacceptable to crack jokes just to get your audience's attention, like some of my colleagues do! And why do they go on strike all the time? Because they don't want to learn! Whereas the young people in such unfortunate countries would give anything to have their opportunities . . .

—I still think something must have happened at that lecture, if you can't even bear to talk about it. If the young men in the lecture hall didn't provoke you, then maybe the young women did! Young women dolled up in the chicest clothes available over there!

—Oh, Lord! Women beautiful half a century ago! The

majority of the female audience members were my age! I'm sorry to disappoint you, but no untoward incidents occurred . . .

—When there are young people in the auditorium you can't help but have incidents!

—There was not one incident because there was not one young person . . . Or hardly any . . . Why did you presume something like that?

—But isn't that what the auditoriums where you speak look like?

—Here! But over there! First of all, there were officials of every rank, people from the Institute, from the university, generally middle-aged, a few young people, but it was hard to tell whether they were students or not; and they certainly weren't the type of young people to ask the speaker trick questions. From what Professor Stan told me, it was a typical audience for such a venue: a consulate hall or foreign library. People over there don't frequent such places, so as to avoid being seen in a bad light. But in the auditorium there were also old acquaintances of mine, elderly people with their families, who had somehow or other found out that I was going to be there. That mix of people caused me additional difficulties, because I didn't know what kind of audience to pitch it to . . .

*

The pink, yellow, gold, white, purple-black cups of the tulips have closed for the evening. But in the earth are swelling the bulbs of those that will open tomorrow morning, when today's tulips will be lopped at the root by the merciless hand of the gardener, careful lest their petals become shriveled. The tulips in this park are not allowed to age.

—Professor Stan had warned me to be wary of political provocations. That is why I gave a strictly scientific talk, and so, as far as an audience of laymen was concerned, it was utterly boring.

She protests: you are incapable of being boring, he insists: yes I am, unfortunately.

—Believe me, I have never ever given such a boring talk! I

didn't allow myself to stray off the topic for one instant! Not one aside, not one digression. Not that I like playing the clown in front of students, but over there you're not allowed to make the slightest joke. Over here, they would have been throwing paper airplanes at me and within half an hour the auditorium would have been empty. But there, they found my speech as natural as could be, not one whistle, but not much applause either. The only thing that confused them was when I announced: "My dears, I regret that we won't be able to take part in a dialogue, as I would have liked. Perhaps you too would have preferred it, but I have come prepared to deliver a boring scientific lecture." In any event, to me Alexandru's wariness seemed exaggerated: nobody had any intention of hassling me. But when I told that I was going to give a boring lecture, they were confused, they didn't know how to react. What did I mean? I heard somebody laugh, I heard a few words being spoken, which, in the embarrassing silence of the others, sounded rather insolent. Over there, they are accustomed to there being a hidden, even a contrary, meaning in everything you say and they look for insinuation in even the blandest words. I hesitated as to whether I should bat the ball back into their court or not. I decided not to.

—And then what?

—And then I spoke, and they pretended to listen.

—Why do you say that? Maybe they really were listening?

—Of course they were listening! My colleagues were listening! The specialists! But the rest? For whatever reason, each of the others could hardly wait for it to end. The journalists because they wanted to besiege me for interviews I had no intention of giving, as I told you before I left. The officials, who, the same as everywhere else were in a hurry, because they wanted to congratulate me and give me invitations I had every intention of declining. And the audience . . .

*

Maybe the music has reinvigorated him. Maybe the excessive tiredness of the last week has mobilized him. Or maybe it is just the irritation that grows in him as his story approaches the unpleasant moment. Forget about it, he feels like telling himself, the same as whenever he dwells on a blunder, forget about it, it's too late to fix it now. Or to forget about it . . .

—By the end, the auditorium was fuller than it had been during my lecture. Punctuality is not the strong point of the people over there, a large part of them had entered while I was speaking, but they didn't seem to be aware of any impoliteness. And so by the end, the same as at the airport, a throng of strangers crowded around me to congratulate me and make themselves known to me. Finally, a disorderly queue formed, moving forward very slowly, and I had to exchange a few words with each, to jot down telephone numbers, addresses, to listen to incomprehensible stories, full of insinuations and pointless details, to promise that I would definitely go to lunch with them, have coffee with them, visit their houses in the country, in the mountains, at the weekend. And since the ladies, as well as the gentlemen, were very talkative and they all had the same kind of confusing story to tell and the same almost unintelligible way of talking, they would blink, like this, they would cough, pause, wave their hand at the ceiling, to the left, to the right, I wasted a lot of time with each of them, with the result that the ones at the back of the queue started to protest, in a whisper at first, and then more and more loudly. It was then I thought that if disorder broke out, it could be unpleasant for all of us, for both them and myself.

*

Before seeing it, she heard it. A brief crunching noise across the gravel of the path. And now Christa espies it: a grey ball darting over the brightly colored flowerbeds, growing smaller, receding into the distance.

—A rabbit, Traian! Not over there, on the right, I said! Next to the statue of the stag! On the right, not the left . . .

His eyes, their bluish green diluted by the thick lenses of his spectacles, wander confused over the orderly immensity of the park.

—On the right? Where on the right? Ah, yes! There he is!

—When I see rabbits, I always think of chocolate figurines rather than living creatures. Probably because I liked it so much when I saw the chocolate rabbits and Easter eggs in the window of the confectionary shop that moved into our house, before Easter . . .

And so it was that at the end of every April you alone remained to see the huge chocolate egg coated in a multicolored pink-white-pistachio glaze, garnished with ribbons, surrounded by chocolate rabbits large and small, in the window of the most elegant confectionary shop on Hauptstraße, which is to say, our old house, where we were so cold, but we were together.

One spring-summer day you will enter the courtyard of the renovated confectionary shop, which is to say, your former garden, you will sit there, the four of you, Hermann, you and the children, at an elegant white table, with huge portions of ice cream topped with mounds of whipped cream. You will show the children your old window, whose panes are touched by the branches of the plane tree, and they will greedily plant their silver teaspoons in the fluffy mounds of whipped cream, it's the first time we've eaten ice cream at such an expensive confectionary shop, Mother, it's the first time!

That is why they can't bear to lift their eyes to the window you insist on showing them, and when Hermann asks for the bill, they will ask you in amazement: what's wrong? why are you crying? why are you crying, Mother?

*

—And so what at first moved me and later amused me began to feel like a chore. It even got on my nerves when I saw them rummaging through their pockets for a scrap of paper, for a ballpoint pen that had run out of ink, turning their poor worn-out handbags inside out in search of something on which to write down a telephone number to give me. Over there, visiting cards are a rarity. And at one point, after I gauged how many people were left in the auditorium and how much time I was going to waste with each of them and I realized it would take at least another hour, I really lost my cool. It was easier on them, they had come to see me and ask me for something specific. What is more, they are used to waiting in queues; it's become a sadomasochistic pleasure for them. And so, in a hoarse voice—you know how I get after every lecture—I told them: "I thank you all, my dears, for having come to listen to me! Unfortunately, I have to go now, but I shall be here for a few more days and I am certain that we shall have other opportunities to talk!"

He pauses, puzzled by the hesitation he reads in her eyes:

—Am I boring you with my stories?

—Boring me? What an idea! I'm listening to you with the utmost attention. But I must say that it was rather inelegant on your part to get rid of them like that!

—It wasn't my intention to get rid of them, believe me. I was determined at least to call the numbers scribbled on those scraps of paper before I left. I put them in my coat pocket and I had no choice but to go to the restaurant with the local bigwigs, with the people from the Institute and, naturally, Professor Stan and his assistants. Nobody from the family came, apart from Cousin Victor, I don't know why. At the restaurant it was terribly hot. I asked if I could take my coat off and put it on the back of the chair, but somebody, maybe the waiter, maybe cousin Victor, kindly took it to the cloakroom, from where I soon recovered it, because somebody had opened the window to let some air in. There was an awful amount of cigarette smoke, given how much people smoke over there, without a care for non-smokers. I must have caught a cold because of the open window or else all the smoke triggered my usual rhinitis. I think it was on the way from the restaurant to the hotel when I took my handkerchief from my pocket to blow my nose, I don't have any other explanation for it, and like I told you, I wasn't feeling at all well!

*

He realizes that what he is saying is muddle, that he can't quite manage to explain what happened. With his handkerchief he dabs his damp cheeks and reaches into his shirt pocket for his box of pills. He is about to take out the box, but then he changes his mind.

—At the hotel, I didn't check to see whether the scraps of paper with the addresses were still there, but they must have been, because if I had lost them on the way from the Institute to the restaurant, they would have returned them to me straightaway: we were accompanied by a whole procession of admirers, from a distance, all the way from the Cultural Center to the restaurant. The distances were not great; the hotel was not far away. But when we left the restaurant, it was late, at that hour there was no sign of any admirers, there were just Victor and I. I went up to my room. I passed a very unpleasant night, with a headache, difficulty breathing, maybe it was rhinitis, maybe it was annoyance, maybe both. As I wasn't feeling well, the next day I didn't go out at all. They brought me cups of willow tea, but I wasn't so exhausted that I wasn't able to drink them.

—You didn't tell me that you were ill over there until now!

—I didn't tell you because it annoys me just thinking about it . . . It was then that poor Victor proved his whole devotion! He kept watch over me the whole time, a great mountain of a man, but he tiptoed around like a cat! I scolded him, told him to go and have a rest, but I couldn't persuade him. Victor insisted that a doctor visit me, but there wasn't any need. By that evening I felt much better. The fog had lifted from my brain. It was only then that I remembered the pieces of paper with the addresses, but all I found in my pocket was my handkerchief. I suspect that when I took it out of my pocket, I must have pulled the addresses out and dropped them by accident. It was bad luck, an unfortunate occurrence . . . If only I hadn't stuffed them in my pocket so carelessly! That was the only moment, absolutely the only moment I could have lost them.

He avoids Christa's eyes, their blueness, so limpid, so intense, so cold in the light. For sure, she would never have crumpled up the precious pieces of paper and stuffed them in her coat pocket and she would never have lost them in the dark on the main street of a huge provincial town. The capital of a provincial country.

He feels even guiltier now than when he discovered his empty pockets in the hotel room. Or perhaps it is only now, as he tells Christa what happened, that he feels the guilt in its entirety?

CHAPTER TWENTY-SIX
The "Scientist" Dossier (5)

Sheet no. 130—131

INTELLIGENCE REPORT

We bring to your notice the following:

Librarian CRISTIAN DOBROTĂ from the Institute of Agricultural Sciences and Veterinary Medicine in Bucharest has been put forward for promotion and to receive the grade of scientific researcher grade III, with a corresponding increase in salary. Even if it is a low grade and a small corresponding increase in salary, we believe the decision to be a mistake.

Regarding this decision and to prevent this mistake being committed, our conscience obliges us to lay out the following so that you can analyze it with your full and appropriate attention and see whether it is still the case that this undercover enemy of the regime should remain in our Institute, and certainly not to grant him a higher scientific grade.

The present-day "researcher" CRISTIAN DOBROTĂ since his days as a student and afterwards has been a notorious member of the National Peasants Party, and was a member of the Peasants Party committee at the Faculty of Agronomy in Bucharest.

Even today he maintains close ties with former members of the political parties. CRISTIAN DOBROTĂ was detained by our investigative organs for more than two years and he boasted that he was released and rehabilitated which isn't true.

And what's more: he maintains relations with a friend of the family, MANU TRAIAN, a fugitive abroad, and he went to listen to him when he came to our country. He claims he writes to him and intends to visit him probably to stay there permanently.

His brother, Anton Dobrotă, was sentenced to life with hard labor as he was an aviator on the Eastern front, in the Soviet Union.

These incontestable concrete facts convincingly mirror the atmosphere in the home of this enemy of the regime. The aforementioned Cristian Dobrotă has sneaked his way into a job as a librarian at our Institute from where he poisons the young researchers with subtle allusions against the regime, especially against the collectivization of agriculture, telling them that the collective farms are hotbeds of infection for the domestic animals and hotbeds of theft, nobody's property, belittling and deprecating leading contemporary experts, who he particularly likes to mock.

None of these things are accidental, because CRISTIAN DOBROTĂ comes from a family of exploiters. It's no accident that his daughter is called Mihaela, he says that he gave her this name in memory and honor of the last king of the former bourgeois-landowning Romania, when he saw she was a girl, because he had decided upon the name MIHAI.

He is always coming up with alarmist rumors, which he peddles among his bosom friends, rumors that he hears on Radio Free Europe, Deutsche Welle, and the BBC.

The Cadres Department at the Ministry of Agriculture and Forestry also knows about some of these concrete facts because in the autumn of

1967 they rejected the appointment of CRISTIAN DOBROTĂ as a "researcher" in our Institute, but after that he sneaked in.

Please take appropriate measures to put a stop to the villainies and defiance of this dangerous enemy, assisted by comrades devoid of even the most elementary sense of vigilance, who help him to sneak into the highest scientific positions.

A group of employees at the Institute of Agricultural Sciences and Veterinary Medicine under the aegis of the Academy of the People's Republic of Romania

Consistent with the original
Lieutenant MATEI SILVIU

CHAPTER TWENTY-SEVEN
Serial Lives

—WHAT HAPPENED WITH the lost addresses is unpleasant, of course, but I think you are blowing it all out of proportion. Even if you hadn't lost the addresses, you weren't there long enough to have time to pay visits or to waste time making polite phone calls to say goodbye. Your disappointments come from unrealistic expectations, which is what I told you when you left: what you think you are going to find there doesn't exist anywhere except in your mind! I know that very well, because whenever I have gone back to the town of my childhood, I experienced the same disappointment as you . . .

—There's no point our coming to this confectionary shop again, said Hermann, holding his arm around her shoulders, not only to save money, although that is not a reason to be overlooked, but it seemed to me that the ice cream is not as good here as it is at the shop in our neighborhood and your memories of this house make you ill.

—But doesn't it make you feel ill to remember your fiancée Klara, who lived right here?

It would have been much better if you had not asked that question, a question you will never forget, what was the point of reminding him he was engaged to your sister, when you know better than he who fathered Klara's child, which was never born, because they both died, suffocated, burned, in the bombing.

—We were different people then and we were living a different life, said the wise Hermann.

You will look at him without seeing him, surrounded by them all you will walk like a somnambulist through the smell of greenness, of freshness, through the golden, velvety light.

It was three weeks and three days before the explosion at the factory in which Hermann was to die.

*

—The places, the objects change at the same time as the people, although they last longer than the people. And our former house, which had become a confectionary shop, changed after the war, for a few years it belonged to the French, we were in their zone of occupation. The new owner fitted out a room for chess, and in our former garden, now the courtyard, he installed expensive furniture of a different design. His prices were very high, and so it was only once that I went there with Hermann and the children, who were all completely uninterested in my memories, no matter how hard I tried to show them things, look, that was my room, look, that was the window to our dining room. I promised never to set foot there again, but I would not have been able to anyway, less than a month later the explosion happened at the BASF factory. The confectionary shop on Hauptstraße closed for renovation; the windows of all the buildings in the center of town had been shattered in the blast.

—But how did it happen in fact? Who was to blame?

—It's a complicated story! The inquiries and investigations lasted for years and in the end the French were found guilty, because they had forbidden round-the-clock production at the factory. If the Americans had not opened the frontier and given a helping hand, the whole of a little town would have been blown sky high, which was what happened to half of the plant.

He notices that her voice has grown velvety now she is remembering how the Americans came to help and he wonders whether Christa will finally tell him more about the young officer from Kansas City.

—That was the hardest period of your life, wasn't it? After Hermann's death, it was harder for you than even after the bombing in which your mother and sister died, wasn't it?

*

It is plain that despite the moments of weakness when she confessed to him, Traian has not really grown close to her, if he is capable of comparing her reactions in moments when she could have lost her mind for grief. Periods of her life? Sooner different lives, serial lives. Because before she met Traian Manu, Christa Döring lived two other lives. And if it was her he wanted, Traian should have incorporated her previous lives within his own affective memory.

The voice with which Christa replies sounds cutting, almost curt.

—Of course it was the hardest! At least after the bombing I had my grandparents and they helped me survive! Of all their children and grandchildren, I was their favorite, because I resembled them: they told me many times that I had inherited their spirit of moderation and vitality.

—I suppose that your grandparents were also affected . . . Their daughter and granddaughter had died after all.

He has stopped walking and he takes off his glasses to wipe them with a handkerchief he chances to find in his pocket. It was as if the question was just one he chanced to ask, in the polite voice he reserves for strangers.

—My grandparents hid their pain as best they could, to help me recover!

Traian looks at her in puzzlement, and Christa lowers her curt voice another tone.

—"Get it into your head that you are not to blame for the death of your mother and your sister!" my grandfather used to say to me every day, trying to snap me out of the shock of the bombing. He explained to me that family members always feel guilty for not having been able to prevent the deaths of their loved ones. "Believe me, I am fighting the same self-destructive feeling too," he told me many times. I suspect he blamed himself for Mother's growing depression, to which he had been a helpless witness. Like he did me, he advised her to lead an active, healthy life and to detach herself from the tragedies around us, but his words never had any effect on her. Mother had always been the rebel of the family, but it was a gentle kind of rebellion, an obstinacy masked by apparent submission. Grandfather used to say that it was a classic case of infantile reaction prolonged into adulthood, when you oppose your ageing parents, whom you confuse with authority, as Mother had done . . .

Traian puts his glasses back on his nose and stuffs the handkerchief back in his pocket. Without looking at him, Christa is convinced that his face is radiant, as ever, radiant with the obtuse satisfaction of a duty fulfilled. And by the tone of voice in which she continues, she wishes to make him understand he has no reason to be. That he can't just enter and leave her, relaxed and sated, albeit more and more seldom, and then return to his sole obsessions: his laboratory, his writing desk, his working hours.

From her partner she also expects something else: that he resemble Hermann . . .

*

—"It is hard to fight against somebody's nature, remember that for the rest of your life, you are not to blame for other people's unhappiness! Not even the unhappiness of people in the family! The time will come when you have to let them go, adults have to be responsible for themselves," my grandfather kept saying until his final years, when his mind clouded. How dreadful old age is! But when it came to me, he achieved his goal: I got into the habit of struggling against myself and I stopped blaming myself. Naturally, my correspondence with Hermann helped me enormously. And my grandparents were so happy when Hermann came back from the front and we got engaged! But by then, I had stopped waking up in the night, screaming and crying. We married very soon after we were engaged. Hermann was so protective and wise. It was as if he had never been away at the slaughter! We never talked about our past, neither mine, nor his. The children arrived, I had a different family, I no longer felt alone.

The irritation in her voice has dissolved. He notices the change with relief. Whenever she goes back to the stories from her past, Christa becomes irascible and unpredictable. The times when she wept in bed after they made love have long since passed. What has remained is the irritation that she refuses to control, even if she will apologize in an hour or two, the depression leaves scars for life, I know you will understand.

*

—Yes, it's true, after Hermann's death, those were my hardest years. Since Hermann was not killed instantly, but died from internal injuries a month later, for a while I had no income. I did not receive a pension until after the trial and the trial dragged on for years. I used to pass that confectionary shop without seeing it, just as you don't see the windows of the expensive shops when you are poor. Grandmother had died, Grandfather was in an old people's home, there was nobody to look after us. How can it not be hard to bring up two children in such circumstances? My depression came back, but I had to fend for myself. And after the war the shortages were as bad as under the dictatorship! The only difference was that the fear was gone . . . but in fact, there was a different fear. The fear of not having enough money, especially given that you could find nothing in the shops, everything was on the black market.

He understands her better than she thinks, doesn't he have the same memories of wartime, when it comes to the prices and the fear of not having anything to eat the next day? But unlike Christa, Traian Manu is convinced that the wounds of the past can heal. And with slight worry, he notices that his wife is increasingly prone to memory lapses: otherwise, why would she give him different versions of the same event, him, who refuses to make the slightest allusion, the smallest comment?

—The prices were so high for food and so low for the things from my grandparents' house, which I sold one by one! For a time, Lily, Hermann's sister, stayed with us, but she was unable to help much with the chores, because she had to study . . . As it was, I had given up university because of the children. And for a time I survived by selling things: for example, I sold five very rare editions of Freud to buy four packs of butter, four kilos of meat and two kilos of genuine coffee . . . does that seem cheap to you? I can assure you that it was a great bargain, a bibliophile American officer . . .

*

That was the American officer who gave testimony at the court case Christa brought against BASF to obtain a pension. She mentions him very seldom. But he does not point this out to her, just as he has never attempted to read any of the neatly ordered letters stored in the erstwhile family jewel box. The jewels survived the bombing, only to be sold one by one after the war, as Christa once told him, with a crooked smile. And he deduced that she kept on selling what her grandparents had left her until fate decided that Christa's new savior should wear the uniform of an American officer. He was a witness to or even a participant in putting out the fire after the BASF explosion. The testimony of the man who had helped to evacuate the offices damaged in the explosion, in which Hermann was wounded, had been central to the court case for the pension.

He remembers the first time he glimpsed this episode from her life: Christa's whispers and her leg curled around his legs, his hands playing with the silky hair of her sex, the damp sheets and the buzzing of a mosquito immune to Autan. A tragedy, a television serial, with a *deus ex machina*: before the court passed its final decision to pay the pension retroactively to the grieving family (a considerable sum, which was invested in a new house), the young American soldier had done all he could to help the young German widow, who had been left without any support in the world. The American supplied the young widow's house with meat and butter and coffee and as a keepsake he had received her grandfather's precious editions of the works of Freud. He was not a bibliophile, but his encounter with the library of that house in Germany mattered to him. He did not return to Kansas City, but went to study psychology at a prestigious university on the East Coast. At least that is what Christa would like to believe.

*

He looked like he was barely out of his teens in the photograph
that Christa removed from the bedside table after their first night
of love and placed in an album of years long past: a gangling
youth in an American officer's uniform, with a Nordic name and
face, probably the descendent of Swedish immigrants.

He must be old by now, too, even if back then he was a few
years younger than Christa. In the intervening decades will he
have become an established psychiatrist, with a growing number
of patients at his private clinic and numerous students on the
course he teaches at the university in Kansas City, or will he have
returned from Korea or Vietnam with a chest full of medals and
a mind broken by traumatic memories?

Traian never allowed himself to ask her, just as now he does
not allow himself to point out to her that new and contradictory
details have appeared in the American's biography. Sometimes
he has the impression that for Christa the image of the young
American has been superimposed upon that of the ever more
divine Hermann, merging with it until the two become one: the
advantage of loves that do not last decades.

Perhaps Christa does not have memory lapses, but merely
wishes to spare his pride: not to arouse retrospective jealousy.

Or perhaps despite her frequent depressive stories, the
wounds of the past have quite simply healed. Without her wanting it. Without her knowing it. This is the most plausible of all
his hypotheses, and probably the most upsetting for Christa.

She will never allow her past sufferings to heal.

CHAPTER TWENTY-EIGHT
The "Scientist" Dossier (6)

Sheet no. 88

Department II

28 August 1986

SERVICE "F," correspondence.
We attach a letter to be franked accordingly and postmarked with the date 5 Sept. 1986.
The letter is to be photocopied and placed in postal circulation in order to reach its destination.
Please send the photocopy of the letter to code no. 242.

Head of Service
DUMITRU TRĂSNEA

Sheet no. 89

Dr. Traian Manu

Via Pavia, 313

Neapole

Italia

Dear Friend,

I thank you cordially for the warm words that you spoke to me on the occasion of your visit to my home. May God grant you health and that you be able to bring to fruition all the things you proposed to me, because, thanks to the plans of my wife, Flori, projects are not lacking. I also thank you for the best wishes you passed on to my daughter, whom you were unfortunately not able to meet. In regard to her family situation, with regret I must tell you that it is *in statu quo.*

I am curious to learn the results of your research published in the American magazine you mentioned to me. Perhaps you could send me an excerpt to my home address, since it might get lost at the institute.

I cannot tell whether my requests have prompted any reaction among your friends. Perhaps endeavors in this respect will not have been successful. In any case, I apologize for the efforts you have made, thanking you for your good intentions. I will not hide from you that I sometimes dream of an eventual trip to Rome, in which you have generously given me cause to hope. You cannot imagine how much I would like it not to remain just a dream like so many others in a life that it would be euphemistic to name banal.

I hope that at least my long-awaited promotion from archives to research will not be just another dream.

My compliments and best wishes to your wife, whom I saw in the photograph that you always keep with you. And it is well that you do so: what would become of us without the warmth of family? I cannot even imagine.

Yours affectionately, Cristian.

P.S. My home address is: Cristian Dobrotă, Cîmpineanca 13, Sector 3, Bucharest.

CHAPTER TWENTY-NINE
The Career of a Castaway

—It may be that some of the people who kept insisting they speak to you just wanted to get something out of you. Given the poverty you say is rampant over there, I don't see why they could care less about your feelings! Good God, we're grown-ups, aren't we, we have our feet on the ground, don't we?

Traian gives her a puzzled look, but remains silent. If he pointed out to her that she was gesticulating too much and that her voice sounded strident on this side street where it is almost as quiet as in the park, she would reproach him, as usual, for being conventional and old-fashioned.

And Christa delays telling him that the cause of her irritation is that she no longer remembers exactly where she parked the car; his anxiety would only augment hers. And the longer she fails to recognize their car in the endless line by the park fence, the more her irritation turns into panic and her voice grows shriller. And although he is unaware of the reasons for her unease, he answers her in the conciliatory voice he uses whenever he tries to calm her:

—The same as on other occasions, it may be that you are the one who is right. Some of the people who managed to talk to me after the lecture did indeed slip in specific requests for things along with all their pointless words and comical gestures. I didn't have time to write the things down and afterwards I forgot what they were. Especially given that, in that way, I discovered a part of the audience had not come because they were interested in the lecture or even because they were curious about me—even here, as you know, that is something I don't like and I always say that I'm not a museum exhibit—but with very precise requests in mind.

*

—But by losing the pieces of paper with their telephone numbers, you rid yourself of the most insistent ones.

—Not at all! The ones who were late in finding out about my arrival or who hadn't had the courage to set foot inside a foreign cultural institute besieged me during the days that followed. I would find them in the hotel lobby, on the street, at the ministry. At one point, Cristian Dobrotă also made his appearance, the brother of my old schoolmate, Anton. I've told you about Anton many times. He had a younger brother, Cristian, who was completely different from him. We never took much notice of each other at the time, you know how it is at that age: the interests of a boy of twelve are one thing, and those of a boy of sixteen or seventeen another thing entirely. Add to that the difference in temperament: Anton was as extroverted as Cristian was introverted. Cristian did not get to benefit very much from the advantages of an influential family, apart from the fact that he had an excellent education, but as you will see, little good did it do him. On the other hand, he had to bear all the subsequent inconveniences. Perhaps he stored up bitterness in his soul at how his older brother had outshone him in his youth, he had been spectacular, but later, from what he said, he became like a ball and chain. Can you understand such resentments?

What a question! How could she not understand? Klara and her good mood when she woke up in the morning and sang in the bathroom so she could pluck up the courage to wash with cold water. Her thick eyelashes that required no mascara and her long legs with her slender ankles and *trotteur* shoes, and the way the men turned their heads to look at her on the street. The chocolate bonbons that Hermann brought Christa and the packages of cakes the lame owner of the confectionary shop made for her, as she was the sister of the irresistible Klara after all. Oh, how infuriating she found that thankless role and how often she had wept because of it!

She nods without saying a word, still on the lookout for the car.

*

—When I was a child, the Dobrotă family was one of the most influential in our town, and in their household I had an ambiguous status: they knew that Anton managed at school mainly thanks to my help and they regarded me as exerting a positive influence over him. As I have told you, he also had problems when it came to discipline. Anton was superficial by nature, but generous and, being a good sportsman, he was loyal and comradely. As is often the case with children born into privilege, he was not very keen on studying, but he played tennis very well, he was a local aviation ace, and naturally he had great success with the ladies. I got on quite well with him, although we were very different. But during adolescence, when even you yourself don't yet know who you are, if a friendship can survive the awkward clashes, then the differences of personality enrich you, they help you to come out of your shell. As an adolescent, Anton was closer to me than his brother, can you believe it?

Can you apply the word friendship to your stalking of Klara, which after a given point became mutual? Can you tell him that your relationship in the final years, as two sisters competing for Hermann's heart, meant you would never have faith in friendship between women, because you expected any one of them to do to you what you did to Klara? And did Hermann really choose you or was he just trying to find Klara in you? Did he really want you or did he use you to punish Klara, postmortem, because another man's child had died in her belly?

*

—Shall I go on telling the story or does it bore you?

—Tell the story! Tell the story!

Her moment of hesitation is at an end: abruptly she remembers where she parked the car and quickens her steps.

—When I saw Cristian Dobrotă again, I recognized him straightaway. He was wrinkled and had bags under his eyes, but the expression on his face had remained the same. When I last saw him, he had just graduated from lycée, with the highest possible mark in his baccalaureate, and when I saw him again, he was a man on the verge of retirement. After all those years, he still looked like an adolescent, but an aged adolescent, with appalling teeth and bad breath. I remembered his shock of black curly hair. Now his hair was white and smoothed over his skull, unbelievably white . . .

—Maybe it was a wig. Why not? To cover up . . .

—You must be joking! If you could have seen his modest clothes, his almost slipshod appearance, you would never have thought such a thing. It was the same hair as in the past, but it had aged, like him. He insisted that I visit him at home. In the end, so as not to keep meeting him in the street every morning . . .

—In the street? Why?

—I never could work out why . . . Maybe the receptionists intimidated him. They exceeded all bounds when it came to servility, as well as impertinence. It depended whom they were talking to. Maybe it was the paranoid obsession that a lot of people have over there, that they are being followed. Cristian kept looking all around him, he spoke in a whisper, he made bizarre signs of warning with his hands. At the hour when I usually left the hotel, I would bump into Cristian, walking up and down on the pavement outside, frantic that he was late for work, but even more frantic at the thought that he might miss the opportunity to meet me. He claimed not to be able to reach me on the telephone, but how then were Alexandru and Victor able to reach me?

—They knew your schedule better . . .

—Yes, maybe . . . Anyway, out of pity, out of compulsion, on one of the last days I agreed to squeeze a visit to the Dobrotă family home into my terribly busy schedule. It was a fleeting visit, because the car provided by my friend Alexandru was waiting outside to take me to the reception at the institute.

Christa's eyes move triumphantly over the other cars in the lot: there it is.

*

—Cristian was living in one of the Dobrotă family's houses, or rather in just two rooms, one of which was a passageway. The house had been nationalized, like all the rest, and they were living there as tenants. The bathroom and the kitchen, from which came a pervasive stench of cabbage, were communal. But I couldn't recognize anything of the elegant house which, in my impoverished youth, stunned me with its luxuriousness. Now, it was dilapidated and dirty. Relatively new, but cheap furniture had replaced the old. The old objects were in bad repair, chipped, everything of value had been sold in the years of hardship, like you did when you had to fend for yourself . . .

—This Cristian must be an old bachelor, full of tics . . .

She says it laughing, without rancor. She is generous, because she is happy. The car is just two paces away. She will quickly find the keys in her handbag, she will put on her seatbelt and make sure he puts on his, she will then put on her glasses so that she can check the map once more, although she knows the route so well. She will do lots of other things that he will sense, will see as if through a mist, convinced without even looking that she is just driving and listening to him.

—No he's not, actually! He's married and as soon as she laid eyes on me his wife proudly announced that they had just celebrated their silver wedding anniversary. Probably the only precious metal to be found in their house! Cristian must have made huge efforts to persuade me to accept his invitation just so that he could introduce me to his wife. He is as wispy and lacking in self-confidence as she is overbearing and uninhibited. She claimed that we had met before, in our youth, but I hardly think so, since she is at least ten years younger than me. But together they form the classic type of the inseparable couple. From her stories, it seems that she had admired the Dobrotă family ever since she was a romantic young girl, a role in which it is difficult to picture her now . . .

—Why are you so scathing about her?

—I have no intention of being scathing! I think she is an

honest woman, on whom my friend's brother, fragile as he is, has been able to rely during his difficult life. I appreciated that and understood it as soon as I entered their home.

—How can you gauge the life of a couple at just one glance? What could you say about us, for example, just five minutes after entering our home? Mind you haven't fastened your seatbelt properly!

*

—I deduced that they were a solid couple when they told me that they had married a month after Cristian was released from prison. Nowhere in the world is an ex-convict a less advantageous match than there! Naturally, you will ask me why he was sent to prison and I have to confess that I didn't really understand the reason and I was embarrassed to keep asking. It seems that up until the mid-sixties their prisons were full: former politicians, the formerly wealthy, people who had had connections with the West, people who had told jokes about the regime, you know the pattern all too well, unfortunately. And the prisons were dreadful, like they are in Latin American countries, but I found out more about that over here, in exile circles, than over there, where the subject is greeted with silence. Cristian told me that he had been "detained without trial," an official phrase that I expect they used in numerous memoranda to the authorities to claim their rights. Without much success—I have heard a lot of complaints about the same thing. Apparently, he still carries the stigma.

He falls silent, because he abruptly gets the feeling that she is no longer listening to him. Or maybe she has not been listening from the start?

—Shall I continue with the story?

—In a minute, let me see which way to go . . . I always miss the slip road to the motorway here. But it's too late now to go in the wrong direction for an hour, two hours . . .

*

—As I was saying, I couldn't understand the need for those memoranda, if the so-called crime of belonging to a once well-off family and of being the brother of an aviator who became famous in a now repudiated war has no statute of limitation. Probably the last Madam Dobrotă is active by nature and this is what impelled her to attempt the impossible. But with or without the memoranda, it was obvious as soon as they got married that things would be hard for them.

On the slate roof, past which the car flashes, a white dove is moving with small, swift, rat-like steps. Behind the roof, a soft, ivory-green sky, warmed by the setting sun. When he looks at it, he is flooded with his customary mood of tranquil calm. It is his sky, a sky he recognizes after so many decades in which at least once a day he has cast his gaze up at it. His favorite hour is approaching: sunset.

He remains patiently silent, so as to spare Christa's concentration while she is driving. But it would seem that this time she has not missed the motorway slip road.

—Why would it be hard for them? Was he arrested again?

—He was arrested only once more, after the revolution in Hungary, but it was preventative; they made massive arrests there, of people who might have had cause not to like the regime imposed after the war. And there were plenty of them! But after his release from prison, Cristian couldn't get a job anywhere except as an unskilled laborer. He had two university degrees and a PhD from abroad! Undernourished and clumsy as he is, Cristian could not cope with unskilled labor. He was sacked or left of his own accord, I can't remember which. In any event for a while they survived on his wife's wages, which I find admirable on her part, especially given the life of shortages they lead there. Ultimately, since she is resourceful, she found him an insignificant job at the institute where he still works. After a while, he even managed to get a promotion, albeit to a position that is still beneath him, because he is bursting at the seams with reading and very conscientious. His wife proudly told me that she has made up for the disadvantages of Cristian's background, because, as they said, she is of "healthy social origins": she comes from a family that was socially disadvantaged before the war, which under the new circumstances became an advantage. I think her mother was a servant in the Dobrotă household, because she knew far too much about them. If you want to understand the situation in that country, which you stubbornly insist on calling mine, think of India. You are born into a caste and you can't escape it, either when getting a job or when starting a family. If you dare to defy the rules, you are marginalized. To me it seemed that society there was organized according to tribal laws of kinship and atonement for ancestral sins. And what is more incredible still is the way the people there accepted those absurd rules: they resign themselves to them like fate. The memoranda they showed me fell back on ridiculous arguments! They complained to me that even their daughter had to atone for "Anton's sins": that phrase appalled me, but I decided not to get into a discussion with them about it, because I was in a hurry.

*

The corners of her mouth have drooped disapprovingly. Her driving gloves are also bothering her; her palms feel damp. It is hot, summer still, she might take them off. But her orderly spirit urges her to be patient; night will soon fall. She must be patient. And she will be.

—I deduce that it was no pleasure to visit the Dob . . . what did you say Cristian's surname was?

—Dobrotă! Don't get me wrong, I was delighted to meet Cristian Dobrotă, although his behavior even at home struck me as bizarre. For example, he kept getting up off his chair, going to the telephone and trying to fix the dial in place with a pencil: the absurd game of an irritating child, which particularly irked me since I was in such a hurry. In the end, his wife, with an exasperated expression on her face, brought a large pillow from the bedroom and plonked it on top of the telephone. When I asked them what was going on, one signaled me not to say anything and the other changed the subject. Later, I told my friend

Alexandru about their behavior and he burst out laughing. "Get used to it," he said, "here everybody is convinced that he is being followed by the secret services. And the household objects they suspect the most are telephones, because they think that there are microphones inside them." So, the Dobrotă family had, by such ridiculous means, been trying to counteract the supposed listening device . . .

—You will tell me yet again that I have a mania for contradicting you, but maybe they were right in a way . . . You don't understand such things . . .

Christa straightens up in her seat. The pain above her buttocks has climbed to beneath her shoulder blades. She cannot be bothered to explain the things he has failed to understand even after that trip of his. She cannot be bothered even to continue the sentence. She is saving her nerves and energy so that she can get to the end of this exhausting day. If only she could lie down with her eyes closed, chasing away the images that keep coming back, all the more vivid the more she tries to distance herself from them . . .

                                *

The rectangular portal of the eleventh-century Romanic church, whose ancient outline keeps watch from on high over the colorful cars rolling along the motorway. Was it this old church that reminded him of the religious discourse of that atheist country?

Traian reaches for a Tic-Tac and pushes the pill into one corner of his mouth so that he can continue talking.

—I was in a hurry, like I said, and so I didn't have the presence of mind to ask who might be spying on them and why. They looked so stressed! Especially Cristian, who, despite the good upbringing he once received and despite his duties as host, kept looking at the clock. Finally, I worked out that he must have been constantly afraid lest I leave before he could tell everything he wanted to. I am convinced that when it came to me they, like the others, had a plan, but as usually happens, when they put it into effect, they got sidetracked: carried away by the pleasure of being first fiddle, his wife wasted the time I was there on telling her stories. More conscious than she was of my busy schedule, Cristian was on tenterhooks: I could sense it because he avoided my eyes, he cracked his knuckles, a coarse habit I don't remember him having had as a child, and at one point he abruptly abandoned our conversation about Anton and broached the subject with me directly. He had a huge favor to ask of me.

He pauses, drinks some water, looks out of the window. The hills, crowned with little white villages from the fourteenth century, narrow streets of stone perched above orange and mandarin groves. The golden fruits lying in the freshly mown grass. Huge cacti, with red flower buds, the tousled crowns of the gnarled, white-trunked olive trees growing from the red earth. His insatiable eye, rejoicing in the picture-postcard beauty, and the thrill of sadness, the recognition of something that comes from just as far away in his life as his memories of childhood in a distant land.

*

—Cristian went into a long and convoluted story, interrupted from time to time by his wife, which made it even more difficult for me to understand it. Although I realized that I was going to be late for the reception, where they were waiting for me, it would have been unthinkable to leave before they finished. Broadly, it was about their daughter's husband, who was supposed to have come up against all kinds of unpleasantness at work because of the Dobrotă family's past—old matters, *long since atoned for*, to use their religious turn of phrase. Some well-informed person is supposed to have told the young man that this was why his career had reached an impasse and why he would never be sent on trips outside the country. Being ambitious and well educated, the son-in-law had lately become more and more irascible and kept threatening Cristian's daughter with a divorce. When they got to this point, Mrs. Dobrotă burst into tears, it would be a great misfortune, she said, their daughter would be devastated and what was more they had a child. The atmosphere is always tense, tears, recriminations . . . "Although you have no children, you have to understand that for a father there can be no greater suffering than to have some harm befall his child," added Cristian. "I understand," I said, "or I think I understand, but what can I do about it, my dears? I have no influence over here." "You have the influence and you can do something about it if you want to," he whispered. His voice was self-confident and he laid his hand on mine. It was trembling slightly and he had an unpleasant smile that I noticed only in that moment, just as it was only then that I noticed his down at heel shoes. "I wasn't able to come to your lecture, unfortunately, but from what I hear, there were a number of very influential people in the audience," he added.

*

His wife then went to the vitrine housing the bibelots and from a drawer she took a piece of paper, obviously prepared in advance, on which a number of names were written in ink. She thrust the piece of paper in my pocket with an air of finality: "Just a single word from any one of these people will be sufficient for my family's sins to be forgotten," she whispered. "And the intervention should be aimed primarily at Cristian's job. At long last he has been put forward for a promotion from archives to research. But the person helping us has told us what difficulties he has come up against and he thinks that without a solid intervention nothing will come of it."

—And so it wasn't to do with the son-in-law's situation at work, but your friend's career!

—No. Or rather yes, to a certain extent. But if it was true what they said, that by helping the father-in-law's career, you solve the son-in-law's problem, then the family situation and the work situation are connected. Let me repeat their argument for you, which didn't really convince me. They claim that merely if Cristian were promoted, it would be a sign that his situation had normalized, which would then immediately be transmitted to the other files. And the son-in-law would realize that he had not become part of a persecuted family with a bad file. *File* was the magic word that kept coming up in our conversation.

*

The little hedge of pink, white, red oleanders, slicing the darkening motorway into the same two steely bands that undulate behind, curling like metal shavings. The wooded hills climbing into the sky, the gnarled white trunks of the ancient olive trees rising from the red earth, the thick-walled houses with windows that are tiny so that the darkness within will preserve its coolness. And the shadow that descends upon them.

—What they were asking struck me as utter madness, me, a foreign citizen, but I was embarrassed to tell them straight out! But even so, I didn't think it was right to encourage them, either. "I shall do you this service with the greatest pleasure, my dears," I said, "if it is at all within my power! But I cannot expect anybody to break the law! And I doubt," I went on, "that such an intervention would have any positive result. But I am convinced that by doing your duty, you will persuade them that you deserve to be promoted. I too have experienced a lot of difficult moments in my life." But poor Cristian and especially his wife tried with all their might, they pleaded with tears in their eyes, to persuade me to "do something." Such was the painfully embarrassing time I endured with them: I can't even bear to remember it!

CHAPTER THIRTY
Categories of Behavior

—DOBROTĂ CRISTIAN . . . the name sounds familiar . . .

—The brother of the aviator, comrade colonel! I read about the aviator, Anton Dobrotă, in a recent study that defined the categories of behavior in prison . . . Anton Dobrotă was category four, the aggressive/intractable type. The evaluation may well be correct, he was an outstanding sportsman, a mediocre intellect, the only man ever to escape from Aiud. I was unable to discover how he died, the case studies didn't provide exhaustive data . . .

—Well, let me tell you then! He died like a dog, in solitary, spattered with blood and shit, and he howled himself hoarse! How else do you want enemies of the people to croak? And we had the Russians behind us as well! But his brother, Cristian, wasn't he in the slammer too?

—Two years, without trial . . . The anxious type, mental blockages . . .

—Leave it out, you and your parrot talk . . . Now I remember that Cristian, they brought him to me, grovels like a doormat when he sees you, but refuses to collaborate . . . Go and have a chat with him, take the network file on him out of mothballs, we didn't have anything to put in it, they told me he never leaves the house, the only person he sees is his wife, they don't come much lower than you, you dirtbag! I told him and he just laughed like an idiot, no, there was nothing he could tell about nobody! Well, now he's got the goods aplenty on the Defector!

—If you will allow me, comrade colonel! His wife is a person we can talk to! She's sincerely devoted, our support person at her place of work, except that she's got a weakness for that man. I had a discussion with her once, about his promotion, family problems, with her daughter, her son-in-law . . .

—You know what my theory is, lieutenant! Women lower themselves easily and in the blink of an eye they grow twice the size! Triple! I can understand why you can't be bothered wasting your time with him, fair enough! Call her into headquarters! It's not like it wouldn't be the first time, eh? Hmm, well! It's not bad, let's see where it leads! Have the procedures been followed? Was the Defector's luggage checked on arrival and departure? Any materials with a hostile content?

—Only on arrival! Exile magazines, with *sămănătorist** titles: *White Flowers* and *Carolers, Awake* . . .

—What do you think this is, Christmas, Easter? You're talking to an officer, lieutenant Matei. You're not attending some lecture by Noica!

—We have an address from the border guards, based on a tip from the cousin, our source "Bădescu," who has been working with the people at the border. Manu Traian brought exile magazines, signaled in the report by agent "Bădescu." On departure, his luggage was inventoried by the same source, "Bădescu," but it was clean. The person for whom the corpora delicti were intended has not been identified nor where said corpora delicti vanished to.

Now he can laugh in his face. It don't matter how high your ma and your pa are in rank, you still don't know all the nuts and bolts of our apparatus, do you, you jackass?

—Don't bother your head about them, Lieutenant Matei! Right now, the corpora delicti are being registered by our archives department, along with the addresses of the sponsors, the printing presses, the editors. They were requested by our source "Emilian," the vice-president of the Academy. That's why the border guards turned a blind eye to them. Anything else? What's with that table?

—It's the table of the telephone numbers and addresses of the people who requested a meeting with Manu Traian on the evening of the lecture. They were made available to us by source "Bădescu." The meetings did not take place, as the addresses were purloined in advance by source "Bădescu," the Defector's cousin, from his pocket.

* Sămănătorism: right-wing conservative and traditionalist literary and cultural movement, named after *Sămănătorul* (The Sower), an early twentieth-century magazine.

—It would have been better if they'd taken place, as long as we knew about them! This agent "Bădescu" of ours is getting a bit too big for his boots, arranging our working schedule for us. Restrain him, so that he doesn't overstep his responsibilities, otherwise we'll have to remind him what he was before we roped him in. And have his expenses claims checked, make sure not too much hard currency sticks to them fingers of his . . . Go on then, have the preliminary files microfilmed and get a move on with the action plan!

CHAPTER THIRTY-ONE
Sins Unatoned For

HE DOES NOT look at Christa. He has twisted around in his seat and is looking through the windscreen at the wooded hills across which the shadow of evening is spreading. Only a little longer and in the bluish, pellucid air the lights at the edge of the motorway will start to float. He is aware that by talking he makes the journey seem shorter along this stretch of motorway, which, after nightfall, is so monotonous. The headlights sweep the little hedge of oleanders, fleetingly illumining the white, pink, red flowers.

—After I left the Dobrotă family home, I realized that half of the time we had talked only about Anton. His sister-in-law knew his life inside-out . . .

—Maybe she was in love with the older brother first. You know what teenage girls are like, who fall in love with famous actors, with their sisters' fiancés. You say that Anton was a famous aviator, that his photograph appeared in the newspapers . . .

—He was a man who had a charisma hard to explain today. The photographs of Anton don't say very much nowadays. In the Dobrotă house there is a photograph album that survived the searches. And of course the three of us looked through it . . .

—Were there any photographs of you in it?

—They claimed that I appeared in a group photograph among the heads of a crowd of unknown people. But I was not at all convinced. I did not even recognize the expression on the face. They offered me the photograph when I left, but I didn't want to take it . . .

—Why? I would have been curious to see what you looked like then . . . I've never seen your parents . . . your mother . . .

*

—What point would there have been in my burdening myself with it if I wasn't sure that I was the one in the picture? And all those unknown people, whom I no longer remember. In any case, it was an amateur photograph, it was dark, unclear. What would I have done with it here? Best leave the photograph in the album, where it belongs, I told them. I am sure that Mrs. Dobrotă will preserve it better than I could. I would probably have lost it by now, like I did with the addresses. Whereas she, the Vestal priestess of the family . . .

—You do have something against her, nonetheless.

—It irritates me when I remember her indiscreet chatter. Why was it she kept reminding me of all those trivial things from childhood? And above all, why did she have to make such a song and dance about them? Even if I am not an expert in adolescent psychology, unlike you, I don't believe she was perverse enough to have loved both brothers. She is quite simply a gossip . . .

—Do you think that it is necessarily perverse to love two brothers? And anyway, I didn't say she loved both at the same time! How outmoded, how old-fashioned you can be!

—Outmoded, old-fashioned, as you like, but I'm almost sure that the whole parade of complicit memories was for a purpose. It served some end . . .

—What end? What end could it serve?

After a sidelong glance, Christa's eyes dutifully return to the road ahead. On the right, the huge Dr. Oetker pudding on an advertising hoarding awaits the imminent moment when its multicolored lights will be lit. On the left, the walls of buildings pass by, darkened in the dusk. On the green-bronze hills swarm round white shapes: scattered flocks of sheep.

*

—All that false, indiscreet familiarity was meant to show that the three of us had remained as close as we were in our youth. And as such I was meant to feel obligated to do what they were going to ask of me. But in my youth it was only Anton who was my friend! I never paid any attention to Cristian! As for Mrs.

Dobrotă, as I said, she did not exist in our lives in any way. You will, I hope, be able to understand why I was so bothered by her chatter when she said things like: "Do you remember when you had scarlet fever?" From the very moment I set foot in the house, she started talking to me with a familiarity that was out of place: "Do you remember what trouble you had getting Anton to learn by heart that end-of-year Latin essay you had composed for him?"

—How could you have remembered, when you can't even recognize yourself in a photograph!

—Imagine, by some miracle or other, I did remember that essay! I had been doing Anton's homework all the more zealously after I started being remunerated for it, to which was soon to be added another incentive, and I felt embarrassed when I had to take the small fee for my efforts.

—So you received money then, did you? laughs Christa. And the incentive, let me guess . . . You started courting his cousin, the pianist.

—You guessed it, my dear. It is probably a universal situation of adolescence. I was very shy, full of complexes, but she divined my feelings. We were both studious, but I, poor me, I had grown up in a much humbler household and I was overawed by the elegant manners, the un-self-conscious conversation, in which I have never shone, as you more than anybody else knows, and by the fascinatingly rich library. Since the future reveals itself to us through chance encounters, I remember, for example, that I always used to look at an album of engravings about the monuments of Italy. Most of all I liked the ones in Rome. Doesn't that seem strange to you?

—Everything you have been telling me seems strange to me. And that Mrs. Dobrotă's memory is also strange. Didn't you ask her how she knew all those things?

—It was obvious how! Cristian must have told his wife about his family, to give himself some ascendency over her. Or perhaps he was simply taking refuge in the memories of times better than the present.

—But why would she have remembered all those trivial details that had nothing to do with her?

—I asked myself the same question and this is what I came up with: Mrs. Dobrotă must have absorbed her husband's memories, because life there is dreadfully monotonous! When the future is so predictable, only the past can provide an opportunity for entertainment.

*

What speculation! Her hand relaxes on the steering wheel, in disappointment. The corners of her mouth are still rigid amid their wrinkles. She remains silent.

—As often happens, my dear, a veritable process of symbiosis occurs between them. They had adopted from one another the same expressions, gestures, words, even each other's memories.

—What do you mean, they had adopted each other's memories?

Her gloved hands are now clenching the steering wheel. Is not this what she has attempted for years and years: to feel he is there beside her in the nightmares from which she awakes bathed in sweat, her heart thudding, her neck taut with the silent screams? Is not this what she has thought, lying with her eyes wide open in the dark, fearful to go back to sleep next to his wheezing, indifferent breathing? Minutes as long as hours, hours in which she got out of bed, went to the bathroom, when she looked at her increasingly haggard face in the misted mirror, at the puffiness beneath her eyes, the wrinkles that score the corners of her eyes, Traian will not agree to a facelift, and the next day, at breakfast, he asks, puzzled: Did you have insomnia, my dear? I got the impression that you were wandering about the house like a ghost . . .

Irritated, Christa presses harder on the accelerator pedal.

*

—In fact, I didn't put it very well when I said that each had adopted the other's memories. The memories travelled down a one-way street, from Cristian to his wife. Never in the opposite direction! The wife told the glorious history of the Dobrotă family—it was obvious she had had the practice! Maybe she uses it to get one up on her friends. On the other hand, Cristian never said anything about his wife's family.

—He was conscious of having made a bad marriage!

—The light at the end of the tunnel gradually expands to reveal a grove of straight, slender trees. Bald hills with clumps of vegetation, the dry beds of the rivers that once filled the now dry valleys with marshes and mosquitos.

Christ came to Eboli. And he has been living here long enough for all these things to become lifelong memories.

But how cutting Christa's voice sounded when she talked about a bad marriage!

*

—Unfortunately, it weighs on me that I wasn't able to help Cristian somehow. I keep remembering how he was arrested, imprisoned. True, as I was leaving, I told them: "If you manage to obtain permission to travel, you will be welcome to stay with us, my dears. Christa and I will do everything we can to make you feel welcome."

—I can but give you advice, the same as my grandfather used to give me . . . But you are the one who has to find the strength to resist the memories from there, which, from what I understand, are getting more and more unpleasant. It wouldn't have been at all good to bottle up these stories, to poison yourself with them slowly . . . Tell them and forget them! Don't blame yourself where no guilt exists! You shouldn't feel responsible for what happened to your family in the past. And nor for what is happening to your erstwhile friends today! From what I understand, your country has always had problems and what I am about to say may well annoy you, but I am convinced it always will!

CHAPTER THIRTY-TWO
To Be or Not to Be an Old Crock

Daniel says:

And I was still in two minds as to whether I should sidle off to the bus if Nagging Cassandra let me out of her sight for an instant, or whether I should stay until he vanished beyond the frontier guarded by the stern faces and starred shoulders of the blue-eyed boys.

For now, Traian was still there, with his bag slung over his shoulder and his coat with all the pockets and zippers, in a nimbus of Hugo Boss, in a hurry to get past check-in, to get a shot of Victor's armored suitcase and us, the rest of the family.

The women on the blue vinyl bench seat, the men around the bench seat with their briefcases and jackets and neckties and undertaker's suits and dirty stories and bellies and metal teeth and interchangeable sentences about who is replacing whom, who is undermining whom, who is backing whom, who is eating whom for lunch, who has got whom a better position, who has got whom demoted, who is under investigation, who has stayed where he is, who sent the anonymous letter, he-he-he. And then another little joke!

No! Never will I accept to make such appalling jokes!

And then there was jolly old Victor, who would slap me on the back whenever he saw me:

—How's it going? Everything all right?

That's the only thing he can say.

—How's it going? Everything all right?

*

And I admit, no matter how insane it might seem now, I still nurtured the hope that at the last moment he would turn to me and call out:

—Don't forget to write! And don't forget that I'll be coming back next year! Don't forget, Daniel, that I'll be expecting you to come and visit me on the *Other Side!*

I was still waiting for a reversal of the situation worthy of Mihaela's bedtime stories, *Good night, children!* In other words, I was waiting for him to realize, at least now, at the very last moment, that I was him, the one in the sepia photograph, speckled with drops of coffee or cooking oil, the photograph from the thirties that Nana kept in a corner of the mirror.

I was him, who had not left, I was him, who was to return. To me, the glass dome of the airport was still full of festive cheer, like on New Year's Eve. What else was our meeting to be than (he recites) *a ritual, the story of passing on the torch and of the desperate attempt to carry it further*, that sentence is from my latest favorite book, *Păltiniş Diary,** Dudu lent me it for a week, his mother has an under-the-counter thing going with the woman at the university book stand.

*

And since nothing annoys me more than falsities and formalities, I did not budge from the spot, I made no gesture. I still believed, albeit less and less, that in order to recognize me all Traian would have had to do would be to take a closer look at me.

That is why I hadn't been worried those two weeks, while Professor Stan and his gang of dilettantes and Victor and his team of black-marketeers were chasing him all over the place.

But now there was no time left, game over, in a matter of seconds he would be going through customs, and I had to choose whether to stay to the last moment and see for myself that he was leaving, with his suitcase stuffed full of Victor's microphones, without so much as giving me a wave, or whether to go

* Gabriel Liiceanu, *Păltiniş Diary: A Paideic Model in Humanist Culture* (1983). Gabriel Liiceanu (1942–) was a follower of philosopher Constantin Noica, whom he visited in Păltiniş in the Carpathian Mountains. The *Păltiniş Diary* is an account of an alternative philosophical education in reclusion, untrammeled by the official ideology and discourse. Although published in the Communist period, the book was not viewed with official favor and was very difficult to obtain.

downstairs to the basement, to the toilets, like a hero, but in fact to go outside, to the bus stop, and to call you, *my dirty Diana,* from the public phone and say: "That's it, honey, I've arranged it, my uncle has promised to fill Victor's suitcase with condoms and send it to us by DHL."*

*

And in the end I decided to sling my hook, so as not to see that he didn't realize who I was, out of that whole flock of ours. I was walking to the bus stop, my ears still ringing with Cassandra's desperate cries:

—Daniel! Where are you, Daniel? Come here and wave to him with your cousin, your uncle, your great-uncle! Daniel! Where are you? Don't make me have to shout after you!

But by then I had come up with another two conflicting hypotheses, that is:

TO BE OR NOT TO BE . . . AN OLD CROCK?

More specifically:

1) No, I will never, never accept to become an old crock, not even an old crock like him!

2) Yes, I would like to be him, even at the risk of ending up an old crock!

*

An old crock, which is to say, standing in the milk queue in the morning; poring over the small ads and funeral notices in *România Liberă*; two drawn chess matches a day in Cişmigiu Park.

Plus the ritual phrases:

—Keep my place for me in this queue, I have to collect my pension today, I'll be back soon, in three hours!

—When we were your age, we didn't . . .

—Keep a civil tongue in your head! The cheek!

* During the nationalist-isolationist 1980s, contraceptives and abortions were made illegal as part of Ceauşescu's drive to increase the national population.

—We were young once too, no matter what you might think . . .

—Give your seat up to that lady! To that man! To others!

—You animal!

—Don't twist your face when you're talking to me!

—Take that cap off! Take your hands out of your pockets!

—You haven't got a clue what happened at Yalta! Compulsory Russian lessons! Prosecutors! Collectivization!

No, no, never, I will still never accept to be that kind of old crock! Option 1.

*

Or else yes, to be him, the way I saw him when he appeared on the first day, with those cool glasses and those quite trendy clothes of yours, old man, and all of them swarming round him, the ladies, the secret policemen, the black-marketeers, the undertakers, and the pockets on his sleeve, and his well-trimmed beard, trailing Tabac Original aftershave, yes, then I would have died to be him! Option 2.

But even then I didn't have any luck, I couldn't even see him very well, he was very far away, and Cassandra, off her nut as usual, had started shouting:

—You too, Daniel, go on, nearer the front! He's quite shy by nature, you know. At home he's bolder, at home he can even be impertinent! The problem with him is that he's not very good in company . . . Go on! Get nearer the front, so that our Traian can see you! Take Daniel with you! Go on, Daniel, darling! Go on, I'm begging you! Do it for me! Do it for Nana! I'm begging you, do it! Iambeggingyou! Go and introduce yourself already! Meet your uncle, great-uncle, great-grandfather, our guest! Go on, Daniel, don't make me have to shout, where are you, don't make me have to shout after you.

It makes you want to kill them all!

As you'll realize, I should have abandoned my post as incisive observer then and there, I should have made my getaway, gone off on the bus, by myself, but not before expressly signaling to

Mother that I was going, because I knew full well what a panic she can create.

*

But to come back to our two choices, the theoretical issue would be as follows: despite the glasses, the wheeled suitcases, his upright gait, everything he has seen, read, listened to, eaten, Beaubourg, Manchester United, the Milan Scala, the Florence Pinacothèque, etc., might Traian Manu be nothing more than an old crock, careful of his eye and nose drops, his blood-pressure pills, his varicose-vein gel? A more stylish old crock, but ultimately still nothing more than an old crock.

But even so, I would still like to be him, even if I will have to take all those blood-pressure pills and get out of breath when I climb the stairs, especially if I am talking:

—Why don't you take the elevator, Professor? At your age *e pericoloso sporgersi!*

And there would be guys to lug Uncle Victor's heavy suitcase, full of my inspired father's wooden spoons, teetering on every step all the way up to the seventh floor.

*

At the time, there in the airport, I did not yet know about all his manias—for example, every evening at a given hour, on the dot, he would start to panic:

—My dears, please excuse me, I notice it has grown dark and I haven't phoned Christa!

And/or:

—My dears, I can't come at that time, it's impossible! Please wait a little, it's absolutely vital that I phone Christa!

And like a shot out of a gun he would dash for the telephone, squirming in the armchair, turning the television on and off, a real sea wolf/caged lion, until those insolent telephonists, hooked up to the blue-eyed boys, deigned to put him through. Crackling, interruptions, appeals to Professor Stan to get us a free line, the red telephone, I have to call her urgently, extremely urgently! I have to call Christa urgently!

And finally, after three hours of inhuman suspense, a feeble chirp. And he rushes to the telephone, almost ripping it from the socket, so that he can say:

—Yes, my dear, I'm fine, don't worry, I feel perfectly fine, my stomach is not aching, I'm not constipated, I haven't got diarrhea, I'm taking my tablets on time, the weather is rather warm, one of my ears is clogged up, but have no fear, there are doctors here too, there are nurses with epaulettes, they visit me on the hour, don't be concerned about me, but take care of yourself, take your tablets, make sure you sleep well, have sweet dreams, dream about me.

And there were other things he said that left you open-mouthed, but I merely deduced them, because although my ear was pressed to the door, he was speaking German, a language in which I had taken only four lessons when Mihnea fell off the balcony and they expelled all of us who were at the party in the hall of residence.

*

And so in the end I chose to be him, even if that meant becoming an old crock.

On the other hand, I'll have a video player all to myself, and cassettes and CDs of Judas Priest, Iron Maiden, Madonna, The Rolling Stones . . .

But if I were him, maybe I wouldn't be able to stand listening to hard rock, only Grieg, only The Beatles . . . I'd fix myself a Campari, just two fingers' worth, enough to cover the bottom of the glass, topped off with a Schweppes Indian Tonic and three glaçons and a blonde who knows her trade . . .

To be him and still to be me, otherwise I might not care too much about any blonde! Although Gionni says his granddad gets a hard-on whenever the nurse arrives with the bedpan!

To be him, even if that meant having osteoporosis, osteoarthritis, arthritis, lumbago, because in exchange I'd be able to wear genuine Todd shoes!

That's the label I saw inside his soft shoes, and the look and the smell of them! You'd think nobody had ever stuck their feet in them! I don't know how it was that the light from the passageway slanted directly onto his shoes, they were by the door when I opened it a crack.

*

I was waiting in the passageway, during those two nights in Cărbuneşti, waiting for the party to finish, waiting to see him enter his room, so that maybe the two of us could talk together. But just my luck, it was a letdown, as usual, because Nagging Cassandra started shouting:

—Daniel, where are you, Daniel? Fetch me a glass of water!

And so returning to my post, I cautiously opened the door, and truth to tell, I wasn't capable of saying a word when I heard him:

—Who is it? Who's there? My dear, now that you've woken me up, come in and turn the light on!

And I can't forgive myself for not having turned the light on or having gone in! Or at least for not having replied: "It's me, Daniel! I'm sorry, wrong door!" Or for not having gone up to him the next day and said: "I hope I didn't wake you up last night." Or: "I'm sorry for having woken you up last night."

Because that was the other thing: I didn't know whether to address him with the formal or the informal "you."*

*

It was a letdown because usually I know what I think, what I feel, what others think of me, and that's why I refused to believe that he could walk past me the same as he walked past all the others.

And not even now can I believe that that is precisely what happened!

* *Tu* or *dumneavoastră*. Unlike the French *vous*, for example, the Romanian *dumneavoastră* (literally "your (pl.) lordship") is used solely as a polite form of address; the second-person plural pronoun *voi* does not imply formality and is used only for addressing more than one person.

In any event Mother claims that he'll be coming again in the summer. But even if he does come in the summer, won't it be the same? Professor Stan and his cronies piling onto him, plus Victor . . .

Maybe I'll catch him if we go to Cărbuneşti and he takes tea in the yard, I couldn't tell whether he realized who I was or not, so that he would remember me afterwards, *je suis aussi un fan du thé Lipton Yellow*, I shall tell him, and he will say: Come over here, Daniel, and let's talk a little while, tell me, toying with those cool glasses, and the way he holds his cup of tea, with those long, bony fingers of his.

*

I think he may have noticed me once, he was at the table with Victor, I was passing, he looked at me and tossed out the following advice:

—Why are you walking all hunched up like that, my dear? At your age it's very important to learn to walk straight! Try to learn, my dear, you'll look taller too, but above all, if you learn to walk straight now, it will be good for your spine all your life.

But it's very hard to walk straight like he said, in fact, I don't even believe it's possible to stay straight all the time. I tried it yesterday, but it didn't work, I kept thinking how I must look: like a parrot.

And my shoulder blades kept hurting.

CHAPTER THIRTY-THREE
An Undercover Officer with Diplomatic Status
or a Scholarship Student in the States?

—*THE ACTION PLAN for the intelligence operation involving the aforementioned MANU TRAIAN, born 3 April 1922 in Cărbuneşti commune, Dolj, son of Ion and Maria, by profession a biologist, currently director of the European Institute . . .*

—What the hell, I thought you was cleverer than that, lieutenant! Leave all that stuff out! Get on with it!

—*In the context of the increase in hostile actions against our state on the part of groups of defectors in foreign countries, the following objectives become necessary: 1) To establish as precisely as possible the connections between MANU TRAIAN and MORA AUGUSTIN, president of the Romanian Academy in Paris, Rome and Munich. 2) To uncover the plans of the hostile group of defectors that go by the name of the Romanian Academy etc. etc. for the year in progress and of defectors in management positions, said defectors having been identified along with all their connections. 3) To establish the defectors' connections in this country. Deadline: 10 November 1986. Responsible: Lt. Matei Silviu.*

*

—Yes, the Academy is a target that needs to be penetrated! And the more we penetrate it, the more work there is to do on it . . .

They both laugh. This is how Nuţi finds them when she arrives with the coffee, the fresh croissants, and the Rémy Martin cognac, for which Colonel Ipsas has had a weakness ever since he went *Outside* for the first time, to France: he was a member of the Comrade's bodyguards.

The lieutenant cannot eat to the sound of the colonel's chomping. But he drinks his mint-flavored green tea, which mummy brings him back every time she goes abroad, along with a bottle of Queen Ann.

—Won't you have some cognac even? What, are you into yoga and vegetarianism now? laughs Ispas. You catch all the same bugs as our targets. You ought to penetrate that Bivolaru,* you become a yogi, keep Noica under surveillance, parrot philosophy . . .

—The documentation, comrade colonel! May I continue reading? *To achieve these tasks the following operational intelligence measures will be taken: 1) Use of agents "Emilian" and "Bădescu," who will intensify their efforts to invite MANU TRAIAN to attend a professional conference in our country and will increase the frequency of visits by MANU TRAIAN's family abroad, with an emphasis on private meetings. 2) Establishment of a personal relationship with MANU TRAIAN's wife, MANU CHRISTA, who is refractory to collaboration with our country. 3) Establishment of contact with support persons in the Institute for the Propagation of Romanian Culture Abroad, the universities of Bucharest, Iaşi, and Cluj, the Academy's Biological Research Institute, publishers, the press. Deadline: 26 January 1987. Responsible: Lt. Matei Silviu.*

—Are you sick of having an easy time or what, lieutenant? How can you give 26 January as a deadline when you know how busy we are with the Comrade's birthday?** Put down 10 February 1987 and it's all right by me. Halt! Don't you start jabbering away again like a broken record. Add: *An intelligence report from our source "Bădescu" about our source "Emilian" will be required, and vice-versa, from our source "Emilian" about our source "Bădescu."* You'll instruct the two to remain in contact with each other and to work together on their future visits. Under our

* Gregorian Bivolaru (1952–), a plumber during the Communist period, he became a self-styled spiritual teacher and yogi. Kept under constant surveillance by the Securitate, he was also tortured, jailed twice, and interned in a psychiatric hospital. Even after the fall of Communism, he continued to have problems with the authorities and in the end fled to Sweden, where he was granted political asylum.

** On 26 January, Nicolae Ceauşescu's birthday, the cult of personality went into overdrive, with mass rallies where attendance was compulsory for many segments of the population (e.g., schoolchildren).

supervision "Bădescu" has already requested an invitation from Manu Traian to visit him as a tourist, and "Emilian" will meet Manu Traian in the very near future on a work trip. Good! Next!

*

4) Identification of the aforementioned Izvoranu Cornel and Izvoranu Daniel, targets of Service "F," who have entered into correspondence with Manu Traian and intensification of efforts to recruit them as our agents to keep the family of Manu Traian under intelligence surveillance. I am now also going to add Dobrotă Florica.

—What about the procedure? What do you have in mind?

—In what respect, colonel?

—In what respect my ass! Apologies, lieutenant, that was just one of our traditional folk sayings. Your mother is a colleague of ours. She hasn't retired yet, has she? Oho, she was a looker, all the men used to drool when she entered the building, not to mention the entrances she used to make! Real lofty, if you get my meaning. You've got reason to be proud, because she had a sharp mind as well as everything else! Hard as iron, sharp as steel, if she got it into her head to do a thing, she could sit on her ass or stand on her head and it would still come off for her! But what were we talking about? We'll suborn this Izvoranu senior and then some! You're good at action plans on paper, but you've got a way to go before you can put it into practice, titch!

—Comrade colonel, with all due respect, Izvoranu Cornel is a Party member. It is therefore not possible to take action. Or else it is possible, but it will require approval from his branch office . . .

—What are you talking about! Haven't you heard of Sector 1 R.C.P. headquarters in Amzei Square? Get in touch with Popescu, the undersecretary for propaganda, our support person, and you'll have the go-ahead in the bag. Summon Izvoranu, have a talk with him at headquarters, he's the kind of family man who'll shit his pants and so recruiting him won't pose any problem. You'll be responsible for that operation! What about

his son? What are you going to do with Izvoranu junior? Have
a think about it.

*

—I have a proposal, comrade colonel! I've examined the file on
Izvoranu Daniel; it's quite thick for someone his age. He was
expelled from university along with a whole group of students
and he was lucky enough to be in with Colonel Bean's son, they
took them back en masse, but he's hanging by a thread. I had
thought of starting a student samizdat magazine, it's a phenomenon that's non-existent in Romania, it gives a good impression
Outside, P.R. via Free Europe, that bunch will jump up and down
for joy, they'll be blaring nothing else! And Daniel as editor-in-
chief, why not, he's got his head in the clouds and he's disorga-
nized, but he's more cultured than the others, and Manu Traian's
visit has made him lose contact with reality even more . . . And
then let him be recruited here, at headquarters, so that it's not
just the university at stake, but something bigger . . .
    —Why don't we put the boot into him, just a wee bit, what
do you say? Maybe there won't even be any need . . . when he
sees he's being roped in, he'll be like a little lamb! If the operation succeeds, you may well see your dream come true, lieutenant: an undercover officer with diplomatic status, probably in
Rome, because new horizons are starting to open up . . . Forget
about your dreams of a scholarship, fieldwork, seniority, that's
everything, mark my words, 'cause I want what's best for you,
and if you don't believe me, just you ask your ma!
    Walking backwards out of the office, lieutenant Matei thinks
to glimpse a cold, sharp gleam in the colonel's hazel eyes.
    But no, when he looks more closely, it is the same jovial
accountant's face he has known since childhood.

CHAPTER THIRTY-FOUR
The Nocturnal Visitor

—POOR CRISTIAN WAS waiting for me with the table laid in the hall, which they converted into an office/dining room/living room after their daughter got married. Yet again I had to cope with *boeuf* salad, which I was served everywhere I went and in which, despite the different recipes, my stomach could always detect the presence of too much poor-quality cooking oil. There were also some sandwiches, which I barely touched, I do have a reception to go to, my dears, please don't take it amiss, I told them. When I arrived at their house, I had already had some unfortunate prior culinary experiences, from when I had stayed with the whole family for a few days in our little home town, at the villa of one of Victor's friends.

—You haven't told me about how you spent your time there. Were you able to take a little exercise, to get some fresh air?

—Exercise? With whom? When? There, the meal is the central moment, the nucleus of the day, and it swallows up everything else. "Moment" is hardly the best way to put it, since the meals lasted for hours and hours. Then there would be a respite, followed by yet another meal! For years and years I missed the traditional feasts of that kind, which begin mid-morning, with aperitifs and strong liquor, and end on the afternoon of the following day, with sour soup to get the feasters back on their feet. People continuously coming and going, the frailer ones vanishing and then returning, partially restored by a few hours' sleep. And naturally, they drink without any qualms whatsoever, and this is something I think you would not have liked. You would have also found the food too rich. As a child, I used to like to get caught up in uninhibited merrymaking like that, with dozens of mouths talking and laughing simultaneously. Of course, as I was too young, the meanings of the jokes, many of which were obscene, eluded me, and likewise I didn't grasp the boredom or the petty conflicts, all the things that pertained to ordinary life and which must have existed there too. But now, when I found myself sitting at the table with them, duty bound to undergo the ordeal of so many different dishes, I myself had to recognize how old I had grown . . .

*

—Because it goes without saying that you're hardly at the age to be going there! And with that diet of yours that you're not allowed to deviate from! If only you had been twenty years younger! And if you were stubborn enough to go there now, at those traditional feasts of yours the sensible thing to do would have been to make your excuses after an hour or two and then to leave the table!

—Absurd, my dear! How could I have stayed for just an hour and then left, when it was precisely my arrival they were celebrating! In any event, I should tell you that I did get up and leave, at a reasonable hour. I think you can imagine how hard I had to fight against the protestations of the others, especially cousin Victor's. But when I reached the critical point, I became obdurate. I would go up to my room and sometimes I even managed to fall asleep without taking my pills. That was why it put me out of sorts all the more when somebody kept ruining my sleep . . .

—At night?

—I told you about it at the time, on the evening of my arrival. You've forgotten . . .

The smile in his voice meeting her smile. The complicity of the night of love that resembled the nights of times past as much as their faces today resemble those in the photograph. But they are still themselves, even if their bodies have shed the smells of which they were once ashamed and they no longer take any pleasure in lying uncovered with the light on.

*

—A number of times I woke up when somebody opened the door a crack and remained on the threshold. You know what a light sleeper I am, even if I do tend to snore. If he had knocked on the door, if he had coughed discreetly, I would have heard. But no. He stood there motionless. "Come in, my dear," I said every time it happened, "come in, now that you've disturbed me, come in and turn on the light." But he didn't, and so I never saw his face.

Christa gives a strident laugh:

—She was waiting for an invitation . . . to come to bed!

—You can laugh all you like, but I don't even know whether it was a woman or a man! At the hotel there were women and you could see at a single glance what they wanted, what they were looking for. They would knock on your door, ask for a cigarette lighter, you kept bumping into them everywhere, they would be waiting in the armchairs in the lobby. The game was clear and you knew what you would have been getting yourself into. But this was something else . . . This somebody would disappear, mumbling something, probably an excuse. I can sense by your silence that you don't believe me, but . . . Does it seem possible to you that somebody could keep getting the wrong door?

*

The little hedge of oleanders that slices the motorway in two, the wooded hills climbing towards the sky, the gnarled trunks of the centuries-old olive trees, the round-trunked pines, the cacti, the palm trees, the pastel-colored houses dotted along the edge of the road, each with a tractor, a truck, a car in the yard. The whole familiar backdrop that makes the story he is telling seem all the more unreal to him.

—Why do you complicate things pointlessly? It was carelessness! It happens . . . Or maybe your room was close to one that was more in demand.

—Naturally they had given me the best room, and so it was the furthest from the bathroom, if that is what you were thinking . . .

—Then, I don't know . . . It depends on what happened after that . . .

—Nothing happened after that! Apart from that, having been woken up, the only thing I could do was to fight against insomnia. Tossing back and forth in bed, I could hear the floorboards creaking up and down, the water dripping from a faulty tap, although the villa was new, doors opening and closing, probably each person making the necessary trips before bedtime. And, of course, from downstairs, from the table, Victor's voice, louder than all the rest . . .

*

—But believe me, to the best of my ability, I agreed to see all the people who sought me out, especially the ones I had promised this and that at the lecture and who hadn't had the patience to wait for me to telephone, as if they knew I had lost the scraps of paper. The same as with poor Cristian, I would find them waiting for me outside the hotel and at the entrances of the institutions I had to visit. They would be negotiating with Victor, trying to reach me. At one point, I'm sorry, but I got the feeling that I was trying to fill the tub of the Danaids, because more and more of them kept showing up . . . and each of them had specific requests: medicines, which as you know, are costly here unless you have insurance and a prescription, clothes, coffee, invitations, books, cassettes, and above all interventions . . . And so in the end, I had enough of it, I rebelled. What am I doing here? I asked myself one morning, when I set eyes on my face in the bathroom mirror.

The thick, damp smell of the bathroom that he has hastily tried to cover up by spraying a cheap deodorant. The strange face, miraculously rejuvenated, since without his glasses he sees it blurred by the poor quality mirror. The bidet without a plug, the overly slippery floor tiles, on which he lost his footing.

—What do I owe them, in fact? I asked myself. When for decades I was alone and poor, when I was a pariah, a nobody, when I endured uncertainty, humiliation and hunger—every night when I laid my head on my pillow I used to wonder what was to become of me—who helped me during those hard times? Who gave me a helping hand, who sent word to me or a few written lines of encouragement in all those hard years when I always had to be the best in order to receive the least, because I was a foreigner?

The exaggerated twang in his voice, which he hears with displeasure but no longer tries to control. And everything he saw there and everything he sees here gliding past the car window and distractedly tries to recognize.

All that remain are words that he is unable to spit out, to spew up. He is nauseous and a pain is climbing his left arm.

loneliness   *cold*   *uncertainty*   *hunger*

*

Always the endless motorway, sliced in two by the little hedge of oleanders from which the searing headlights pick out pink, white, red flowers. On the left, the huge cross that he divines more than sees in the dark, in the hurtling car, the cross that points the way to the endless Polish cemeteries. *Bloodshed like at Montecassino.* The white gleam of the rebuilt Montecassino abbacy. The German officer who took the documents to the Vatican a day before the bombing.

What was I doing then? Where was I? Who was I with?

Past the car window glide the stunted, frail olive trees and their foliage glints whitely, the same as the willow tree left behind—how many years ago?

More and more numbed, he dozes in his seat, trying to remember, managing to glimpse fleetingly a blurred photograph that dissolves into confusion and sleep when he tries to grasp it. Always the endless motorway.

The blindingly white sunlight through which the woman and the man in black are moving: two eternal silhouettes, frozen, solemn. And outlined ever more distantly, in the blinding heat, the silhouette, equally strange and equally familiar to him, of the man riding a donkey, with two huge wicker baskets hanging on either side of the animal's belly.

And Christa has a long way to drive, with her gloved hands, just as determined, just as relaxed, gripping the steering wheel.

And they will both pass at speed among the white, neutral lights, among the huge, multicolored advertising hoardings that pierce the night.

*

I fell asleep in the car, my dear, and I dreamed that we were both walking through a park with colorful tulips, around us were hopping doves as tame as hens and domestic rabbits. But at one point, I don't understand why, I was suddenly alone, I was running desperately through a train, I hadn't managed to buy a ticket in the station and I kept hiding under the bench seats. Up to here it was a dream, now I am awake, I am standing in front of the old house from when I was a child, I am standing at the gate, under a cypress.

But was there a cypress? Was there a fir tree in our yard?

I cannot remember whether to dream a cypress is a good or a bad omen, what I know for certain is that I do not like the dream. To have a fir tree in your yard brings misfortune, they say. And I have seen cypresses only in Rome.

To wake myself up, I dig my fingernails into my flesh as deeply as I can, I clench my fists as hard as I can, but my fingernails are also flesh and my clenched fists are cotton wool, I clench my teeth as hard as I can, my fists, and like this I am sure I am awake, I am not dreaming. I am here, I am home, and I cry out:

*

—You at least recognize me! You at least recognize me, you at least look at me, Mother . . . In every story, your mother is the one who recognizes you, only you turn your head and the cypress casts its shadow across your face.

If you don't say a single word to me, it means you are angry with me! That's what you always used to do and I knew what I had done wrong, I suspect even now why you don't want to answer me. You always liked long letters and I wrote to you seldom and sparingly, sometimes nothing but a few lines on a postcard. But I always talked to you in my mind. Sometimes I was so tired that I would no longer be able to hold the pen in my hand. What point would there have been in my putting down on paper all the things I said to you in my mind? If I was happy, I would put it off, if I was sad, I would no longer feel like it.

Remember that after a while you yourself started to write more and more seldom, less and less. Latterly, it was not even your handwriting anymore, somebody would write to me that you were well, in good health, but your fingers were stiff with arthritis and you could no longer hold the pen in your hand.

In the end I stopped receiving any letters. Imagine how uneasy I was! No matter how hard I tried, for months, decades, years I was unable to discover any news about you! Much later, in a different, unknown hand, I was sent an announcement, a *faire-part*. That was all.

It was hard for me to imagine that you really were no longer anywhere. From morning till night I wandered the streets, I could not reconcile myself to the thought that thenceforth nobody would keep a faded photograph of me in an old leather handbag. It was raining, I think, because my cheeks were wet, and with whom could I talk in my mind thenceforth?

It was the only day in my life when I thought that you were dead. Within me I knew that in fact it was impossible, because at night I dreamed of you so often! Therefore, somewhere you still had to exist.

And now that we have met again at last, there is no point in your being angry anymore, believe me! One thing still remains unclear to me, whether then, in the train, when I was hiding from the conductor, I was awake or dreaming . . .

*

—Life is hard enough as it is, we shouldn't make it harder for ourselves by wracking our consciences. I know you won't want to admit it, but in fact you have been troubled ever since you came back, your mind keeps wandering elsewhere. I still think that belated trip was a dangerous shock, just remember how much I tried to talk you out of it on the way to the airport . . . But at least now listen to what I say: you shouldn't keep thinking about things that give you no pleasure! Look, look . . .

Christa breathes a sigh of relief. Now, on the bend, she sees the huge coffee cup, projected against the deep blue sky, with stars lighting up around the advertising hoarding. Lavazza. The red letters with a gold accolade. She'll fill the tank first. And then a decaf for him and an herbal tea for her. Or an espresso?

She tenses her numb muscles—she used to be able to stand up in a flash, but now her body moves sluggishly. Traian has fallen asleep again, his head lolling to one side, propped against the window, and he is breathing rather strangely, his snoring is too loud . . .

—Wake up, Traian! Come on, make a little effort and wake up! How quickly you fell asleep, I didn't even notice! Come on, unfasten your seatbelt, you don't want to stay behind in the car, do you? What's with you . . . what's with you . . . Traian? It can't be! It can't be! Wake up, please!

May 1985–July 1989
January 2001–June 2003
January–June 2007
2008
April–May 2013

GABRIELA ADAMEŞTEANU was born in 1942 in Târgu Ocna, Romania. She is a novelist, short-story writer, essayist, journalist, and translator. She is the author of the acclaimed novels *The Equal Way of Every Day* and *Wasted Morning*, and is the editor of *Revista 22*, the weekly publication of the Group for Social Dialogue (GDS), a Romanian non-governmental organization whose stated mission is the promotion and protection of democracy, human rights, and civil liberties.

ALISTAIR IAN BLYTH, a native of Sunderland, England, has resided for many years in Bucharest. Among his previous translations are *Our Circus Presents* by Lucian Dan Teodorovici and *The Bulgarian Truck* by Dumitru Tsepeneag, both published by Dalkey Archive Press.

MICHAL AJVAZ, *The Golden Age.*
The Other City.
PIERRE ALBERT-BIROT, *Grabinoulor.*
YUZ ALESHKOVSKY, *Kangaroo.*
FELIPE ALFAU, *Chromos.*
Locos.
ANTÓNIO LOBO ANTUNES, *Knowledge of Hell.*
The Splendor of Portugal.
ALAIN ARIAS-MISSON, *Theatre of Incest.*
GABRIELA AVIGUR-ROTEM, *Heatwave and Crazy Birds.*
DJUNA BARNES, *Ladies Almanack.*
Ryder.
DONALD BARTHELME, *The King.*
Paradise.
SVETISLAV BASARA, *Chinese Letter.*
MIQUEL BAUÇÀ, *The Siege in the Room.*
RENÉ BELLETTO, *Dying.*
MAREK BIENCZYK, *Transparency.*
ANDREI BITOV, *Pushkin House.*
ANDREJ BLATNIK, *You Do Understand.*
Law of Desire.
IGNÁCIO DE LOYOLA BRANDÃO, *Anonymous Celebrity.*
Zero.
BONNIE BREMSER, *Troia: Mexican Memoirs.*
CHRISTINE BROOKE-ROSE, *Amalgamemnon.*
MICHEL BUTOR, *Degrees.*
Mobile.
G. CABRERA INFANTE, *Infante's Inferno.*
Three Trapped Tigers.
JULIETA CAMPOS, *The Fear of Losing Eurydice.*
ANNE CARSON, *Eros the Bittersweet.*
ORLY CASTEL-BLOOM, *Dolly City.*
LOUIS-FERDINAND CÉLINE, *North.*
Conversations with Professor Y.
London Bridge.
MARIE CHAIX, *The Laurels of Lake Constance.*
HUGO CHARTERIS, *The Tide Is Right.*

ERIC CHEVILLARD, *Demolishing Nisard.*
The Author and Me.
MARC CHOLODENKO, *Mordechai Schamz.*
JOSHUA COHEN, *Witz.*
EMILY HOLMES COLEMAN, *The Shutter of Snow.*
ROBERT COOVER, *A Night at the Movies.*
STANLEY CRAWFORD, *Log of the S.S. The Mrs Unguentine.*
Some Instructions to My Wife.
RENÉ CREVEL, *Putting My Foot in It.*
RALPH CUSACK, *Cadenza.*
NICHOLAS DELBANCO, *Sherbrookes.*
The Count of Concord.
NIGEL DENNIS, *Cards of Identity.*
PETER DIMOCK, *A Short Rhetoric for Leaving the Family.*
ARIEL DORFMAN, *Konfidenz.*
COLEMAN DOWELL, *Island People.*
Too Much Flesh and Jabez.
ARKADII DRAGOMOSHCHENKO, *Dust.*
RIKKI DUCORNET, *Phosphor in Dreamland.*
The Complete Butcher's Tales.
The Fountains of Neptune.
JEAN ECHENOZ, *Chopin's Move.*
FRANÇOIS EMMANUEL, *Invitation to a Voyage.*
PAUL EMOND, *The Dance of a Sham.*
SALVADOR ESPRIU, *Ariadne in the Grotesque Labyrinth.*
JUAN FILLOY, *Op Oloop.*
ANDY FITCH, *Pop Poetics.*
GUSTAVE FLAUBERT, *Bouvard and Pécuchet.*
KASS FLEISHER, *Talking out of School.*
JON FOSSE, *Aliss at the Fire.*
Melancholy.
FORD MADOX FORD, *The March of Literature.*
MAX FRISCH, *I'm Not Stiller.*
Man in the Holocene.

CARLOS FUENTES, *Christopher Unborn.*
Distant Relations.
Terra Nostra.
Where the Air Is Clear.
TAKEHIKO FUKUNAGA, *Flowers of Grass.*
WILLIAM GADDIS, JR., *The Recognitions.*
JANICE GALLOWAY, *Foreign Parts.*
The Trick Is to Keep Breathing.
WILLIAM H. GASS, *Life Sentences.*
The Tunnel.
The World Within the Word.
Willie Masters' Lonesome Wife.
GÉRARD GAVARRY, *Hoppla! 1 2 3..*
C. S. GISCOMBE, *Giscome Road.*
Here.
WITOLD GOMBROWICZ, *A Kind of Testament.*
PAULO EMÍLIO SALES GOMES, *P's Three Women.*
GEORGI GOSPODINOV, *Natural Novel.*
JUAN GOYTISOLO, *Count Julian.*
Juan the Landless.
Makbara.
Marks of Identity.
JACK GREEN, *Fire the Bastards!*
JIŘÍ GRUŠA, *The Questionnaire.*
MELA HARTWIG, *Am I a Redundant Human Being?*
JOHN HAWKES, *The Passion Artist.*
Whistlejacket.
KEIZO HINO, *Isle of Dreams.*
KAZUSHI HOSAKA, *Plainsong.*
NAOYUKI II, *The Shadow of a Blue Cat.*
DRAGO JANČAR, *The Tree with No Name.*
MIKHEIL JAVAKHISHVILI, *Kvachi.*
GERT JONKE, *The Distant Sound.*
Homage to Czerny.
The System of Vienna.
JACQUES JOUET, *Mountain R.*
Savage.
Upstaged.
MIEKO KANAI, *The Word Book.*
YORAM KANIUK, *Life on Sandpaper.*

ZURAB KARUMIDZE, *Dagny.*
JOHN KELLY, *From Out of the City.*
HUGH KENNER, *Flaubert, Joyce and Beckett: The Stoic Comedians.*
Joyce's Voices.
DANILO KIŠ, *The Attic.*
The Lute and the Scars.
Psalm 44.
A Tomb for Boris Davidovich.
ANITA KONKKA, *A Fool's Paradise.*
GEORGE KONRÁD, *The City Builder.*
TADEUSZ KONWICKI, *A Minor Apocalypse.*
The Polish Complex.
ANNA KORDZAIA-SAMADASHVILI, *Me, Margarita.*
MENIS KOUMANDAREAS, *Koula.*
ELAINE KRAF, *The Princess of 72nd Street.*
JIM KRUSOE, *Iceland.*
AYSE KULIN, *Farewell: A Mansion in Occupied Istanbul.*
EMILIO LASCANO TEGUI, *On Elegance While Sleeping.*
ERIC LAURRENT, *Do Not Touch.*
VIOLETTE LEDUC, *La Bâtarde.*
EDOUARD LEVÉ, *Autoportrait.*
Newspaper.
Suicide.
Works.
MARIO LEVI, *Istanbul Was a Fairy Tale.*
DEBORAH LEVY, *Billy and Girl.*
JOSÉ LEZAMA LIMA, *Paradiso.*
ROSA LIKSOM, *Dark Paradise.*
OSMAN LINS, *Avalovara.*
The Queen of the Prisons of Greece.
FLORIAN LIPUŠ, *The Errors of Young Tjaž.*
GORDON LISH, *Peru.*
ALF MACLOCHLAINN, *Out of Focus.*
Past Habitual.
The Corpus in the Library.
RON LOEWINSOHN, *Magnetic Field(s).*
YURI LOTMAN, *Non-Memoirs.*
MINA LOY, *Stories and Essays of Mina Loy.*

MICHELINE AHARONIAN MARCOM,
A Brief History of Yes.
The Mirror in the Well.
BEN MARCUS, *The Age of Wire and String.*
DAVID MARKSON, *Reader's Block.*
Wittgenstein's Mistress.
CAROLE MASO, *AVA.*
HARRY MATHEWS, *Cigarettes.*
The Conversions.
The Journalist.
My Life in CIA.
Singular Pleasures.
Tlooth.
HISAKI MATSUURA, *Triangle.*
ABDELWAHAB MEDDEB, *Talismano.*
GERHARD MEIER, *Isle of the Dead.*
HERMAN MELVILLE, *The Confidence-Man.*
AMANDA MICHALOPOULOU, *I'd Like.*
CHRISTINE MONTALBETTI, *The Origin of Man.*
Western.
WARREN MOTTE, *Fables of the Novel: French Fiction since 1990.*
Fiction Now: The French Novel in the 21st Century.
Mirror Gazing.
Oulipo: A Primer of Potential Literature.
GERALD MURNANE, *Barley Patch.*
Inland.
YVES NAVARRE, *Our Share of Time.*
Sweet Tooth.
DOROTHY NELSON, *In Night's City.*
Tar and Feathers.
WILFRIDO D. NOLLEDO, *But for the Lovers.*
FLANN O'BRIEN, *At Swim-Two-Birds.*
The Best of Myles.
The Dalkey Archive.
The Hard Life.
The Poor Mouth.
The Third Policeman.
CLAUDE OLLIER, *The Mise-en-Scène.*
Wert and the Life Without End.
PATRIK OUŘEDNÍK, *Europeana.*
The Opportune Moment, 1855.

BORIS PAHOR, *Necropolis.*
FERNANDO DEL PASO, *News from the Empire.*
Palinuro of Mexico.
ROBERT PINGET, *The Inquisitory.*
Mahu or The Material.
Trio.
MANUEL PUIG, *Betrayed by Rita Hayworth.*
The Buenos Aires Affair.
Heartbreak Tango.
RAYMOND QUENEAU, *The Last Days.*
Odile.
Pierrot Mon Ami.
Saint Glinglin.
ANN QUIN, *Berg.*
Passages.
Three.
Tripticks.
ISHMAEL REED, *The Free-Lance Pallbearers.*
The Last Days of Louisiana Red.
Ishmael Reed: The Plays.
Juice!
The Terrible Threes.
The Terrible Twos.
Yellow Back Radio Broke-Down.
JASIA REICHARDT, *15 Journeys Warsaw to London.*
JOÃO UBALDO RIBEIRO, *House of the Fortunate Buddhas.*
RAINER MARIA RILKE,
The Notebooks of Malte Laurids Brigge.
JULIÁN RÍOS, *The House of Ulysses.*
Larva: A Midsummer Night's Babel.
Poundemonium.
ALAIN ROBBE-GRILLET, *Project for a Revolution in New York.*
A Sentimental Novel.
AUGUSTO ROA BASTOS, *I the Supreme.*
DANIËL ROBBERECHTS, *Arriving in Avignon.*
JEAN ROLIN, *The Explosion of the Radiator Hose.*
OLIVIER ROLIN, *Hotel Crystal.*

SELECTED DALKEY ARCHIVE TITLES

ALIX CLEO ROUBAUD, *Alix's Journal.*
RAYMOND ROUSSEL, *Impressions of Africa.*
VEDRANA RUDAN, *Night.*
PABLO M. RUIZ, *Four Cold Chapters on the Possibility of Literature.*
GERMAN SADULAEV, *The Maya Pill.*
LUIS RAFAEL SÁNCHEZ, *Macho Camacho's Beat.*
SEVERO SARDUY, *Cobra & Maitreya.*
NATHALIE SARRAUTE, *Do You Hear Them?*
Martereau.
The Planetarium.
STIG SÆTERBAKKEN, *Siamese.*
Self-Control.
Through the Night.
VIKTOR SHKLOVSKY, *Bowstring.*
Literature and Cinematography.
Theory of Prose.
Third Factory.
PIERRE SINIAC, *The Collaborators.*
KJERSTI A. SKOMSVOLD, *The Faster I Walk, the Smaller I Am.*
JOSEF ŠKVORECKÝ, *The Engineer of Human Souls.*
GILBERT SORRENTINO, *Aberration of Starlight.*
Blue Pastoral.
Steelwork.
Under the Shadow.
MARKO SOSIČ, *Ballerina, Ballerina.*
ANDRZEJ STASIUK, *Dukla.*
Fado.
GERTRUDE STEIN, *The Making of Americans.*
A Novel of Thank You.
LARS SVENDSEN, *A Philosophy of Evil.*
PIOTR SZEWC, *Annihilation.*
GONÇALO M. TAVARES, *A Man: Klaus Klump.*
Jerusalem.
Learning to Pray in the Age of Technique.
LUCIAN DAN TEODOROVICI, *Our Circus Presents...*

NIKANOR TERATOLOGEN, *Assisted Living.*
DUMITRU TSEPENEAG, *Hotel Europa.*
The Necessary Marriage.
Pigeon Post.
Vain Art of the Fugue.
ESTHER TUSQUETS, *Stranded.*
DUBRAVKA UGRESIC, *Lend Me Your Character.*
Thank You for Not Reading.
TOR ULVEN, *Replacement.*
MATI UNT, *Brecht at Night.*
Diary of a Blood Donor.
Things in the Night.
ÁLVARO URIBE & OLIVIA SEARS, EDS., *Best of Contemporary Mexican Fiction.*
ELOY URROZ, *Friction.*
The Obstacles.
LUISA VALENZUELA, *Dark Desires and the Others.*
He Who Searches.
BORIS VIAN, *Heartsnatcher.*
LLORENÇ VILLALONGA, *The Dolls' Room.*
TOOMAS VINT, *An Unending Landscape.*
AUSTRYN WAINHOUSE, *Hedyphagetica.*
DIANE WILLIAMS, *Excitability: Selected Stories.*
Romancer Erector.
MARGUERITE YOUNG, *Angel in the Forest.*
Miss MacIntosh, My Darling.
REYOUNG, *Unbabbling.*
VLADO ŽABOT, *The Succubus.*
ZORAN ŽIVKOVIĆ , *Hidden Camera.*
LOUIS ZUKOFSKY, *Collected Fiction.*
VITOMIL ZUPAN, *Minuet for Guitar.*
SCOTT ZWIREN, *God Head.*

AND MORE...